# Inhuman Beings

## Monsters Myths & Science Fiction

## By Richard May

© 2016, 2017 by Richard May



"Fire and Pain" was first published in a slightly different version in *Best Gay Erotica of the Year, Vol. 1*, Cleis Press, 2015.

"The Horned Man" was first published in *Hyacinth Noir*, Imbolc 2013.

"Inheritance" was first published in a different version in *Enter at Your Own Risk: Fires and Phantoms*, Firbolg Publishing, 2012.

An eBook edition of 15 of these stories is available under the title *Inhuman Beings: Erotic Encounters of Men and Not-Men* from mlrbooks.com. The three stories in this paperback edition not included in the eBook are "Kakouhthe: Cyclone Man," "Shen Lung and the Old Farmer," and "Ticket to Ride."

Version: 2.0 – 20170611

ISBN: 978-0-9989007-9-7

Library of Congress Number: 2017907688

# waynegoodmanbooks

waynegoodmanbooks@gmail.com
Twitter: @WGoodmanbooks

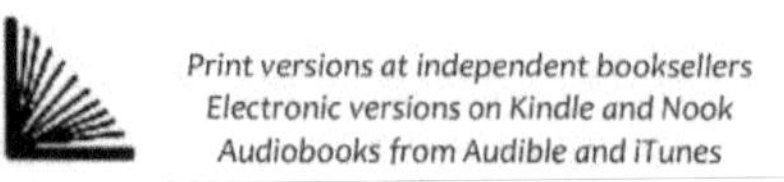

"With *Inhuman Beings*, May seductively crosses the boundaries of time and space, the real and the imaginary, in these spellbinding tales of love and lust and things that go bump, not to mention hump, in the night."
– **ROB ROSEN**, editor of the *Best Gay Erotica* series

"*Inhuman Beings* is an enormously imaginative, genre-crossing work in the tradition of Peter Cashorali's groundbreaking *Fairy Tales* but with greater breadth and franker eroticism; an impressive achievement."
– **MICHAEL NAVA**, author of the Henry Rios novels

"*Inhuman Beings* represents a seminal work in gay male erotic literature that draws on the threads and yarns of our cultures and civilizations. Tales from many countries and eras transport you across the globe and through the years, making this book one that will stand the test of time."
– **WAYNE GOODMAN**, author of *Better Angels*

– **JUSTIN HALL**, author of *Hard To Swallow*

# *Dedication*

Dedicated to my partner, Wayne Goodman

# Acknowledgments

Thank you first to my fellow writers in the biweekly free-write group led by Michael Aleynikov. You were there at the beginning of many of these stories, helping me off to a good start. My special thanks to Michael for his friendship and continuing personal and literary encouragement.

Thank you to my partner Wayne Goodman for listening to first, rough edits of each completed story, for giving always constructive suggestions and comments, for being the publisher of the paperback edition of this book, and for his love.

Thank you to MLR Press for having the faith to publish an eBook edition of 15 Inhuman Beings stories, especially to Publisher Laura Baumbach.

Thank you to San Francisco and Oakland reading series curators Jon Sindell (Rolling Writers), James J. Siegel (Literary Speakeasy), and James Warner (InsideStorytime) for believing my stories are worth reading to an audience.

And thank you to the Readers of the expanded, paperback edition—Wayne Goodman, Justin Hall, Trebor Healey, Jeff Mann, Michael Nava, and Rob Rosen—for reading and commenting. You have given me renewed belief in my ability to tell a story.

# Table of Contents

# MONSTERS

# INHERITANCE

Enscombe was just as I remembered: ugly, dark and huge. It squatted on the edge of the Daberley Moors, our moors. The house, moors and estate had belonged to us for 300 years.

Father inherited after Grandfather's death. After the funeral we left for London straight away. We didn't even stay overnight and never went back. Infrequently, when I thought of Enscombe, I asked my father why. He always just stared into the distance, leaving the question unanswered. My mother was no more help.

"I don't know why, my dear. Your father just doesn't like the place."

Now my parents were dead as well—killed in a horrendous train wreck in northern India, hundreds of lives lost—and Enscombe was mine. The eldest son always inherited. I was the only son and I would be the last, having no intention of fathering children nor any need for a monolith in the middle of nowhere.

I was selling Enscombe and hoping to make a lot of money. Most of ours had gone into the house. Father paid continually to repair and restore it, heaven knows why, so it was in as perfect a condition as a 300 year old house could be. I had no sentimental attachment to it, no attachment at all. I barely remembered my grandfather, a large formerly handsome man, although I do have a clear picture of him sitting by a fire in his library, reading a book. He did that a lot when we were there.

During the scant days of our obligatory visits, I wandered empty rooms full of furniture and dust and the sound of ghosts. Having ghosts never bothered me during the day but after dark I woke up sometimes, lost in the huge bed of my father's boyhood room, sure I was being watched. I never saw anything of course so at the precocious age of 11 decided ghosts didn't exist, no matter what my friends said.

One place I never went was the moors, which lay north of the house and immediate grounds. My grandfather warned of bogs and quicksand and my father looked queer so I made sure not to go. I was an only child and already felt my biological responsibility. Now however I was responsible only to myself, biologically and otherwise.

I looked at my cell phone. The buyer's agent wouldn't be at the door for hours. I had to pass the time somehow and didn't want to disarrange anything inside of Enscombe. The Taylors had the house in excellent order. A walk on the moors seemed a good alternative therefore. I would never have the chance again; everyone expected the sale to go through quickly.

I decided to stop at the Taylor's cottage to let them know.

Their family had a long history with ours, having lived at Enscombe about half as long as we: 150 years of excellent service. The first of them had been stable servants; then they graduated to the house. Mr. Taylor, the last, became estate manager when my father promoted him from butler slash handyman. Mrs. Taylor cooked and cleaned.

They were retiring when Enscombe sold. I seemed to remember they had children somewhere else in Scotland or England or maybe America but I didn't really know.

Mrs. Taylor met me at the door, cheerful cheeked as always, and asked me in for tea. I refused politely, explaining where I was going and my fear of being late coming back to greet the Pierces, the large rich family who proposed to take Enscombe off my hands. We said goodbye.

Once I left the manicured grounds, the world immediately changed, becoming natural and wild. I had walked many such places in England, Scotland and Wales but the contrast here was sudden. I laughed at myself for being frightened. "Of what?" I asked out loud, there being no one to hear but the birds and small furry creatures hiding in the thick broom and brush. I set out on an overgrown path. No one had been this way for a long time.

Around a turning I was pulled up short by the sight of a tall young man in old fashioned clothes. He was sturdily built and looked like he was used to vigorous exercise or hard work. He couldn't have been more than two or three years older than I. Since he was glaring at me, I apologized for intruding.

"No need, Andrew," he said in a still angry voice. "I were expecting you."

I started. "Excuse me," I said. "Have we met?"

"No, sir, we haven't but I know all about you. Pardon my familiarity." He doffed his cap in an ironic show of servility, displaying the thick and curling copper hair so many Scots have but which, sadly, I do not. I couldn't quite tell the color of his eyes but thought they might be grey. "Stephen Taylor," he said, bowing histrionically.

I could tell he was putting me on and, more alarming, there was an edge to his voice which was clearly meant to menace. Maybe he was angry I was displacing his grandparents, forcing them to retire. Whatever his reason I thought it might be good for me to return to Enscombe.

"Fine day, sir, out on the moors," Stephen Taylor said to keep me with him. "You haven't been here in a while, have you, sir?" He was openly sneering, for all his polite words.

"Not since I was eleven. Is that when we met?" As much as I wanted to retreat, his eyes held me in place, as well as something in my groin. Stephen Taylor was a very handsome man.

"Yes," he agreed, with a nasty chuckle. "It were about that time." His accent was difficult to understand, even for me, a native Scot. "Are you planning a long stay?"

"No, I'm afraid. Hasn't your grandfather told you? I'm only here to sell the estate. My father's passed away and it's of no use to me. Better it go to a family who needs all those rooms."

He frowned at me. "Sell Enscombe?" And then his look hardened even more. "Your father's dead, you say? I hadn't heard. My sympathies, Mr. Andrew." His tone wasn't sympathetic at all. If anything, he sounded glad to hear the news.

We stared wordless at one another until a wind came up and Taylor seemed to think it was time he be away. I was inordinately glad. But I asked in any case, "Shall we walk back to your grandparents' house together?" It seemed only polite.

He looked at me oddly and said, "No, thank you, sir. I'm not going that direction. Good day." I watched him stalk off on long legs right through the brush, farther onto the moor. Astonished, I hurried back to the cottage.

When I knocked Mr. Taylor answered. "Oh, sir. Come in, come in. We've just had a call. The Pierces put their visit off until tomorrow. A sick child, I was told."

"I'm sorry to hear that. About the child," I explained. "It's just as well though. Gives me more time with the old place. Oh, and I met your grandson out on the moors."

They looked at each other with surprise. "None of our grandsons is here, sir."

"Oh. Hmm. He introduced himself as Stephen Taylor so I assumed…." The look they exchanged now was one of horror. "What?" I asked them.

Mrs. Taylor started to speak but her husband shushed her. "You know it's silliness, Anne. Nothing worth bothering Mr. Andrew with."

But they were so pale I urged them to tell, whatever it was. Mr. Taylor would not but Mrs. Taylor said in an audible whisper: "He deserves to know, Edward." Mr. Taylor scrutinized me with an open stare I'd never seen from him before. He looked a bit like the Stephen Taylor who wasn't his grandson.

"Sit, sir, if you please." He indicated the best chair, which I knew was his. I placed myself on the ancient couch. His wife nodded at him and he began.

"It was, folks say, over a hundred year ago. Before the First World War. Victoria was still the Queen. Before there were cars."

"Edward," his wife cautioned.

"Yes, anyway, late in the 19th Century. My family had just come on at Enscombe a generation before. All three of the sons then were stable boys and one was especially keen on horses."

"Stephen," I suggested.

"Yes," Mr. Taylor agreed, nodding slowly, his eyes analyzing me again. "Stephen Taylor. The family's oldest son was just as keen. Stephen Taylor became his groom. He and Mr. Andrew were out riding almost every day, especially on the moors."

The first Daberley son had been an Andrew for at least 200 years. Hearing my name and Stephen Taylor's connected gave me chills but I urged Mr. Taylor to go on.

"One day it was, in June I think, Mr. Andrew came back from his ride alone, leading Stephen Taylor's horse. He told my great-great-grandfather that there had been an accident. Stephen was hurt. He might be dead. My great-great jumped on a horse bareback and called for his other sons. The three of them followed Mr. Andrew in a hurry back to the spot.

Stephen Taylor was dead. It looked like he'd fallen off his horse and his head had struck a rock."

I remembered a Stephen Taylor's gravestone in the servants' graveyard. I had thought nothing of it. Why would I? I looked at the two Taylors in front of me now, both so solemn. "But what does this have to do with the Stephen Taylor I just met?"

"It's a child's ghost story," Mr. Taylor said and then was silent. His wife looked exasperated and told me the rest.

"It is indeed a ghost story, sir, but it isn't childish. I have seen Stephen Taylor myself. Where were you today, sir?" I described the spot. "The turning, yes. That's where I saw him too. That's where he was killed." I was struck by her choice of verbs.

"Now, Anne."

"Don't Anne me, Mr. Taylor. The boy has a right to know."

Mr. Taylor shrugged. "You've told him now."

"Not all," Mrs. Taylor muttered.

"That's enough," her husband said sharply.

"What's the rest? My father never said anything about this."

"He wouldn't," Mrs. Taylor said mysteriously.

"Anne," Mr. Taylor warned again.

"Tell me, please."

Mrs. Taylor ignored her husband's warning. "The story goes that the ghost of Stephen Taylor has haunted every Andrew Daberley who's lived at Enscombe since. Your father used to have terrible nightmares."

"When he was a child?

She looked like she was trying to remember. "No, I think it was when he came back from university. He must have been 22."

"How old was the Andrew in the story?"

They looked at each other, alarmed again. I knew what the number was. After that, they said nothing more about the ghost. We talked of the sale and their retirement plans. They invited me to supper and to spend the night. They urged the latter on me especially but I had dinner plans in the village with the only friends I had nearby and wouldn't be back for hours. If at the end of the evening I was afraid of Stephen Taylor's ghost, I could just stay with my friends and not bother the Taylors or disrupt the social order.

After goodbyes, I returned to the empty house and began to walk the rooms. The Taylors had done a magnificent job of removing years of dust: the furniture looked almost new. My furniture and my rooms, I thought, for one night more. I sat in as many chairs as possible and played both pianos, wondering if any of the previous Andrews had been musical. The sounds of the keys reverberated strangely. The Pierces would need to have the pianos tuned if they kept them. Or perhaps it was just the high solitude of the house. Strangely though, I didn't feel alone. As in my childhood, I could feel all the ghosts around me.

I finished my tour in time to shower, change and ride off on my Triumph. It was very late when I returned; my friends hadn't wanted to let me go. "Are you sure you're all right on your own?" they asked. That seemed funny to me so I laughed but they didn't. They had known Stephen Taylor's story.

The narrow lanes were empty, dark except for my head-light. The cottage windows were also dark so I cut the motor and walked the bike up the mall. Trees stirred with a breeze as I passed. It seemed unusually cold, which made me glad for my leather jacket.

Enscombe loomed even more oppressively in the dark. I remember being scared of it when I was a child. I was scared of it now but secured the bike and walked inside.

Clocks told me it was after midnight, the new last day for the Daberleys at Enscombe. I climbed the central staircase, thinking of all the feet which had trod before me.

My father's bedroom felt freezing so in quick order I stripped, not bothering to hang my clothes, and slid under the heavy blankets. Sleep came quickly but I was awakened soon after, or so it seemed, by the sound of footsteps in the hall outside my room. I was groggy and pulling myself into sitting when the bedroom door opened and the shadow of a tall man stood in the doorframe.

"Aren't you afraid?" he asked in Stephen Taylor's voice.

"No," I lied, jumping out of bed and turning on the lamp, only belatedly covering myself with underwear tossed aside. "But I do want to know what you're doing in my house in the middle of the night."

"I come here often," was all he said as he entered the room and closed the door. I made ready for him as he came across the carpet but he just sat, slumping in the armchair.

"He killed me, you know."

"Killed you? Who?"

"The Andrew that was then. Let me see. He would be your fifth great grandfather. Maybe four. Anyways, he killed me. I thought he loved me. Told me how good I looked on a horse. How good I looked off it. I tried to keep my place but he went on about me every day that spring and June. Finally, I tried to kiss him and he hit me with a rock. I died straight away.

"I'm sorry, Stephen," I said, because I was. It was my ancestor after all. I didn't think till later how bizarre it was to be apologizing to a ghost, but Stephen Taylor didn't look like a ghost. He wasn't transparent or wavering or squiggy round the edges. He looked like a man, flesh and blood, muscle and bone.

"Warn't your fault," he said, looking up at me with startling grey eyes above his folded hands under a blunt chin.

"I still feel guilty."

He looked at me with a sudden sneer. "That's your inheritance from him. He felt guilty the rest of his life. I saw to that."

"You haunted him!"

"Every night he were here, which wasn't much towards the end. It never is."

"Did you show yourself to my father?"

"Course. I come to all the Andrews when they reach the age. You're 22 now, ain't you, sir?" The room grew colder. He rose and came to the bed. I moved to get away but he pushed me back down.

"What are you going to do to me?"

He made a fist as if to strike. I put my hands up. He took both, gently. "Nuthin', sir. I never do nuthin'."

"Why?" I asked, trying to pull away.

"Hopin', I guess," was his sad answer, holding on. His hands felt strong and warm. Did all ghosts have hands like this?

"Hoping?" I asked, relaxing in his grip. His touch was gentle now. I wasn't afraid any more: I knew what I could do for Stephen Taylor. I pulled out of his hold and lay back down under the blankets, making room for him. He stared a moment, unbelieving, then undid his shirt and pants. I watched him pile each article neatly on the chair.

He was powerfully built and fully erect, a young man in the prime of his life, a life another Andrew Daberley had taken. He slowly inserted himself next to me. His body was as strong and warm as his lips were gentle when they pressed against mine. I remember logic asking how could this be, but experience said it was. I felt his hardened cock against my thigh. His large hand cupped my chest while his tongue explored my mouth. I felt the weight of his long body as it slid on top of mine, the definition of muscles, the manipulation of fingers and teeth. I massaged the real width of a wide back as he kissed me more frantically. I felt the strength of arms push my legs back and settle them on his shoulders.

When Stephen Taylor entered me, I felt a joy never felt before in all my dealings with men. A cock had been an instrument of pleasure–that was all–but Stephen's was something else, something more. There was no discomfort, no need of condoms. He was a ghost, wasn't he? He fit inside me perfectly as if we were missing parts, found at last and refitted.

As Stephen fucked me, I lost the feel of my own body. At first the cock was plunging and pulling inside me and his mouth was against mine and his arms were on mine, holding them down, but then I disappeared. I wasn't and Stephen wasn't. There were no endings or beginnings, no edges of being. We floated and flew in the freedom of the fuck.

Then suddenly I was back. I was coming; he was coming. I was screaming; he was shouting. And then with an emotional thud we were two bodies again, man and ghost, chests heaving, hearts pounding, his cock still up my ass but something known again, something definite out of the infinite.

Stephen softened and pulled out of me. He wiped me down like a horse. I took the shirt from him—was it mine or his?—and soaked the sweat of him into it. I smelt the good fragrance of his body, and my mind began working again.

"How…" I began to ask. He put one very real finger over my lips.

"Shhh," he said and pulled me close again. I fell asleep in his arms.

Light coming through open curtains woke me. Surely I had drawn them the night before. Stephen was gone but I could see the impression of him beside me in the mattress and feel it lingering on and in my body. My ass ached pleasantly. I felt the small scratches of his skin and beard on mine. I stretched in happiness and rolled onto what was left of him. I kissed the pillow where his head had lain.

But the day was advancing, and I felt it coming. The Pierces would be here, and the house would be sold. I would never see Stephen Tayler again. Would they? I felt a heavy sadness settle on my back and a terrible loneliness enter me but heard something like Stephen's voice say clearly through the gloom, "Come to me."

Dressing hurriedly, I pulled on my boots and combed my hair haphazardly, remembering to grab a heavy coat. I ran from Enscombe towards the moors, avoiding the Taylors, and crashed along the path, scaring pheasants and grouse and scrambling creatures. I rounded the turning and there he was, as real as yesterday, as real as last night.

"You're here!" I told him stupidly.

"And where else would I be, sir?" he said, with happy mouth and eyes.

"Andrew."

"Andrew," he repeated, his voice amazed.

I walked to him, saying as I went, "I thought you'd be gone. I thought I'd set you free."

He opened his arms for me, enclosed me in them and brushed the hair out of my face. "You did, my bonny bairn. You did."

"Why didn't you go then?"

He leaned back to look askance. "I thought I daren't now you come to me." And then he laughed and we kissed. After a night of kisses, it was just one more but it was the one that made my decision.

"I have to tell the Pierces not to come!" I said loudly, pulling away and starting a rapid walk towards the cottage. He didn't follow. "Come with me," I said, turning back.

He gave me one more kiss. "Later, love. I don't want the others seeing me. It disturbs them. But you go." He gave me a little shove and a warming smile to set me off.

I stumbled back the path. I would tell the Taylors they could still retire. I would be fine on my own. Stephen would be there with me. I couldn't tell them that of course, but the knowing of it made me happy.

That other Andrew had done a terrible thing but Stephen had forgiven us. I felt lighter, free of something myself but more than that. I felt loved, the freest of feelings.

A breeze followed me, warm and encouraging. I prepared my reasons, hoping no one would see my joy.

# **O**ni and **T**engu

After a plane, train and taxi I arrived in Kogen Onsen. It wasn't much more than an inn. The front desk clerk Taro, asked me in halting English if I were going to hike Daisetsuzan National Park. When I answered *"hai,"* he beamed and began a soliloquy in Japanese that lasted through the main floor and up to my room.

Taro took root just inside my door, filling my mind with stories about local monsters. I sat on the bed, enjoying the view of his sturdy body and wondering whether he might fill me with something else.

"The Tengu, they are bad. You know Tengu?" I shook my head no. "Yeah, they are bad. Big nose, really long, and wings and teeth. They eat you up." He looked at me oddly. "They do other things with that nose, too."

"Is there anything else I should look out for?" I asked impatiently, meaning real dangers like bears or poisonous snakes.

"Yep. Oni. Blue oni, red oni. Big muscles, big horns." Taro pumped his impressive guns in a muscle man pose and held forefingers to either side of his spiky black hair. He saw my interest in his biceps. "Maybe you like them too. Big muscles," he repeated, puffing out his already generous chest.

I dreamed of Taro that night. He was naked except for a fundoshi—Japanese free form men's underwear—and turned into an oni before my eyes. The oni was blue, with the predict-ed muscles and horns, and he fucked me raw. My sheets were as disheveled as my hair the next morning. What a dream, I told myself.

At breakfast, the human Taro made a point of sitting with me while I ate my sticky rice and four ounces of salmon. He was very familiar for a Japanese guy, patting my shoulder and leaning in confidentially, lodging his thigh against mine under the table. It felt good but not good enough to delay my hike. I was on a schedule: hike Daisetsuzan, soak in Sounkyo hot springs on the other side of the park, return to Tokyo, pack, fly back to Denver and my real life. My Japanese sabbatical was just about up.

Regretfully, I pulled myself away from Taro's meaty thighs and went upstairs to pack. I returned clothes and toiletries to my backpack, except for yesterday's underwear. Somehow, I had misplaced it. Oh well, I thought. I have two more.

I did find a blue fundoshi cloth left in a drawer. I tried to turn it in when I paid my bill but Taro told me to keep it. "A souvenir," he said with a very unJapanese wink.

Outside, I found the trailhead and began walking towards home. After an hour of tall trees and thick bushes, sounds of wood-chopping rang through the forest from up ahead. I'd chopped enough back home in Colorado to know. When I turned the corner, I saw another strongly built young man, na-ked except for a tiger print fundoshi around his cock and matching hachimachi band around his head. Seemed pretty fashionable for the middle of nowhere. His deep tan glistened reddish brown with sweat.

I spoke to him in Japanese and he answered with a greeting and deep bow. When he looked up, his plain face surprised me with its interested eyes. I had seen men like him in Tokyo, young farmers new to the city. They thought they could make money in construction and maybe find a big city boyfriend.

The illegal woodcutter introduced himself as Buta. "Buta?" I asked.

"Yes," he confirmed, looking back at me calmly.

I couldn't believe anyone would name their child "Pig." It must be a nickname. I wondered about that for a few seconds before I noticed Buta was waiting.

"Michael," I said quickly. Buta nodded as if I had told him a great secret. I barely heard what he said next; his eyes wouldn't let mine go.

"Maikeru-san, are you thirsty from your walk? Would you allow me to share my water with you?" He spoke in a formal, old-fashioned way and held out a jug. I said *domo* and drank. Buta watched my Adam's apple swallow his water.

As I handed back the jug, our fingers touched and held. I heard seconds ticking off my mental clock. "Well, then, good-bye," I said at last and made to leave. Buta's voice stopped me.

"There is a very good place to camp by a stream and under thick trees ten kilometers away. The sign says Camp Three." I thanked him and bowed again. Buta returned the bow, our heads almost touching. As we rose, he smiled. I smiled back, straightened and walked off without another word. I could feel his eyes following me. I tried hard not to look around. There was no time for this either.

After the next turn, I was alone again and felt the fear of it. I tried to focus on sounds. Buta did not return to chopping wood but the forest around me was full of noise: birds calling, the rustling of unknown creatures through the brush, the crunching of my feet on the trail. The sexy images of Buta and Taro faded. Daylight faded also, ending at the sign Buta had mentioned. I turned in the direction of the arrow.

The woodcutter was right. Thick fir trees protected the campground from any cold Hokkaido winds. A sizable stream flowed musically over large rocks and around small boulders. The flat ground would be good for camping.

I set up my tent and spread a tatami inside. Reflexively, I tried my cell phone to check messages but there wasn't any coverage. *Kamaimasen.* No matter. I wrote in my journal while it was still light and fixed my dinner in Japanese proportions. After eating, I sat quietly, listening to the night around me. Was that a rush of giant wings or just a breeze through the fir trees? Were those heavy footsteps coming down the path or just wishful thinking? I laughed at myself and went to bed.

I dreamed again of the blue oni with Taro's face and woke up wet, my chest heaving, my cock starting to soften. I looked around the tent, surprised I was alone, sure I hadn't been and laughed at myself a second time.

My underwear and I were soaked so I crawled into the warm night air to wash. There was someone in the clearing. I could feel them. I whirled right and left, front and back, calling out in Japanese. My answer was leisurely footfalls and the sound of brush being parted. An animal then. I washed myself and my Jockeys quickly and laid the underwear on a bush to dry. Back in the tent, I had trouble falling asleep again but finally did.

Bird calls woke me, sounding cheerful and reassuringly small. I stretched, rolling onto my back, easing into the day. In the middle of my daydreaming, a voice from outside said *"Ohayou,"* good morning. I sat up quickly, answered *"Chotto"*– just a moment–and slid into my shorts and shirt.

Outside the tent I saw the smiling face of the illegal woodcutter. He was standing close by with apples in hand. "I thought I would see how you were doing," he explained. I replied that I was doing very well, thanked him and bowed. Buta returned the bow quickly. Our eyes met again at groin level.

"Why don't I make us some tea?" I suggested, straightening quickly.

Buta organized a little fire while I pulled out the tea and implements. He sliced apples with his pocket knife while the tea steeped and I cooked oatmeal. We shared breakfast like we had forever.

"How did you happen to be here today?" I asked, hoping I didn't sound suspicious.

"I'm cutting wood nearby."

"Is that wise? I mean, what if the authorities find out?"

He laughed from deep inside. I looked at the middle of him, to see where the sounds came from. The horizontal lines of his abs showed through his tight red tee shirt.

"It's not illegal, Maikeru-san. I am the official destroyer of brush in these parts. I remove dead wood and cull trees." He stood and reached into his baggy cargo shorts for his wallet. The ID announced: Buta Sasaki, Ministry of Agriculture, Forestry and Fisheries. I handed it back to him, avoiding his steady gaze. Did they allow you to use nicknames on official documents?

We finished breakfast talking about ourselves. He explained his first name. "Our parents named us after animals. My brothers are Dog and Dragon." I thought his brothers had come out ahead on the deal.

During a lull Buta looked at his watch and I reflexively looked at mine. Both the lull and our watches said it was time to go. I washed dishes while Buta made sure the fire was out. He helped me tear down my tent and pack it away. We crouched together to roll the tatami.

"Oh!" I said, remembering my drying underwear, and jumped up, knocking heads with him. He rubbed his forehead ruefully. "*Sumimasen deshita!*" I'm sorry! I forgot my underwear." That made Buta look at my crotch. I hurried to the bushes circling the clearing before he could see my red face.

The briefs were gone and in their place was another blue fundoshi cloth. "Oh!" I repeated. "My underwear's gone." Buta came up beside me and looked at the cloth. "I don't wear fundoshi," I explained, feeling even more embarrassed. Then I told him the story of the first lost Jockeys and first blue fundoshi and Taro saying to keep it. He took each word seriously, asking questions, mainly about what Taro had told me.

"Do you know him?" I asked.

"Of course. We grew up here together." He looked around the clearing like it had been this very spot. "He is right though. This *is* tengu territory. They might not be happy you are here."

"Do you really believe in oni and tengu?" I asked, expecting to hear a no. Instead, he nodded yes. "Have you ever seen one?" He nodded yes again. I couldn't believe him and watched his face for the lie. My eyes drifted to the breathing in and out of his substantial chest, then back to his face. His strange eyes were stranger now. The whites of them seemed as if they had turned a light yellow.

"*Saa*–well," he said, looking down quickly, a light red himself now. "I better get to work." He turned and almost ran down the path to the trail.

"Thanks for the apples," I called after him but there was no reply. I shrugged and started towards Sounkyo.

It was another lovely day but, after my conversation with Buta, I listened more carefully to birds calling and looked up at any rustling of wings or trees. Of course nothing happened, at least involving man-birds. I walked miles through unmolested peace and beauty.

Just before dark I followed another turnoff to another camp Buta had mentioned. There was stream passing by this one too, not as wide as the first but just as musical.

That night I dreamed a third time of Taro and woke panting and soaked with sweat and cum. While I caught my breath, I overheard a conversation between the trees and the stream. The sounds calmed me. Reluctantly, I crawled out to wash myself and underwear. The trail had climbed in elevation so the air was not so warm here.

I ran through the clearing to splash chilly water all over myself. I soaked and wrung out my briefs. I made sure to take them back into the tent with me. They were my last pair. Animals were way too acquisitive in Japanese forests.

I hung my clean underwear from a tent pole near my head. The night was so quiet I could hear drips hitting the tatami, but I listened past the water torture to the night around me. The quiet sounds outside worked as a sedative.

The dream returned. The blue oni was on still top of me, my legs back against my chest. It fucked me more slowly, taking its time before flooding my insides with cum, making me come with it, then cleaning us up with my underwear, which was still damp. Our sex was wordless, as it had been before, the only sounds my gasps and the oni's grunts and final elongated bellow.

I woke unrested, rubbed my face and reached for my underwear. It was gone, replaced by a third blue fundoshi cloth. I felt a quick terror. Someone had been in my tent, someone with an underwear fetish. How? I rushed outside, almost into Buta's arms.

"What…what are you doing here?"

He looked alarmed until he noticed I was naked. "I thought I better check on you again," he explained as his eyes drifted down to my cock. I could see his own growing inside his fundoshi. I gulped, turned quickly and crawled back inside my tent. I considered the blue fundoshi, then pulled on my shorts and shirt. When I rejoined Buta, he was already starting a fire for tea.

Squatting beside him I realized my ass ached. Too much walking maybe. But my legs and feet felt fine. Over tea, I told Buta about my third oni dream and missing underwear. His yellowing eyes flashed. His face was angry when he declared, "We will camp together tonight." He told me which campsite to stop at, then stood and hurried out of the clearing, again without a goodbye. I watched his short, thick body speed away from me, muscular ass churning.

I watched the path for several moments, hoping Buta might come back, fantasizing sex between us if he did, but that didn't happen so I considered my hiking apparel for the day. I tried tying one of the fundoshi cloths around me but it fell to the ground. I tried again and this time it held, if only just barely. Maybe Buta would give me instructions later on. My hopes and cock rose at the thought.

The trail became steeper, the air colder and the wind stronger. I put on another layer against the chill. The trees thinned steadily, and clearings increased in circumference. At lunch I came to one that was almost a meadow and decided to rest.

I drank cold tea and ate beef jerky, nori and dried fruit until I was full. The sun and a full stomach made me sleepy. Why not sleep? My fears were silly. I had seen no one but Buta since Kogen Onsen, except in dreams.

I dreamed again but this time of tengu. I was being lifted into the air, held in the talons of a man-bird. Its nose was nearly a foot long and pointed ahead of us as we flew up into the pines. I could see my pack below, growing smaller.

I struggled and the tengu tightened its grip; the points of its talons pierced my clothing and skin. I screamed and the tengu squawked, flying higher. I told myself it was just a dream. I will wake up and remember this with a shrug or laugh or not at all.

I didn't wake up though, and the dream continued.

When we had almost reached the treetops, the tengu settled into a wide nest and released me, standing and calling and flapping its large grey wings. It had talons for toes but otherwise was a man, with all a man's body parts. Its cock was erect and longer than any I had ever seen.

I flung myself against the side of the nest and looked over for escape. We were a hundred feet in the air; my only hope was to wake up. I slapped myself several times. The tengu squawked and squashed me against the floor of the nest with a heavy foot, screeching loudly into the air. In seconds another tengu came flying. I could see it was male too, with a bigger body, longer nose and even longer cock. It screeched back at its mate and they began to rip my clothes off with their hands and talons. They tied me up with shreds of cloth and suspended me from a branch above the nest.

The larger tengu positioned himself behind me, his nose entering my ass, plunging in and out, more rapidly the more I cried out. I thought of Buta and hoped he would save me but how could he? It was just a dream. In any case my screams were soon muffled by the smaller tengu's long nose entering my mouth. I gagged but the tengu held me fast, front and back.

After long minutes they switched from fucking me with their noses to pounding me with their cocks. They changed positions without resting and changed mine as well. I was on my back and on my side, no longer suspended. My body was scratched and torn. I felt as if I were shrinking. They would keep at this until I was completely gone.

Through their screeches and squawks, I heard a sound from far below, the clang of it mighty. I felt the huge tree shudder like an earthquake with each clang. The tengu stopped their torture, looked at each other and then over the nest. Something roared up at us, a gigantic sound, louder than the wind. The tengu flew down to it. I leaned over to see, my mouth and ass aching, dreading their return.

On the ground below was a gigantic red beast, an oni with long horns and a heavily muscled body, wearing only a tiger skin loincloth. The creature swung a huge axe at the tengu as they flew around it, warding them off as they screeched, roaring at them as they swooped to tear it with their talons.

While the monsters fought, I looked frantically around me. Could I escape? How? Climb down? I looked over again at the ground beneath me. The height made me dizzy but it was the only way.

I made myself clamber onto the nearest branch and begin to find footholds down. The tengu saw and flew back, making a horrible noise. The red beast roared more loudly than ever and started banging again at the tree. I lost my grip and fell, sure now I wasn't dreaming.

I screamed as I thudded against a hard surface, opening my eyes not to death but to a hideous red face. I was in the arms of the oni. I screamed again and struggled against its grip but, in my thrashing, somehow I heard Buta's voice telling me to be calm. His words came from the red oni's mouth.

"Buta?"

"Maikeru-san," the monster answered before it began running with thunder steps out of the forest, past the tree line, up into boulders and rocks and colder air. The tengu flew after us, squawking angrily and swooping low. The Buta oni held me tightly against his deep chest. I could feel his heart. I felt terrified and safe at the same time.

We charged up the mountain into a hole in its side, the tengu at last giving up their chase. Inside the cave the oni set me down and began to transform. The monster's red face became Buta's ruddy one, its red body his brown, the loincloth his fundoshi. I held onto the cave walls, wide eyed, not believing what I saw. In minutes, Buta the man was back, as if Buta the oni had never been.

Without looking at me, Buta brought water and a cloth to wash my wounds. They weren't deep: pecks on my chest, bruises on my ass and scratches everywhere. I watched the care he took, wanting to thank him but unable to speak. When he was done, Buta prostrated himself at my feet.

"Maikeru-san, I didn't keep you from harm. A thousand apologies, a thousand."

He repeated his apology while I sat, amazed. When he started a third time, I stopped him. "You saved me, Buta. You saved me." I tried to stand but fell heavily onto the cave floor.

"Maikeru!" Buta shouted, leaning over me. The sweet musk of him was overpowering, the scent of a man, not a monster. "Here," he said, helping me to a tatami. I felt so weak, so tired. I must have fallen asleep immediately because suddenly I was dreaming again.

The red oni was making love to me and I was enjoying it. We were both wild, like animals, fucking on all fours. In the middle of the fuck, I woke up. Buta was at the opposite edge of the tatami, about as far from me as he could get. I had a thick blanket over me. He had none. In the cold and just his fundoshi, he was shivering.

"Buta," I said once and then again more loudly. His head jerked up, eyes wild. "Come here," I told him and threw open the blanket. He hesitated but I repeated my invitation and he slid closer, arms crossed over his chest to separate us. "Sleep," I told him before falling back asleep myself, hoping for no more dreams.

When I woke a second time, Buta was half embracing me, one arm across my chest, the hand holding my shoulder in place. I didn't move. His warmth and strength felt good. I smiled at his closed eyes and soft breath and brushed my hand lightly along his forearm to his bicep. He had an erection and so did I.

Buta jumped as if I had stabbed him and pulled away from me, looking ashamed. "I'm sorry, Maikeru."

I patted the tatami between us. "Come back. It's all right." His expression was doubtful but he did as I said. When he was close and I had rearranged the blanket over us, I put my hand on his shoulder to keep him with me. He fell back asleep in moments. I stayed awake a while longer, thinking.

The next morning we discussed what to do over tea and oranges and decided I would continue my hike to Sounkyo, accompanied by Buta. It was too far to go back to Kogen Onsen. I wasn't sure what would happen next but at least I wasn't afraid any more.

"I need my pack," I said.

"We have mine," Buta answered, pulling shorts and a shirt from it.

"But mine has my passport, keys and phone. Everything."

So we returned to the forest to retrieve it. We heard the tengu overhead in the trees but did not see them. Buta held my hand so tightly I had to tell him it hurt. He loosened his grip but would not let go.

Once we had found my backpack and it was on my shoulders, Buta led me on a trail circumnavigating the mountain. The path was narrow so we walked single file, me in front. "I want to keep you in my sight at all times," he said. It sounded like a promise.

At last, we reached a small clearing and Buta said we should stop to rest and eat. Our lunch was cold and quiet. Buta seemed unable to look at me. When he got up, I got up too and we walked on.

It was several more kilometers and after dark before we reached Camp 7, where Buta said we would stay the night. He built a small fire and in its light we set up the tent and spread the tatami like people who did this together every day. Our meal was dehydrated vegetables from my pack and edible roots Buta had dug along our way, a forest stir-fry. I talked until Buta relaxed and began to look at me again and smile. When I grew sleepy, he cut fir boughs and shaped them into a flat rectangle on the ground near the tent.

"I will sleep out here tonight," he said.

"You don't have to. We can both sleep in the tent."

"It is too crowded," Buta mumbled, looking down.

"No, it's not."

"It will be when I change," he said, eyes downcast. "I'm sorry, Maikeru."

"I'm not," I replied, waiting for him to look up. He looked back a long time before nodding.

"It still will be too small," he said quietly.

I took the tatami out of the tent, and we laid it on the fir boughs. When it was straightened and re-straightened, there was nothing left to do but get ready for bed.

I pulled off my shirt and shorts. Buta soon added his to the pile; he was eager now. When we both were naked, I lay down on the tatami. Buta lowered himself onto me and we began to make love. He was Buta while we kissed, Buta while he sucked my cock and I sucked his and Buta when he entered me the first time, front to front, and began to fuck. But, when he withdrew and shifted me onto all fours, he changed. His arms alongside mine became red; his face over my shoulder grew hideous. Horns thrust above my head, mimicking the thrusts of his cock up my ass. I heard his grunts and groans grow louder in my ears. I willed myself not to be afraid, to give myself to the oni.

I turned my head, my mouth reaching for his, our tongues playing like lizards. He kissed my neck and pumped more furiously into and out of me. I lifted my ass to the oni's fucking, and a gigantic hand reached under me for my cock. I felt myself coming and bellowed like the blue oni had in my dreams. When the red oni roared, it reverberated through my head and across the forest. I felt his cum projecting into me, more deeply than I could imagine, even further than the tengu with their monstrous cocks. I took it all, I who had always been so careful about protection, holding my ass up to receive it.

When the oni finished, I dropped my head, exhausted. His chin rested on my shoulder. His hand still held my shrinking cock.

He pulled out of me, and I turned onto my back. I saw a red monster looming over me, staring down with yellow eyes, enormous chest still gasping for breath. Slowly, the color drained out of him and Buta returned to his natural body, face and flaccid cock.

"Maikeru…," he began in a shaky voice.

I covered his mouth with mine and his ass with my hands and pulled him down to me. He was Buta. Whatever he became in sex, he was Buta before and Buta after. I massaged the hard muscles of his ass. He began again.

In the morning I woke up startled. I had been dreaming but couldn't remember about what. Buta was already awake, human head propped on human arm. He looked up at the sky with me.

"No tengu," he verified. He ran a stubby human finger down my face and neck, across my chest from nipple to nipple, down my abs to my cock, which he took in hand. He bent over to kiss me while he jerked it gently, then pushed away.

"We should go," he said as his cock lengthened and rose and his body reddened slightly.

"After," I told him, rolling him onto his back and squatting over him. I lowered my ass onto his cock and began a rhythmic up and down. His hands reached for my nipples, and I accelerated as if he had shifted gears.

The change in him came more slowly this time. His rosy skin deepened reluctantly into red. His body, including his cock inside me, gradually expanded into the oni's monstrous proportions. His face wrinkled, his teeth elongated and grew pointed, the whites of his eyes turned yellow. His ass began to push cock up into me. I writhed above him. When he came, roaring, I roared too.

We locked eyes, the oni and I. I waited for Buta to reappear. When he did he was smiling.

"You were not afraid," he said. There was wonder in his voice.

"I knew you were still Buta. You were Buta before and Buta after," I told him, as I had told myself.

He cupped my ass with both hands in a caress and I bent to his kiss. The caress became a playful slap. "We are going now. Get off me, you monster." We laughed at that. And then, like an old married couple, we folded the tatami, Buta started a fire and I started the tea.

We stayed naked while we ate. When Buta began to dress, I pulled one of the fundoshi cloths out of my pack.

"Oh, I almost forgot!" He dug in his pack and produced three pairs of underwear.

"Mine?" He nodded. "Did you take them?"

"No, but I knew who had."

"Taro," I guessed.

Buta nodded. "He is a blue oni."

"But how did you get them?"

"Oni run very fast. It didn't take long." I remembered how he had charged up the mountain.

"Did you fight?" Two men–much less oni–had never fought over me.

"No. Taro does not fight."

"Oh," I said, trying not to sound disappointed.

Buta laughed and gave my ass a proprietary slap. "Get dressed before the red oni comes back." I thought about saying that sounded like a good idea, but Buta started dressing so I did too. We shouldered our packs and walked again towards Souynko.

The trek took two more days. We hiked, camped and made love both nights. I began to look forward to seeing the oni because it meant Buta was losing control. The oni fucked like no man had ever fucked me, the kind of fuck you read about in books or stories. It seemed to me though that each time we made love the oni appeared more slowly and disappeared more quickly.

We arrived in Sounkyo right on time and checked into my room at one of the hot springs inns. We made love in the shower. The oni tried to stifle his grunts and groans and final roar. I had to keep quiet too. Japanese soundproofing is inconsistent.

For three more days, we soaked together in the pools warmed by the springs, ate restaurant food, made love in various parts of our room and tried not to think about where I would be going at the end of the week.

On my last night, we held each other, sitting on the small couch. I felt the connection love is. Buta looked as if he did too but neither of us said the word. He gave me soft kisses and lowered me onto the floor, spreading my legs with his. When he entered me, I waited for his color to change, his horns to appear and his body to expand, but he stayed Buta the whole time. He looked at himself after we finished, even more amazed than I was.

"I did not change!"

"I noticed," I said, kissing his human face. He kissed me back perfunctorily, distracted.

"The story is true then."

"What story?"

"True love...."

"What?"

"True love will make me human."

"True love makes us all human," I said automatically, thinking about the moral and feeling his kisses down my body. I stretched to receive them, thinking maybe I would not leave Japan just yet. And then Buta took my cock in his mouth, and I stopped thinking altogether.

# **T**HE **H**ORNED **M**AN

A young man sat reading by a comfortable fire late one winter night while his father and mother and younger brothers slept fast away upstairs in their fine house made of stone. A loud knock, urgently struck, brought him up from his chair. Thinking it must be a neighbor and not wanting his family to wake, the young man moved quickly to the stout oaken door and undid the heavy iron latch.

When the door was wide open, he immediately saw a handsome stranger with coal black eyes and coal black hair and a body wondrously wrought. The body was naked except for black hair again at his chest and crotch and down his forearms and legs but, even more remarkable, the man had one horn on the right of his brow, which gleamed white in the darkness.

"Who are you?" the young man asked, both startled and drawn.

"The Devil with One Horn," the handsome man replied. "May I come in?"

Without a thought why not, the young man let him cross the threshold, standing aside to make the way open. The devil brushed against him in a casual way as he strode in and took a chair, spreading his muscular thighs. He smiled up at the young man, whose name was Ruairi.

"Bring me some beer, young Ruairi," he said with a smile.

The young man jumped at the soft sound of the devil's voice on his name. "How do you know me?"

"I know a great many things," the devil replied, spreading his legs wider so Ruairi could see for certain what he was meant to see. "You are well named," the devil noted, his eyes on Ruairi's flame red hair and down his body as if he could see the pale skin beneath the clothes. "And well made," the devil added, with a smile. He put a hand up to Ruairi's chin. "What about that beer, my love?"

"Of course, sir," Ruairi said, waking from his dream and leaving the room for the kitchen. There he quickly took up two tankards and dipped them in his father's cask. He hurried back to the Devil with One Horn waiting in the parlor.

In that room, to his surprise, there were now two devils, the handsome one with a single horn and a second not quite so handsome but bigger in body and wearing two horns, one on either side of his forehead. The devils were sprawled across the floor, having congress with one another, both their cocks erect and huge. They stopped their play and took the two tankards from the boy.

"More beer, Ruairi!" the second devil cried before pushing the first devil back upon the floor. Ruairi took up the two tankards from where they sat and hurried back to his father's barrel, returning to the parlor with three sloshing pints and his own erection.

On the floor of the parlor three devils were now thrashing, two fucking the first front and back. The devil in front was bigger still but a hair less good looking than those before. He had a third horn, smack in the middle of his forehead. Still, he was handsome in Ruairi's eyes and the young man began to remove his shirt.

The three devils noticed Ruairi, their strange dark eyes appreciating his own muscular chest, but they did not invite him to join them on the parlor floor. They grabbed and drank the three pints and when they were done the third devil hissed "More beer, Ruairi!" as he put his great cock back into the first devil's mouth.

This went on until Ruairi was naked and there were 12 devils filling the parlor, all having every kind of sex with one another on every bit of furniture and floor but none with Ruairi. Each time he came back with more beer, another devil had appeared, larger and uglier than the rest, with one more horn than the last. Ruairi grew more frustrated each time he returned, unable to join the devils in their frenzy. All they wanted from him was more beer, and all they allowed was a look.

When the 12th devil with 12 horns demanded more beer, Ruairi flung back with all his frustration, "There's none left! You've drunk the barrel!"

"Then, bring us water for we have a great thirst," the Devil with 12 Horns declared, stepping close to Ruairi, the heat and strength of his body making the young man almost faint. But he gathered himself and said in a firm voice that he would not. There was nothing for him in any of this and he wanted them gone. It would soon be light and his family up. What would they think, and what would they say?

The Devil with One Horn, completely disheveled and more handsome than ever, rose from his place at the bottom of the heap and stood between the 12th devil and Ruairi so their naked bodies all touched and rubbed all three. In a cooing voice, he whispered, his hands reaching around for the young man's fine ass, "Sure now, Ruairi, you'll do this for me? I'll be here for you when you come back. You may have from me all that you wish." And then the Devil with One Horn fondled Ruairi's chest and held his cock until it grew taut again. He smiled at Ruairi as it swelled against his own and gave the young man a deep kiss with his long pointed tongue.

Ruairi gasped and agreed, "Yes then, I will."

The Devil with One Horn smiled again and pushed him towards the kitchen, then went back to his tribe. Ruairi, dazed but excited, ran quick for his clothes and hurried to the village well, rolling the empty beer barrel ahead of him. He uncovered the well and lowered its bucket to pull great draughts from its depth.

A voice came up from the water, making Ruairi peer down. The face of a man neither young nor old looked back at him from the gloom.

"What are you up to, lad, so early a morning?" the Spirit of the Well asked in a deep voice.

"I've come to raise water for the twelve demons having congress in the parlor of my father's house," he said quickly, thinking of the handsome devil with one horn who would be waiting for him. The Spirit of the Well could see he was excited and breathing hard.

"This is evil work, young Ruairi," he said after a moment. "While you are here, they are killing your family."

The red-haired young man looked back where he came and asked in great agitation, "But why? I have done everything they asked."

"They mean to live in your father's house and sleep all day and have sex all together each night, with you as their servant," the spirit answered before he paused and asked, "Is sex with these devils worth the death of your family?"

"No," Ruairi firmly said and began to pull away.

"Wait!" the spirit cried, calling him back. "Do this I'm telling you. At your father's house, stand at the north angle and cry loudly three times, "The mountain of the Fenian men and the sky above it are all afire!"

Ruairi repeated the words and again pulled away.

"Wait!" the spirit cried a second time. "Take a bucket of my holy water back with you."

"But why?" Ruairi asked, nonetheless untying the bucket from its rope and filling it to the brim from the water already in the barrel.

"Go!" the spirit commanded with no explanation and Ruairi flew, wanting to save his family.

When he came to his father's house, he stood at the north angle of it and cried aloud three times, just as the spirit told, "The mountain of the Fenian men and the sky above it are all afire!"

At that, all 12 devils stormed out of the house and stomped off for Slievenamon, which was their home, their heavily muscled legs and huge bodies making deep impressions of their wide feet as they ran, the marks of which can still be seen today.

As soon as the last one vanished, Ruairi ran fast into the house and up the stairs. There was his family, all bloody and dead, as the Spirit of the Well had foretold. In anguish the young man wailed, "Spirit, Spirit, what have I done?"

A deep voice from somewhere replied in soft words, "Hush, young Ruairi. 'Tis not what you have done but what you must do. Take the holy water from my well and bathe each body head to toe, then dry each of them from foot to face with its own fresh cloth."

Ruairi leapt to do all that the spirit had instructed, carefully and with great tenderness cleaning each of his loved ones of the blood shed by the twelve devils, until their deathly pallor was like ivory in the dim dawning light.

"Now, Spirit," Ruairi asked, "Please, please, what should I do?"

"Wait," the spirit's voice answered him and just then each body took a new breath, slowly as if sleeping, which they all were.

Ruairi raised his arms high, crying in happiness, and whispered, "Thank you, oh, thank you, Spirit of the Well!" He dropped to his knees but the spirit raised him up and guided him from the upper rooms with a soft breeze up his body, down the stairs, into the parlor, where havoc was shown. Every table and chair was overturned, his mother's knickknacks tossed, candles broken. Ruairi began setting everything to right but the Spirit of the Well interrupted with more urgent tasks.

"They will return, I am afraid, once they see there is neither fire on their mountain nor in the sky above it, so you must hurry, young Ruairi. Take my holy water, which you used to waken your family and sprinkle it across the threshold of the door. They cannot cross my water colored with the blood of your family, blood which they themselves have shed."

Ruairi did as he was told and then barred the door with a heavy beam. Not a second later came a pounding which shook the house. "Open!" the 12 devils said loudly together, but Ruairi kept silent, no matter how they pounded and yelled.

"Open, door!" they demanded but the door replied it could not.

"I am locked tight and strong and a heavy beam is jammed across me. I cannot move."

"Open, blood!" the devils shouted.

"I cannot," the blood answered. "Since I am mixed with holy water from the well I cannot do your biding."

"Open, water!" the mad voices screamed together in a clap of thunder and fall of rain.

"I cannot," said the water, "For you have brought the rain and it carries me now down to the lough."

At last it was quiet except for one soft voice which said in an insinuating way, "Open for me, young Ruairi, and I will keep my promise."

At the seductive sound, Ruairi did open the door, though the Spirit of the Well warned against it in whispers. There on the doorstep, all by himself, was the handsome Devil with One Horn. He smiled at Ruairi and his cock rose thick and broad headed. Ruairi's also grew to its full and straining length, and the devil smiled to see it.

He held out a beckoning arm and hand, spreading his legs and arching his back as if making ready to receive Ruairi's long cock. "I cannot cross the threshold but you can," he said with a leer, "So come, Ruairi. Come to me now. I want you in me."

The Spirit of the Well speaking against it in his ear, Ruairi watched and debated. The devil was more handsome than any man he had ever seen, and the memory of his muscled ass and the other devils pounding into it made his breath come short. But the more the devil entreated, the more the Spirit of the Well spoke against it until at last Ruairi sighed and closed the door. He set the heavy beam back in its place and listened until he heard the devil take his leave. Only then did he open the door once again. There was no one waiting.

"But they will be back!" he said in alarm to the air and could not be sure if he thought that was good or bad.

"The dark night is over, the sun has returned, and you have defeated the demons of darkness," the Spirit told him. "Be proud of yourself."

"But night comes again and I am just one man, a human, against all of them."

The Spirit of the Well settled close round the skin of Ruairi, making it tingle with delight. "I will share all I know with you, my young hero. You will defeat them. My love will show you how." And in the tingling of his skin and the brush of the breeze against it, Ruairi felt himself loved and made love to and joined with the Spirit of the Well in their own congress on the floor of the parlor.

The sun in its travel had reached quarter sky before they were done. Ruairi now knew the twin mysteries of love and of sex and was eager for more but the spirit said, "Be patient, my love. I must leave now, but I will return. That is my promise and it is a better one than that given you before."

"When?" Ruairi yelped, hearing only the word *leave* and afraid to lose all that he had gained.

"Whenever you want me," the spirit answered, withdrawing.

"How?" Ruairi asked, clutching at the air around him.

"Just come to my well," the spirit replied in a disappearing voice.

Ruairi heard his family rising so dressed himself to hide his lust. He stirred the hearth embers and added a log, sitting back in his chair and taking up his book once again. He smiled with the knowledge he had gained that night and day, sure there would be all the more that he wanted.

# **H**air

"Camping?" my voice squeaked. First bikes, then jogging, now lost in the woods. What was he turning me into?

"It'll be fun," he promised, those icy blue eyes saying something to me. Was it *I like you* or *I want to eat you*? Lucas had that kind of look.

We had been dating a few months, after his bicycle brought us together.

He was leaning over it, helmet off, dark curly hair hanging across his ears, face unseen. My eyes were focused on his spectacular ass anyway. It was made for Lycra. He looked up suddenly with a fierce suspicion that made me retreat, hands warding him off. Then he smiled and I took a step back towards him.

He was almost handsome, with those aquamarine eyes and all that hair and a full beard, neatly trimmed. The *almost* was because of the nose. It was long and wide and blunt, more like a snout than any nose I'd ever seen.

"Lucas," he said, introducing himself and smiling. You forgot the nose when Lucas smiled.

"Nate," I mumbled, distracted by the feel of his coarse hand and thick fingers. They were stubby for someone so tall but I began to like them when they held mine for a moment too long for a casual greeting.

After the usual who's and what's, he invited me for coffee if I'd wait while he finished fixing his bike. To pass the time, I chatted nervously and watched his muscles in motion. He looked at me frequently, checking out what I had to offer and smiling into my hungry eyes.

Over coffee at the Ugly Mug we talked bikes, about me being new to Portland and him being a native and what we did for money. Over a second cup, I heard myself agreeing to buy my own wheels and take the Tour de Portland with him. We set a second date for bike shopping and riding. Come the day, we met at Bike Gallery and I bought a used blue Surly bike, approved by Lucas. The brand name appealed to me.

After purchasing helmet, locks and my own Lycra, we set out, riding single file down narrow Portland streets, Lucas in front and then me. "Hot ass," he growled as he eased by, retaking the lead.

Between his ass and mine, we cut the tour short and rode to his house, a funny little place in the middle of a triple lot in Northeast Portland. It was obscured from public view by the tall evergreen trees surrounding it.

"Woods in the city," I said, nervous but eager for what we were about to do.

"We call it a forest here, Nate," Lucas said, turning his smile and eyes on me. I nearly had to have him carry me over the threshold.

We stripped as soon as he closed the door and got down to it without preliminaries, beyond the obligatory condom. He fucked me on the living room floor doggie style, wrapping his arms tightly around my chest as he crammed his cock inside me. I heard him grunt when he pushed in and groan when he pulled back. I felt the power of those hairy thighs and that now Lycra-less ass. One of his hands moved to my cock, timing jerks with his thrusts. Much too soon I began to come, bringing him off inside me, me yipping to his roars. When our aftershocks ended, Lucas kissed my back, pulled out and left the room. I stayed on all fours, panting and wondering at how quickly sex had happened.

When he returned I was still on all fours. His cock swung half flaccid left and right as he took long strides towards me, carrying two beers.

He stopped and laughed. "You want more, boy?"

"Yes," I barked in a strange voice, raising my ass like a bitch in heat, feeling the air enter me. He placed the beers on an end table and pulled a fresh condom over his cock. Nine inches at least. I hadn't had anything that big inside me before.

Lucas took more time with the second fuck, sniffing my ass, tugging my cock back through my legs and sucking it in noisy slurps, kissing up my back to lick my ear. Wide hands pawed at my chest and spongy abs. Thick thighs pushed my legs farther apart, letting his cock further in. His legs and arms locked me in place underneath him and he began to fuck, accelerating in an elongated rhythm, his groin landing against my ass gently at first, then banging towards his climax.

Lucas shot first the second time, yowling into my ear as he came, licking my neck and jaw in thanks as I spurted into his fist. In seconds he pulled out again, discarded the condom, and fell against the couch, his deep breaths swelling his chest and expanding his tight abs. He grinned at me, large teeth showing. "You've earned this," he said, handing me one of the beers.

"So did you," I told him, snuggling under an arm that slid around my shoulder. In an instant, I recognized a comfort I hadn't felt before. It promised protection against all harm. I let myself be encircled by the feeling.

We talked until we got hungry. Lucas cooked steaks and we sat naked at his table. He ate his rare. The blood oozing out of it revolted me but I just kept chewing my well done and said nothing. I slept over, cradled in the coarse hair of his arms, bound by his furry legs.

From then on we did almost everything together, in and out of bed. We biked, hiked and jogged my way into better health. I even joined 24 Hour Fitness in the Pearl District because Lucas got his muscles there. My own muscles grew, especially my chest and ass, which were Lucas' favorite body parts.

I was becoming something new with Lucas. The stranger in the mirror had my face and someone else's body, but Lucas liked him. I had to remind myself I was still me underneath the new muscle mass and decreased body fat.

We stayed at his place nearly every night. Lucas and I were always naked, not necessarily having sex but naked nonetheless. And when we did have sex, Lucas was loud: grunting and growling, howling and yelling. He was wild and made me wild as well.

Early on, we did spend one night at my place and bounced and bumped and yelled our way around my bedroom for hours. Neither Lucas nor I–nor my roommate–got much rest. I promised Gary it wouldn't happen again.

After that I slept in my own bed only two other nights that first month, while Lucas was away on business. It shocked me how much I missed him–him, not just the sex. When we met for lunch the day he was back, he looked very much worse for wear.

"Rough trip?"

"Um hm."

"Where'd you go?"

He didn't answer and the look on his face made me not want to ask again. Lucas had his moods.

We resumed our daily dates and nightly fucks. His first night back Lucas was rougher than usual, biting and clawing, pounding me like a jackhammer. The hickey on my neck, scratches on my chest and pulsating ache in my ass were all reminders the next day at work.

"I'm sorry," Lucas said that night at dinner. We were at an expensive Northeast restaurant, a surprise, especially when Lucas paid.

'You missed me," I answered, more upbeat than I felt, still nursing my bruises and bites.

"It won't happen again," he promised. My disappointment surprised us both. "Unless you want it to," he added, the look in his eyes fierce. He didn't wink or grin to make it easy for me. I left my yes or no for another day, or night.

The night came a second month later. Lucas was back from another business trip and looked like he needed sleep, not sex, but at his house, behind the closed door, he again became another person. He slammed me against the wall and almost ripped my clothes off he was so ready. I could smell the musk of his arousal.

"Lucas?" I said, as he yanked off his own clothes. He froze, ripped shirt on the floor, pants at his knees.

"I'm sorry," he said softly, taking me in his consoling arms. We dressed and sat on the couch, holding on to each other. I was afraid to let go and wondered if he was too. I debated what he wanted vs. what I feared. My decision made, I stood and began to remove my clothes.

"What are you doing?"

"I'm taking off my clothes."

"I can see that, Nate, but shouldn't we talk about this?"

"No, we should not," I said, pulling his shirt back off and unbuckling his pants. He waited while I took off his clothes, his slanted blue eyes intently watching each piece disappear. When he was bare, I knelt between his legs and moved my face towards his groin. He spread his legs, leaned back and let me suck. When he took over, sex was wild, all across the living room, knocking over lamps and tables in our path. Sometimes it hurt, sometimes it scared me but by the time we climaxed all of it felt good.

We spooned on the carpet, feeling each other's heartbeats.

"Are you cold?" he asked.

"Not with my cozy blanket of Lucas," I answered, snuggling against the fur of him.

He pulled my head around to his lips. "You're really special. I think we're going somewhere." For a month I wondered where this might be but, in all my daydreams, Viento State Park in the Columbia River Gorge was not among the possibilities.

"Let's go Wednesday and Thursday. There won't be anybody else there," he said. I told him I'd ask my boss and Lucas underlined his urgency, which made me nervous. Why was it such a big deal? It was just camping, right? I began to hope my boss wouldn't say yes, but he did–reluctantly–and so did I. At least Lucas was happy.

We left Wednesday after his lunch meeting with a client. Lucas took the freeway through the Gorge in his ancient Jeep. Traffic was sparse and he drove well over the speed limit, hands white-knuckling the steering wheel, intense blue eyes staring straight ahead. When we pulled into the empty parking lot at Viento, Lucas rushed the Jeep into a spot near the trailhead and got out, telling me to hurry. I bit back the why while he yanked our equipment out of the storage space.

We shouldered backpacks and limited camping equipment and started off for Starvation Creek. There was a waterfall he wanted me to see. It was only a mile on an easy trail and we reached it in no time, my shorter legs almost running to keep up with Lucas's long strides.

The fall was bigger than I expected and gorgeous. I tried to send photos to my family back east, but of course there was no service. I figured we'd camp near the waterfall but Lucas put his pack on again and headed off into the brush without a word.

"I hope you have a compass," I joked as I watched him go.

"I know the way," he replied without turning around. I had to hustle to catch up before I lost him in the trees.

It was almost dark before we got where Lucas wanted us to go. We had hiked several miles, sometimes on a trail, sometimes not, always at a fast pace. I was breathing hard and truly hoping he knew the way back since I had no idea. We hadn't seen another human since the freeway.

Wherever we were it was a great spot: a wide flat clearing surrounded by tall trees, almost like we were back at his place. There was a brook close by, talking to itself in the deep woods silence. Make that forest.

"You've been here before?" I asked, rotating to take it all in.

"Yes," he said as I whirled by.

"Do you come here often?"

"Once a month," Lucas answered, throwing down a dark grey tarp that looked as if it had had frequent and abusive use. I stopped whirling in front of him. Once a month? The only times he'd been gone were on business. What business did he have in the middle of the forest? But I trusted Lucas so I helped him straighten corners of the tarp without asking any more questions. We spread the two sleeping bags across the tarp. I watched while he zipped them together.

About the time I was going to say I was hungry, Lucas pulled steaks and potatoes and corn on the cob out of his backpack and set up the Coleman. He cooked while the sun set through the trees.

Lucas ate his steak especially rare that night. It barely hit the grill before he flipped it and then set it on a paper plate. Mine took a little longer but was still bloodier than I preferred.

After dinner we drank a second warm beer while the night deepened around us. I remembered sleep away camp. There were always bird calls and animal sounds in the night but not around our clearing. Oh well, I figured. Lucas and I would be noisy enough for the whole damn forest.

I asked if I could help when Lucas began bagging dishes, utensils and all the remaining food but he just said no and kept working with a strange intensity. I watched him hang the bag by a rope looped over a lower tree branch.

"In case there are animals," he explained, busying himself with securing the rope around the tree trunk and not looking at me.

"Animals?" I yelped, scanning the black around us, glad Lucas was with me. "Like bears and wolves?"

"Maybe," he replied with a strange look. I gulped. If there *were* bears or wolves, I wasn't sure how we'd handle them but when Lucas put his arms around me I believed he'd take care of me somehow.

We began making love on top of the sleeping bags, which I didn't expect, but the air felt warm in our protected spot so I didn't stop Lucas when he took off our clothes and lowered me onto the bags, rather than us getting into them. There was no one else around anyway and it was exciting–out in the wild, naked and alone with a hot man. We could do anything. I felt less human and more animal than ever.

Lucas wasn't quite into it though. He seemed distracted and kept looking up at the sky. "What's wrong?" I asked once but his mouth busied mine again with his tongue. I decided he had reasons for this too and didn't ask again. Maybe we'd talk about whatever it was in the morning.

Suddenly, Lucas stopped kissing. His long arms pushed his body up and held mine down, his thighs gripping my legs tight like a vise, slitted blue eyes staring down at me without ex-pression, wide mouth open, showing his teeth. He looked up again at the sky through the trees. I looked too. The moon was high and full. And then it happened. I saw it all, although I couldn't believe what I was seeing. His nose became a snout, bulging out of his face even further. Hair grew from his beard up his face and down his body, quickly covering him with a thick black fur. His teeth elongated, especially his canines. Body parts swelled. Fingernails became claws; ears stretched long and pointed, covered in the same black hair as the rest of his body. In moments all that remained of Lucas were his eyes, still aquamarine but staring down at me now in awful intention, frightening in their familiarity.

I screamed and twisted side to side, trying to roll out from under whatever he had become but his hands, paws now, crushed me in place. Lucas was stronger than I on a regular night and this creature was stronger than Lucas. I pushed up; I twisted. My heart felt as if it would burst from my chest. My mind seemed about to explode. I thought I was going crazy. I thought I was going to be killed.

I kept trying to fight, trying to think, but it did no good. I was held fast to the ground and there was no way I could comprehend what was happening. It had to be Lucas though, inside the manwolf's body. It had to be.

"Lucas? Lucas, please."

At his name the eyes softened, and the manwolf leaned down towards me. I jerked my face away and screamed in anticipation of the slashing bites but all the creature did was lick, first my neck, then across my chest from nipple to nipple, and finally down my abs to my cock, which it took in its snout. I flinched, afraid of its teeth. I froze when it began to suck me. Its tongue was thick and long and swirled around my erection, making it swell more than it ever had. Terror vanished in the sex. I writhed now in pleasure.

The manwolf must have felt me relax because it looked up from my groin to my face, mouth still working my cock, paws still holding my arms down. The eyes belonged to Lucas. He *was* still there, somewhere inside this thing. I focused on them as it moved its paws to my chest, thick pads rubbing my achingly erect nipples, claws toying with them, points expertly manipulating the buttons. I yelped in fear of what those claws could do but, when the feeling was only good, I arched my back and yelped in pleasure.

The creature above me seemed to smile, like dogs do, and pulled itself up on all fours, staring down at me. I looked up, trying to understand. What did he want from me?

I found out. The manwolf reached with its mouth for the lube and condoms Lucas had set out before we'd started and dropped them onto my chest, still wet with its saliva. It set my arms free and waited. I looked up at it, debating, then tossed the package and tube away and lay back on the sleeping bag, spreading my arms and legs. The manwolf seemed to consider this intelligently before turning me onto my stomach and pulling me up onto all fours underneath it. Its weight settled heavily on top of me, a blanket of hair scratching down my back and ass, front legs parallel with my arms, hind legs spreading mine further apart, opening me to it.

I realized the manwolf's cock was thicker than Lucas's. I whimpered in fear with just the head of it inside me. Paws reached under me to rub my chest and erase my fear. I arched my ass, giving it to the manwolf, and the cock inched further inside me, hairy haunches locking my legs into place. I yelled from the pain, whimpering again, until the familiar push and pull began. I knew this motion: this was Lucas fucking me. My body relaxed, and my mind disconnected. But the fuck accelerated, becoming something more than just Lucas. More power, more desire, faster and deeper inside me. The manwolf fucked like the wild animal Lucas and I never quite became. It banged my ass with abandon, not asking how I felt or whether it was okay for me. I jerked my cock just as freely, intent on my own pleasure, feeling the manwolf take his as I took mine.

The cock expanded inside me, joining us like a lock and key. I ached all over, trembling, wanting to come but trying to hold back, not wanting the feelings to end, enjoying the thick hair scratching my back, the coarse paws on my chest, the union of lupine cock and my ass, the feeling of thought suspended. Then I came, gushing, my sphincter tightening, bringing the manwolf off inside me.

I had never felt cum inside my ass before. It was a wonder and a joy, warm and liquid, seeping into my body, the other becoming me. I heard myself yip repeatedly, happily, so happily. I heard the manwolf howl, wailing at the moon so white and huge above us. I leaned my head back and howled along with it.

At last, we stopped and the forest was quiet again. The creature collapsed, exhausted, on top of me, my body bowing under its dead weight. I managed to hold us up while our mouths panted towards the dark all around, the manwolf's head and snout nestling alongside mine, hair against hair.

After a few moments, I felt its tongue lapping my neck, as if in thanks. I stretched for it, liking the warm wet rasp. Its ass began to move again, the cock hardening inside me, its paws rotating me onto my back. I raised my legs onto the thick fur of its shoulders and felt for its tail, holding on to that long softness while the manwolf fucked me front to front, like we were humans after all.

Throughout the night our fucking continued in different positions and different spots around the clearing: me standing and holding onto a stump, me splayed across a boulder, the manwolf pressing me against a tree and nudging me back onto all fours. We were one beast most of the night, until the dark became light.

Birds were chirping when I awoke. I saw through bleary eyes slithering creatures work their way past us to the brook. I turned to the thing beside me. The manwolf was Lucas again, the thick body hair thinned to its normal abundance, pointed ears rounded, the snout reduced to Lucas's large nose.

He slept in my arms. I stroked the human skin of him to reassure myself he was really back, which made him wake up.

He lurched out of my arms, sat up and looked away. He wouldn't see me, even when we washed ourselves in the snow water of the stream. The icy cold of the water was like a slap. Full consciousness returned. We stood dripping in the middle of the clearing, naked and human. Lucas was as wordless as the manwolf. I made myself say something.

"Does it always have to be like this?"

His blue eyes stared, without expression. Now they seemed all that was left of the manwolf, not of Lucas. I made myself not look away. Finally, he answered in a monotone, "Unless I go away."

I looked down my body at the claw marks and teeth indentations the manwolf had left. I felt my ass ache from the power of sustained fucking. I looked at Lucas and felt his trust. He didn't go away alone this time. He wanted me to know, and telling would not have told. I pondered this and all that had happened. I had one more question.

"Only at full moons?"

"Only at full moons," he repeated. Whether it was a promise or a warning, his eyes didn't say.

"All right then," I told him and Lucas yanked me close, his hairy human arms holding me against his furry human chest.

"But you don't have to leave. I mean, when…."

Lucas waited for me to finish. When I didn't he asked hesitantly, "Did you enjoy it?"

"Yes."

He smirked. "It *was* good wasn't it?"

"It was," I assured him as I spread my legs.

"I don't know if I can compete."

"Don't worry about it," I said, finding his hardening cock and pulling it towards me. "Besides," I added as Lucas slid inside me, "There's always the next full moon."

# **S**and

He was the most beautiful man I could have imagined. I named him Chaim. Leaning over, I breathed life into him, saying the unsayable into his mouth.

Nothing happened, of course. Did I really expect the man of my dreams to rise out of the sand at Hilton Beach in Tel Aviv, in front of everyone and their Speedos? I lifted my hand to destroy him.

"Don't do that. He looks so real."

I peered up at the sound of Israeli accented English and saw the outline of a body stretch above me into the sun. I shaded my eyes and details came into perspective: impossibly wide shoulders, tightly narrowed waist, full crotch in a blue speedo, flaring thighs and a camera case dangling down a deep chest, against a flat stomach.

"Usually people make sand castles," the voice said without expression.

I stood. "Netan'el," I said, pronouncing my name in Hebrew.

"Chol," my visitor answered.

"Pardon me?"

"Sand," he said in English. "My last name is Chol. Sand." I knew what the word meant.

I looked at the inert form below us and back to Chol's tanned skin and whitened smile. The resemblance wasn't a delusion. My explanation might be but the resemblance was not.

Chol and I stood together for a moment, staring at his likeness at our feet, until I spoke. "Would you take our photo?"

"Our?"

I dropped to my knees and lay down beside my sandman.

"Good! Good!" Chol said and snapped off a dozen shots.

"One more," I said, placing my wet lips on Chaim's sandy ones. "Hashem," I whispered again, breathing the word into him.

"What did you say?" Chol asked, his forehead frowning over his camera.

"Nothing," I muttered. I sat up and brushed the sand from my lips.

"No. You said the name of God. I heard it. You are trying to make your sandman come alive. He is a golem!"

I stood, brushing sand off my ass and as much off my back as I could. "Would you mind?" I asked, turning my back to Chol, amazed at how forward I was. Without hesitation, he brushed the parts of me I couldn't reach. His hand felt coarse and abrasive against my skin.

"Would you mind if I took a photo of you now?" I asked. He smiled lopsidedly and lifted the camera over his head, looping the lanyard over mine. It settled against my bare chest. Chol's hands held on a moment, as if they were waiting, but he stepped away before I could react and went through a series of phony strongman poses, smiling a goofy smile. His face was more boyish than handsome but his muscles were anything but boyish.

"Excuse me," I said, stopping man in his parade down the beach. "Would you mind taking our photo?" He agreed reluctantly and with ill grace. I pulled Chol close with an arm around his shoulder. Our hips met with a jolt that thickened my cock. The man clicked once and handed the camera back to Chol, not to me.

"Could I see the shots?" I asked Chol. He put them on slide show. "Slower," I told him and he complied. I especially liked the one of us together. Chol's Speedo was bulging as obviously as mine.

"You're good," I told him.

"I hope so," he said, pulling a business card out of the camera case. "Avram Chol, photographer," it announced. I felt the raised letters and slipped it into the waistband of my board shorts. Chol followed the motion of my hand, looking long enough at where it went to prove he wasn't heterosexual.

"Could I buy copies?"

"Pick your favorites. I will make some prints. For free," he added, grinning, which displayed his perfect teeth. He was perfect in every way, everything I had tried to create in Chaim. Could it be? Was he here?

I heard a faraway voice. "Netan'el?"

"Yes," I answered, focusing again. Chol was smiling in a knowing way. "I'm sorry," I said, feeling sheepish.

"There is nothing to be sorry about, Netan'el."

His voice was warm and soft, but his eyes were oddly vacant. I stared at his otherwise ordinary face with its "Jewish" nose and the requisite day or two of beard. "When would you like to meet?" I asked the eyes.

"When do you have time? You are visiting, no?"

"Yes. From Philadelphia."

"Philadelphia," he repeated meditatively.

"I have time now," I said, surprised again at how forward I was. Maybe it was the time constraint. In a few days I would be back in my office, meeting with my clients. I wanted sex with a nice Jewish man before I left. I wanted someone to talk about back home.

"Good," Chol said, turning to go. His ass was perfect too, stretching his Speedo, outlining the crack inside. He looked over his shoulder. "I have a car," he said. He seemed to wait for me to tell him what to do next. I thought Israeli men were supposed to be aggressive.

Sitting next to him in his roadster made me all too conscious of how nearly naked we were. Swimsuits and sandals, that's all either of us wore. My fingers itched to clutch his thigh, situated so invitingly just across the gearshift. Then, he started the engine and shifted into first.

We drove across Tel Aviv, down streets I didn't know until we turned onto Shenkin. Outside an apartment building no different from the rest, he pulled into the garage and found a space. As the door automatically closed, Chol leaned close to me. I could feel his breath on my face.

"What do you want?" he asked.

My mouth opened and we kissed with teeth and tongue until the garage door screeched again behind us. Someone else pulled in, parked and walked to the elevator without a greeting. Perhaps it was our situation, so obviously *in flagrante*. Chol looked at his hard-on and at mine and produced two towels from a storage compartment behind us. We wrapped them around ourselves for the walk to the elevator. Inside his apartment the towels dropped, and we squashed against each other.

"Tell me what you want," he said again. My fingers slid down his back, making him shiver. I felt the fabric of his swimsuit and the beginning of the cleft between his cheeks. His ass muscles tensed. I slipped both my hands inside the swimsuit and ran fingers over his ass, feeling the few hairs growing across its mounds.

"Oh, Tani," he whispered.

As if he'd said the magic word, I dropped to my knees and yanked the Speedo down his legs and off each foot. His cock had no foreskin of course but also no circumcision scar. I inspected it briefly before taking it into my mouth and sucking happily.

"Do you have condoms?" I asked after he began to breathe heavily. He fetched them at a run, bringing lube as well. I applied the lube, then slid a condom on. I eased him onto his back and pushed his legs back with one hand, fingering lube into his ass. When I was done, he wrapped his legs around the small of my back, my cock entered him and I began to fuck. I pounded into him, coming with my head and neck stretched into the air, my mouth open in an extended groan, like wind through time. He jerked off to my groaning. I rolled him on top of me before he finished. His pecs hung down, hairy, with small pink nipples. I reached up to yank them and his mouth opened wordlessly. I handed him a condom, which he eagerly put on, and he began to fuck me. I lay back, happy with his work.

When I let us get up, he removed the condom. "Let me have it," I said, taking it from him. I wasn't sure how I'd get it past El Al screening or through customs but I wanted it. It would be my favorite souvenir from Israel.

We moved to his couch and sat, naked and erect, while I chose my memories of the beach from his selection. I watched him make prints for me, thinking he should never wear clothes. I told him this and he said seriously, "Then I won't," before he winked and added, "While you are here at least." I thought again of how few days I had left. The thought made me bold.

"What are you doing tonight?" I asked him.

"Nothing. What do you want me to do?"

"Let's have dinner together."

"Only dinner?" he asked, with another wink.

"Definitely not," I replied.

We made love again, moving to his bedroom. Chol did whatever I wanted. I had never been so free in my wanting. Afterwards, we lay back against his pillows, holding hands.

"Show me more of your work," I said.

He slid a huge leg across me. "Yes, master."

I pushed his leg away. "Photography."

"Oh that."

He stood and walked out of the room, his stride exciting me, the ass pneumatic, as it was when he fucked. I thought about calling after him, yelling that I'd changed my definition of work but decided to let whatever might happen, happen.

While he was gone, I looked around the room. It was spare of decoration and detail, more like a hotel room than the Hilton was. There were no family photos, just professional shots of landscapes and the sea, sunsets and mountains.

He returned with his laptop and settled back beside me. We spent the rest of the afternoon looking at his beautiful moody photographs of people and surreal landscapes and marine views. When my stomach rumbled, I said I was sorry.

"I am sorry! Let me make you something," Chol said quickly.

"Too close to dinner. I'll survive. Maybe we should shower and get dressed." He pointed out that I had no clothes, beyond my swimsuit and shoes. We compared waist sizes. His pants would fit me well enough, and one of his shirts would do to cover my skin. Neither however would look as good on me as they would on him.

We showered together, washing each other's back, and each dressed in his clothes.

While I threaded one of his belts through my borrowed slacks, Chol sat on the bed with his hands crossed in his lap, watching me, eyes again vacant, mouth again silent.

"What?" I asked as I sat beside him to pull on his socks and my shoes.

"Nothing," he said and I believed him.

We went downstairs to one of his favorite restaurants, nearby and filled with Israelis and the sound of Hebrew. We ate falafel and shwarma and washed them down with a good cabernet from the upper Galilee. After a finishing coffee, we spent the rest of the night and most of the morning making love in Chol's wide bed.

When Chol asked what I wanted to do the rest of my stay, I said, "Take me places I might not find on my own."

We walked down crowded back streets and ate at hole in the wall cafes. We shopped in Arab men's stores and wore the same clothing. We trolled through immigrant markets and bazaars.

At a goldsmith I selected matching chai necklaces for Chol and myself. I hoped they would help us remember each other after I was gone. We wore them in bed, mine hanging over him as I worked my way down his body and while I fucked him. His bounced against his chest as he rode my cock or held itself against mine while he took his turn inside me.

My last night I asked if we could go from dinner to a nightclub. We hadn't really been with other people. I hadn't met any of his friends. Chol looked disappointed but, as usual, didn't object.

"Where can we go?" I asked.

"There are places," he mumbled.

He was moody and depressed, just what I'd hoped to avoid. I wanted us to have fun before my flight back to Philly left in the morning. My bags were all packed and waiting in Chol's apartment by the door.

"Where do you like to go?" I insisted.

Chol looked at me with yearning eyes. I knew what he wanted but ignored it. "Come on, Chol. Let's have fun."

He sighed. "Evita, I guess. It opens early."

"Can we dance?"

"Oh sure," he replied not very enthusiastically. I jumped up and pulled him after me.

Evita was on a side street off Rothschild. The music was loud and the bar was almost empty when we walked in. "It's

Glitter night!" Chol yelled over the noise. I looked around for evidence.

He bought us drinks, which we sipped at a high table near the dance floor. We sat knee to knee, listening to excellent house music. At least I was listening. Every time I looked at Chol, he looked back glum and withdrawn. I finally yanked him off his chair.

"Come on!" I yelled over the music. He barely moved at first but I kept smiling and bobbing in front of him and eventually he got into it. He even started smiling back. I gave him kisses as a reward and he shifted into a higher gear, turning to shake his beautiful ass at me. I moved in close. "So sexy," I tried to whisper into his ear.

More people joined us, mainly men and mainly young. They had their shirts off or removed them on the dance floor. I pulled Chol's off and then mine. I was proud to be with him. Other men looked at him, down his body, but he seemed to have eyes just for me.

Dancers began to jostle us. It was the typical gay club scene: plenty of skin, sweat and smiles. We began "talking" to a couple dancing next to us, one tall and dark, the other dark and short. When they signaled us time for a drink, Chol and I followed them to a table of their friends. They'd chosen to be as far from the dance floor as possible, and we could almost hear each other. They bought us drinks, and then I bought a round. I was having a good time, talking to fun people, leaning on Chol's muscles, partying against the dawn.

"Let's go home," Chol said suddenly, standing up but not taking my hand.

I fumbled for my phone. ""It's still early! Isn't it?" Chol showed me the time: 2300. "Oh, let's stay a little longer. We're having fun." I didn't notice that "we" weren't.

A good song came on and I pulled Chol back to the dance floor again. When that song was over, another really good one began and I kept dancing. Our new friends joined us, squeezing in close. Chol frowned at them and yelled into my ear.

"Let's go home!"

"What?" I asked. He pulled me away. Our companions grabbed at us and yelled we should stay. I tried to stop our forward momentum but Chol kept pulling me. I dug my feet in. He stopped and faced me. His eyes were blazing. The anger in his face scared me, so brutish, so dark.

"I said, 'Let's go home!'"

"I don't want to!" I said more defiantly than I felt. "Since when do you decide what we do?" This new Chol frightened me.

He dropped my hand violently, wrenching my arm. "I have let you decide."

"Then, let me decide now."

"No!" he thundered over the music, making most of the dancers stop mid step. "You like your new friends better than me?" he snarled. "Okay, faggot, go to them!" As he spat the last words out, he pushed me backwards. Hands tried to catch me but I landed on my butt. Someone not Chol helped me up. People were restraining him. He spat words at them too, unintelligible to me through the music. Angry faces shouted back. Chol pushed someone else, and several guys jumped him. I tried to stop the brawl but two of my new friends held my arms.

"Stay out of it," one of them said.

"I can't!" I told them, trying to pull away again. They let me go.

I rushed towards the scrum in time to see Chol erupt from it, a monster of anger and might, pulling strong men off him like they were pieces of lint. He saw me and I held my arms out to him. He grabbed one and yanked me towards the door.

Outside, away from the noise and crowd, he began to calm down. Over and over he said, "I'm sorry," in his normal soft voice. I didn't know what to say so I just enclosed his wide body in my arms and held on. We moved to his car like a single organism.

In Chol's apartment I removed his clothing and mine. He was docile again. We held each other until we fell asleep.

Much too quickly his alarm clock woke us with bird chirps. We kissed until he said, "We have no time," and got up.

We showered together, washing each other's back one more time, like we'd done each day of our almost week together. Chol asked if we had time for coffee. I let him decide.

In between sips he apologized again for the brawl. I needed neither apology nor explanation. I knew the why of the what. I just held his hand and looked into his sad dark eyes.

We dressed in his bedroom, moving together in the easy way we'd developed so quickly. Holding hands, we walked to the door. Chol lifted my bag and backpack, waiting. I looked around his apartment one last time, then opened the door for him. I closed it behind us and set the lock.

We waited for the elevator without speaking and drove in his car to Ben Gurion just as silently. I wanted to say something but no words came to mind that didn't sound extraneous. "I'll miss you" was unnecessary. "Thanks" was unforgiveable. But the unsaid words hung very heavily in the air as we walked to El Al.

Chol saw me to Security. I took my roller bag and backpack from him, then set them down. We hugged and held on for a long time, which was not long enough. My phone gave me its three hour warning. I slung my backpack over one shoulder, grasped the handle of my bag again and turned to walk away.

"You take my life from me!" he yelled. I turned around very slowly.

"You don't have to pretend to be my golem any more, Chol."

He looked at me through his strange, expressionless eyes. "Who said I was pretending?" he asked flatly. "What do I do now? What am I when you're gone?"

He was taking this too far but I understood in his mind I had something to finish. There was a later flight to London. If I couldn't make my connection, there were worse cities to be stuck in. I gave him my bag and took his hand.

We returned to his car. "Shall we go to the beach?" I asked. Chol knew which one I meant. He turned the key in the ignition, the engine started and we drove.

At Hilton Beach Chol followed me to a secluded section. He removed his clothes and lay down at my feet like a dog at his master's, opened his mouth wide and held up his arms to me. I settled onto him, our lips close. I could feel the breath of his life push up into me. I wasn't sure what to say but, staring down at him, it came to me.

My mouth went to his. He closed his eyes. "I love you," I said and kissed him, feeling grains of sand on our lips. His eyes opened, full of doubt.

"Go ahead. Say it."

"No."

"But..."

"There is no but," I interrupted, trying to give him tongue to shut him up, but he pulled his face away.

"I am to live?"

"Of course," I said, reaching for another kiss, which he gave me abstractedly, his mind processing.

"Am I coming with you?"

I could not imagine Chol in the Gayborhood. "No," I told him.

"What then?" he asked.

I fingered his chai necklace, feeling mine against my chest inside my shirt. "I don't know."

"Are you going back to Philadelphia?" The name of my hometown sounded so foreign on his lips.

"I don't know that either. What do you want me to do?

Chol squeezed me tightly. "Stay," he said, breathing the word up into my open mouth. I inhaled the dark and weight and might of him.

"All right," I whispered. There would be other flights on other days. And then I felt my new life enter me, and I waited for whatever was next.

# Fire and Pain

I went back to Mesopotamia after the Great War to dig for history, part of an archaeological expedition sponsored by the University of Pennsylvania. France had changed me. Before the war I had been tentative and unconscious. I was neither in 1919.

As a graduate student and dig veteran, I was given charge of my own archaeological site. It wasn't an important one so my resources were sparse. I had only two undergraduates and barely enough money to hire a handful of local men. The published report, however, would have my name on it.

We were at a small tell in western Iraq, a mound created by human occupation and abandonment over many centuries, a few miles from the Euphrates. Our area was under British control but there was still distrust among the locals and fighting in the south. Even so, Penn had decided to resume work at our site and elsewhere in Iraq on projects in progress before the war.

We had been sifting through dirt and debris at Amayia for weeks, finding bits and pieces left by the peoples who had lived there, one group succeeding the others for millennia. We had found nothing of importance but I appreciated the stories hinted at of Sumer and Akkadia, Babylonia and Arabia.

During the day the sun was almost unbearable so I had adopted the thawb and keffiyeh, which protected me from both sand and sun. I sweated under the long sleeves and ankle length tunic of the thawb but it was better than burning. I wanted to avoid the leathery skin of older hands in the Middle East. I was blond and thought myself good looking.

We rarely saw strangers. We had helpers from nearby villages but they always left before dark. They seemed to be afraid of the site after sunset, but they wouldn't say why. Even Mustafa, our Baghdad guide, couldn't get the truth from them.

Each evening, we three Americans and Mustafa were left on our own, talking around the campfire over which Mustafa had prepared our meal. As the embers began to darken and die, Mustafa would announce he was going to bed and look meaningfully at Eric, one of the undergraduates. At first, Mustafa had been interested in me–he called me Ashqar, blond in Arabic–but he had settled on Eric, because of his youth I assumed. Arab men seemed to like their partners young.

After we all went to our tents, Mustafa would move from his to Eric's. I said nothing when David, the other undergraduate, reported this to me. We were a long way from home, and men must find their comfort somehow. That was something else I had learned during the war.

One night I heard Mustafa tread carefully past me to Eric's tent. I felt restless, envying Eric his Mustafa, knowing David had no interest in male genitalia. I decided to smoke and left my tent wearing only the izaar, a sort of kilt Arabs wear as underwear beneath the thawb. The night was warm. I didn't even drape a keffiyeh around my shoulders.

I lit my cigarette when I was well away from the tents. The match sparked bright. The desert night is a blacker black than you have ever seen, I'll wager. The skies are full of stars and a fullish moon can provide some light, but this was a moonless night and the sky was clouded over.

I puffed in each direction, making a 360 degree survey. When my circuit reached the ruins, they seemed oddly outlined. I realized they were illuminated. I dropped the cigarette, brushed sand over it with a bare foot and loped quietly but quickly to the site. Looters were common at digs in Iraq, like jackals at a kill.

The light was coming from inside the walls we had uncovered. The last few yards, I lowered myself onto all fours and crawled along the southern wall to what, we believed, had been the opening for a door. Carefully, I peered around its edge. There were no looters but there was a fire, dancing in the constant wind. Why would looters start a fire?

I stood and looked all around me, then again at the fire. I couldn't see what fuel was burning. The flames seemed to come directly from the ground.

And then I heard the singing. The voice was deep and within the fire. Its song sounded vaguely Arab, not that I considered myself an expert on Islamic music. I tried stepping closer to the fire, but the unusual heat kept me away.

As I watched, the tall and slender flame stretched to each side into what looked like arms ending in fiery fingers. Flames coalesced upward between the "arms" into an oval mass resembling a head. A lower portion spread and bent to the left, like an upraised leg. The leg settled back to the ground and another leg appeared on the right side and raised and bent. The fire was dancing.

A face slowly appeared in the head as I stared, dark eyes in the flame staring back at me. I wanted to run, to wake up our small camp, but the eyes of the man of fire held me fast. It *was* a man. That was clear.

The head became flesh, then the neck, shoulders, chest and arms. The shoulders were wide, the chest well defined. The upraised arms were slender but long muscled. The abdomen and belly appeared, tight and trim. The mouth was also tight: the face was angry.

In another second the fire vanished entirely and in front of me was a lanky Arab man perhaps in his 30's, clothed in an izaar similar to mine. He looked at me imperiously.

"Who are you?" he asked. "And why are you here?"

I was taken aback and stammered a reply. "My name is Tobias Ventry. I'm head of an archaeological excavation of this site. From the University of Pennsylvania…"

He waved his hand to shut me up. "Tobias? That is a Jewish name."

"I'm not Jewish. I'm Presbyterian." I sounded like an idiot.

"Are you ashamed of being Jewish?" the man asked, slowly advancing in sinuous steps. His hips rotated towards me, legs moving forward loosely from the hips. I felt my cock begin to swell. In no time it was pointing out of my izaar directly at the man. He was close now. He looked down at my erection and in an instance tore my izaar off and tossed it away. He appraised my cock.

"No, you are not Jewish," he announced. "You have a fine cock, Tobias Ventry. Kneel!" he shouted and pushed me to my knees. He removed his izaar and dropped it beside us. When he turned his erection hit me in the face. I opened my mouth in surprise and he shoved inside me. He plunged rapidly into and out of me. I choked and sputtered and tried to protest but nothing stopped him. When I tried to lurch away, the stranger grabbed my nipples and twisted them hard. The pain sent a shock wave through my body.

"Be still, boy," the man hissed. I wanted to say I was no boy but his cock fucking my mouth and his fingers wrenching my nipples prevented my speaking. I had no choice. I held myself still, and his voice grew softer. "You like this, I think. That is good. Do as I say and enjoy."

"Suck me!" he said suddenly, twisting my nipples until I did, then rubbing my shoulders in appreciation. "You do this well. Your master is pleased." I looked up at the word. "Keep sucking!" he spat out, with hatred in his face. He grabbed my chest with both his hands and clamped them hard. "You like this. What else do you like?" He pulled out of me. "Spread my izaar on the sand." I did as he directed. "Lie down." I lay back against his izaar, the sand warming me through it.

He kicked my legs apart with his feet and stared down at me for a time. He nodded to himself, then snarled, "Turn over!" I turned onto my stomach, alarmed but eager. "You have a delectable ass. Up on all fours, boy," he commanded. I heard him kneel behind me and felt him spread my legs wide with his long thighs. I felt the tip of his cock find my asshole. I screamed when it rushed inside me.

"Please! It hurts."

"Quiet!" he hissed and began to fuck me, as fast as he had fucked my face. I cried out again several times, hoping my colleagues would hear. He settled his body onto my back, one arm landing parallel to my right, the hand of the other reaching around to cover my mouth. "I said be quiet. I will fuck you like the dog you are. Do you hear me?" He yanked my head back violently. "I said, do you hear me, boy?" I screamed out a yes.

At that, he seemed to relax and his cruel slamming slowed. He removed his hand from my mouth and slid his left arm next to mine. We were like dogs then, one atop the other, both on all fours, our only motion his resolute pumping into and out of me, the only sound the slapping of his groin against my ass. He rested his head next to mine and began to pant. I did too.

"Yes, I like that sound, boy. Your ass is good. Very good." He groaned and writhed inside me, grinding in pleasure. "Oh, it has been a long time, such a long time." He groaned again into my ear, his breath hot and moist. He sucked and bit my neck. I stifled moans of pleasure. He seemed to know.

"Moan for me, boy. Let me hear you."

I let myself moan then and he fucked me faster, short jabs against my prostate. My cock ached to come and suddenly I was. My mouth fell open in surprise and joy. It had been a long time for me as well. His right hand pushed my head around to his mouth and his tongue fought with mine while he fucked wildly in and out, in and out and then with a tremendous groan spasmed inside me. I felt his sperm, warm and wet.

He withdrew immediately and rose above me, his cock softening. I was still catching my breath, still wondering at the events. "Look at me, slave!" he yelled down at me. "You are mine now, only mine!" My head jerked up. His eyes were full of fire. "You may go now but return tomorrow night when you see the fire. I want more of you, slave. Do you understand? I nodded. "Speak!"

"I understand!"

He kicked me backwards onto the sand. "I understand, Master."

"I understand, Master!"

"Another thing. Do not touch yourself. Your body belongs to me only. Do you understand?"

"I understand…Master," I said, with hesitation.

"Do you understand?" he repeated, taking a step forward and placing a foot above my genitals.

"I understand, Master!" I repeated with much more conviction.

He folded his arms, beautiful and awful above me. He glared, as if he hated the sight of me. "Get out!" he said, taking up my izaar and wrapping it around himself.

"But…"

"Get out!"

I rose to run but he restrained me with a long arm. "Wear this," he said, picking up his izaar from the ground. I stood, amazed and frozen. "Put it on. Now!" I did, immediately. He looked at it, turning me around, patting me on the ass and fingering my nipples. He smiled to see my cock rise again. "Good boy. Until tonight." And then I heard the crackling of flames and felt a sudden intense heat. I staggered away from the fire and ran out of the ruins through the sand, not daring to look back.

All the next day I hardly accomplished anything. I thought only of nightfall. I wanted the strange man's hands on my chest, his tongue in my mouth, his cock up my ass. I had an erection off and on all day. I wanted badly to relieve myself but remembered his command. By the end of the day, I was frantic.

That night, after Eric and Mustafah had begun their play and David was in his tent, reading I suppose, I ran to the ruins, even though the fire had not shown itself as yet. I smoked while I waited.

The fire appeared first as a single, tiny flame and then grew into the sky, spreading tall and wide. The eyes showed themselves in the flames before the body appeared. They flashed angrily.

"You disobeyed me!"

"But…"

"I did not tell you to speak. You disobeyed me. I told you to wait for the flames."

My head dropped. "I…"

"Shut up! You will learn to obey your master. Go! You sicken me."

I couldn't believe we weren't going to have sex. I had barely gotten through the day; I had to have him inside me. I dropped to my hands and knees and crawled towards him. The fire was scorching but I kept crawling. I kept my head down. I felt the fire decrease. I sensed the presence of the man, like a scent.

"You are a dog," he hurled down at me but less angrily than I thought he would and, like a dog, I began to hope. There was silence. I couldn't keep it though. I whimpered in spite of myself. "The dog speaks. He wants his master's attention." I looked up. "All right, dog. Take this." He held his cock out for me and I crawled to it, taking its full length in one gulp, not choking or gasping. I held it there, waiting for his command.

"Good," he said, while he thickened inside my mouth. "I will teach you how to suck a man's cock. Follow my instructions or this bone will be taken from you." He removed his cock from my mouth. I whimpered again.

"Stop this whimpering, dog. Lick the length of my cock, from the base to the head. Slowly." I did as he commanded and heard him groan with pleasure. "Now, back down to the base." I did this and repeated what I had learned. When I reached the head the third time, he commanded, "Lick the head, all around it." I did this carefully and slowly, loving the feel of him and becoming excited by the pleasure I was giving him.

"Suck the head, boy," he said in a raspy voice. A shudder went through his body when I did. His fingers clamped onto my nipples and he began to face fuck me again. He sneered as he did. "See, your master is kind to his dog. He pays attention to your breasts." He twisted and pulled my nipples. I yelped. "Keep your mouth tight, slave!" He yanked my nipples and clutched at my chest more wildly, the faster his cock pumped in and out of my mouth. The pain became pleasure. I pressed my chest out to meet his hands.

"That is good, boy. You are ripe," he said, with an evil laugh. He withdrew his cock. I knew now not to protest.

I waited while he spread his izaar on the sand. "Lie down," he commanded. I crawled onto the cloth on all fours. "I said lie down! On your back, fool!" I turned over as quickly as I could. "Undo your izaar." I opened it like a package. He stared down at my upright cock. He knelt and I spread my legs. "Wait! I will tell you what to do and what not to do!" I put my legs back together and he placed a thigh on either side of them, holding me in place. I watched him bend his head to my cock and take it into his mouth. He sucked gently, cupping my balls in his hands, before lifting my legs into the night air. I felt joyous, knowing his cock would soon be inside me.

When he entered I could hardly keep myself from coming immediately but I did as he said, wrapping my legs around his back, letting my arms be held down by his, holding still beneath him as he fucked, slowly this time, letting me feel each inch as he eased cock in and out of me. I could not keep myself from roiling beneath him, although I was afraid it would displease him. But, on the contrary, he smiled.

"You are excited, boy?"

I moaned.

"Tell me, boy. Tell me," he commanded. I moaned freely as he withdrew and cried out as he plunged himself back deep inside me. I heard his groans above me and knew he was pleased. I felt fire travel down his body and through his cock into me. He banged against my prostrate repeatedly and I shrieked, begging for release.

"Come, boy," he commanded at last and I pressed up against his groin as I shot and shot. His release was timed to mine; I felt his seed eject inside me. We rode together like a ship on waves of sand.

When he came no more, I expected he would pull out of me immediately, as he had before, but he stayed inside and settled himself onto me, letting our bodies meld together. I heard the night wind of the desert. I felt his hands grip my shoulders and his beard scratch at my clean shaven face. When he did withdraw and stand, he pulled me up with him.

"You did well today, boy. You kept yourself for me. Now," he said, slapping me hard on one cheek. "Tomorrow night wait for the flames!" He turned his back on me and strode away, his body beautiful in its retreat, pale olive in color and lightly covered with dark hair. He picked up my izaar and wrapped it around his body. His head and shoulders turned to me and his black eyes flashed. "Why are you still here, slave? Go!" I grabbed his izaar and ran out of the ruins back to my camp.

The next work day was easier. I thought of him all day but knew we would have the night. If I did as he said, we would have the night.

After dinner, through stupid conversation, I waited for my men to go to bed and then waited hungrily for the flames. When they appeared I hurried towards the ruins, kicking up dry sand as I ran. I charged into the dig, chest heaving. He was already becoming a man.

He smiled at me for the first time. "You are eager, Tobias. So am I. Come here." I walked, then ran to him. Tobias! He had called me by my name!

He held me at arm's length, looking down my body. "You are beautiful. I have known many men. You are beautiful among them." He pulled me to him and held me close. His voice rumbled from his chest to mine with his next words.

"Tonight we will try something new. You are ready." He reached for an object on the ground and, rising, attached a clamp to one of my nipples. I stifled the yell, which pleased him, so I made sure to take the second clamp without as much as a grimace. He held my shoulders and kissed me as my reward before beginning a tugging at the clamps. I grit my teeth and tried not to think about how much it hurt. I hoped pleasure would follow pain. It did, like none I'd ever felt before. It was better than the common nipple play of other men, better even than his fingers at my chest.

He smiled again at me, a real smile, not a sneer. "Good, Tobias. You see? Pleasure from pain. There will be more. You will feel worse pain this night—and greater pleasure." He pushed me to my knees, reached down for the clamps and yanked them hard. I opened my mouth in a silent scream and his cock entered it. My reward! I sucked him happily and the pain in my nipples blended with the pleasure of his cock.

After too short a time, he pulled his cock from my mouth and began to bludgeon my face with it. I lifted my chin to take each blow. "Good," he said. "You like a beating. Stand, slave. Turn your back to me. Bend over and hold your knees."

While I did I heard him moving behind me. I knew not to look around or ask what he was doing.

When the first lash hit my back I yelled involuntarily, loudly, loudly enough so that he stopped and we both listened for any sounds from my camp. There were none. He gagged me to prevent more yelling.

"You will learn, boy, to welcome this and not to cry out but for now…." And then the second lash hit and the third and fourth. There was a pause between each one while the wind brushed the wound and made its sting linger. I kept myself crouched over and tried to welcome each blow. He said there would be more pain *and* more pleasure. I relaxed the muscles of my back and ass and began to welcome the blow. He could tell this and removed my gag.

"It is good, is it not, my beautiful boy?" His hand caressed my back, fingers sliding along the slits in my skin, making each tingle with pleasure–and pain. He pressed his groin against my ass and entered, beginning the fuck.

Afterwards, he held me gently against him and said loving words in an Arabic I could barely understand. He applied salve to my back. When he dismissed me, it was without anger or threat. I walked away that night and dared to look back. He was still a man, watching me leave him.

In the morning, I felt no pain at all from the beating. I looked at my back with a small mirror. There were no marks. The salve had worked a miracle.

That night, after applying the clamps and playing with my chest for some time, he beat me with a short whip, like a riding crop, across my chest and legs, taking care not to hit my erection or my testicles. Somehow, it hurt worse than the lash. I could not help crying out. He stopped.

"You do not want this, boy?" He forced my head down and held his cock for me to see. "Here, I will give you a taste to encourage your better efforts." He pushed me to my knees, and I eagerly took his cock. One, two minutes passed and then he pulled away. "There will be more. Take the pain, boy, and there will be more."

I did my best not to scream, not to anticipate or feel the pain or think about it after. I went into a kind of trance in which I heard the crack of the whip and felt its touch but did not acknowledge pain. He stopped and lifted my chin with two thick fingers and smiled down at me. "Very good. Your reward, slave," he said, sliding his cock into my mouth. "Suck!"

This time, he came in my mouth and I tasted him and swallowed. He patted my head affectionately. "That is good, Tobias. Take all of me you can. Each swallow, in your mouth or ass, makes you mine."

I kept swallowing, threading my tongue into his foreskin, letting it search for every drop of him. I wanted to be his. I needed it now.

He beat me again, across the back, then rode me as he beat me more, like a horse he was spurring on. And I was spurred on. I held my back up to take the beating, my ass up to take the fucking. He pulled my head back by my hair as he rode and beat me. I had been his dog. Now I was his horse. I came when he said I could and felt him come inside me. More of me was his now. I waited for his next command, still panting from the ride.

He knelt behind me, gently running his fingers over the marks of the lash. They soothed the burn. Then he rose and left. I turned to see him walking into the ruins. My eyes watched the syncopation of his walk, the swing of his ass, the proud lift of his head, and yearned for his body back on mine. He disappeared into the farthest walls we had so far excavated.

I waited, hopeful for his return, fearful he would not. I waited on all fours, my welts stinging in the night air, my tits aching with the clamps. He hadn't given me leave to get up.

I heard him come back before I saw him.

"Good! You didn't move. My boy learns quickly." He knelt beside me and his hands began to spread the soothing salve across my back. His touch was as healing as the ointment. "You did very well, Tobias. I am proud of you. Your master is proud of you. Do you hear? You may speak," he added.

"Thank you, Master. I hear." I wanted to say more. There was begging inside my mouth, but I was quiet, waiting, feeling his hands gentle and warm. My cock grew large again. He reached under my body for it and chuckled. "My boy wants more." He kissed my back. "There will be more, beautiful one but not tonight. You must heal again. Tomorrow, Tobias. Tomorrow there will be more. Stand up."

He removed the clamps and put salve on my nipples and in the places on my front where the lash had licked, then wiped his hands on my izaar and held my face up for one kiss, the softest he had given me, sweet and full on my lips. "Go now," he said gently. "Heal and keep yourself for me again." He took my izaar, his izaar, I didn't know any more, and vanished in the flames.

Our excavation and examination continued during the day and my pain and pleasure during the night over several weeks. When it came time to make my next report, my superiors in Baghdad received it with small smiles. "You've done well, Toby. Very well. We didn't think there would be much at Tell Amayia, but you've found more than we expected. You've earned a better assignment. Go back to Amayia to finish up and then take a few weeks back in the States. You'll hear from us what's next for you." They stood up and shook my hand. I did not smile and barely thanked them. I would be leaving Tell Amayia. I would be leaving my master.

I spent the night in Baghdad at a fine hotel, under clean white sheets and an overhead fan to keep the heat away. I thought of my master. I had told him I would be gone a night. He gave me permission but instructed me to save myself for him even so.

The next night, in the ruins, when he appeared in the fire, he saw immediately something was wrong. He commanded me to tell the story and I did.

For some time he thought. I waited in silence, daring to watch him. Finally, he asked, "You do not want to leave, to return to your home, to go on to some better dig, as you call it?"

"No."

"And why is that?"

"You, Master."

"A good answer, boy." I felt something like love cross from him to me. "I have reached my decision. Dig tomorrow as usual but in a further place than you have reached before." He took me to the exact spot.

The next day I did as my master instructed. At first, there was confusion among my students. Why were we digging so far from our last point of excavation? But when the hurrahs were raised, I knew they had found the answer. Eric and David came running from the spot to my table, where I was working on my written summation of the dig.

"Come quickly, Toby!" they yelled at me together. I trotted after them as they ran.

At the exact spot my master had shown me, the men had found a cache of clay tablets in what looked like Akkadian script and numerals, as well as vessels of copper, silver and gold. It looked as if this mound of sand and debris was something more than a poor outpost after all. I calmed everyone down and directed a careful uncovering and cleaning of the finds. We would need more help and more time to deal with these fantastic new discoveries.

That night, my Master asked how my day had gone, which he had never done before. I described the discoveries, and he smiled in amusement.

"There will be more, boy, many more," he predicted. "I give you leave to go to Baghdad to tell your superiors, as you call them. But do not stay the night. Return to me, Tobias. I did not like the parting last time." His eyes showed more than I had dared hope for, even in dreams.

"Master, may I…"

"Yes," he answered, as if he knew my thoughts. I stepped towards him and we embraced, the dark of his body against the light of mine. "You see, you will not need to leave after all," he said into my shoulder. "And I will have time, much more time to teach you more delights. Does this make you happy?"

"Yes, Master."

He pulled himself to arms length from me, his eyes serious. "My name is Jinn, Tobias. Say it."

"Jinn," I croaked out.

"Jinn," he repeated firmly.

"Jinn," I responded in a stronger voice.

"Good," he said softly, folding me back into him. "We are master and slave, Tobias, but we are more now and will be for the rest of your life." He caressed my back that he would soon be beating and fondled my breast where the clamps would soon pinch and be pulled. I felt impatient for the lash and the clamps but knew I must wait. My master would give me what I needed when he knew best. I made myself relax into the strong clasp of his arms and the heat of his body.

The silence was thick around us. The stars gave light from above. Jinn removed my izaar and discarded his. Then, he began.

# MYTHS

# Kakouhthe: Cyclone Man

The land under my feet is still new to us. Indian Territory, the whites call it. We Shawnee came to it reluctantly from Kansas and, before that, Ohio. Kansas was about the same as here: not many trees, flat, a huge empty sky. My parents talk about Ohio, the hills and forests, the many rivers. I dream their stories.

My name is Weyapiersenwah but that is too long so most people call me Hokolesqua, Cornstalk, because I grew so tall so fast. Cornstalk is better than Lalewthika, He Makes Noise. My grandfather named me that because I came crying out of my mother. I'm glad everyone forgot that name after I was five or so.

I am 16 now, the oldest of five children, the first to live. I was born to be a hunter, like my father and his father, but it is hard to hunt with so little land and so little game. We farm now like the whites told us to, my father working alongside my mother, my brothers and sisters and I alongside them. I hear the stories about our warrior grandfathers and feel sorry for my father and for myself. Is he less of a man than they because he does not hunt or fight in battle? Am I a man if I have not taken scalps for the French? The French are gone anyway.

I think a lot these days about what it is to be a man. My mother talks of finding me a wife; she says I would make a good husband. She never explains why. I do work hard in the fields and am already allowed to sit in council, as long as I sit in the back and keep quiet. I am, people say, good looking and built strong. People say I am a man, but I am not so sure. A man takes a woman, they have children, they make a life together.

I will tell you this because you are no one, just sky and earth. I do not want to take a woman. I am two spirit; I know this. From early days I have known it, playing with Strong Heart, my best friend, touching him in ways he allowed me then but not since his manhood ceremony. I do not touch boys or men like that these days, but I see them and still want to.

I am talking to you, sky and earth, because there is no wind today, no wind to carry my foolish words to ears I do not know. The sounds will fall from my mouth to you, earth, and be trampled by my feet.

But in the distance, as I say this, I see someone coming. He is moving fast. As he approaches, I can see that he is dancing. He must be crazy to be dancing out here on the empty plains. Doesn't he see me? As he comes close, I can see he does. His eyes are fixed on me, dark like night. His skin is tanned and his body well muscled. He wears only a breechcloth and a thong to hold it in place low on his hips. My stare does not offend him; he sees and does not look away. I feel my penis harden inside my pants and I am shy, afraid he will see it too. I turn away from the dancing man, but he whirls around me and laughs.

"Don't be afraid of me, Cornstalk. I won't hurt you."

"How do you know my name?" He doesn't look like a Shawnee but he speaks our language. He looks like a wild Indian from the plains to the west and they *are* crazy. They still fight. Of course, this was their land before we came. I would be crazy too and fight if another people invaded my land. I think this and realize I would not. We Shawnee fought the whites when they invaded our land. It did no good. We still wound up here.

The whirling man laughed again when I asked my question. He *is* crazy. I decided to go back to the village or at least the fields where people were working, but the long fingers of his hands held my shoulders from behind. My cock grew larger, with this handsome, almost naked man just inches behind me.

"Stay, Hokolesqua. I have a secret to tell you."

His hands felt good on my shirt and on the skin beneath it. He turned me in his hands to face him. I stood waiting and silent. When someone tells you a secret it is important. It is trust. I was determined to listen carefully, no matter how good his hands felt.

"First, my name. I am Kakouhthe."

I had never heard of anyone with this name. It means Cyclone Person. I had heard it before, however, in a story my mother told us about the whirlwind. I wondered if this were the secret. Kakouhthe laughed as if he could read my thoughts. I liked the sound of his laughter and the opening of his lips to make it. I liked the dance I saw in his eyes.

"No, that is not the secret. I didn't say it was my secret. It is yours, Hokolesqua. Shall I tell you?"

I tried to squirm away, wanting to run. I only had one secret. How could this stranger know it? He held me fast though. I fought him with all my training, tripping him and landing on top of his body when he fell, holding his arms and legs down with mine. I could feel his cock; he was as hard as I. I relaxed and he pushed up and whirled me onto my stomach, settling first his legs on my legs, then his cock along the crack of my ass, holding the rest of himself above me with brown arms while he rubbed his cock up and down. I tried to roll away but only managed to turn to face him. His cock aligned itself with mine and continued its rubbing. My breath grew heavy and Kakouhthe grinned.

"This is your secret, is it not, Hokolesqua? Don't worry. I won't tell anyone. It will be just between us." He laughed as if he had made a joke. With no more words he ripped my shirt off in shreds, his mouth finding my chest. I tried not to like his lips on my nipples, his hands on my breasts, squeezing roughly. It did not matter. Kakouhthe paid no attention to me beyond my body, pulling down my pants and nodding approvingly at my erection. He kissed and licked it. It was impossible now not to moan, not to want more. He knew.

Kakouhthe released my arms and stood up, his bare legs standing on either side of my hips, the feet holding me in place. I watched as he untied the breechcloth belt and as the cloth floated down to me. It covered me as it uncovered him. He was pale only in a thin line across his abdomen and around his cock. He let me appreciate his body and his manhood for a few moments before he bent to remove my pants completely in one sudden yank over my boots. He smiled again and leaned down, picking up the fallen breechcloth where it lay across my groin. He knelt and held it against my face.

I smelled the musky smell of a man, strong and not unpleasant. No, not unpleasant. I drew in this good smell with a deep breath and held it in my lungs for as long as I could. When I exhaled Kakouhthe tossed the breechcloth aside and pulled me up with him.

"Come," he said, dropping my hand and beginning to run. "Bring your things."

I grabbed my clothes and his and ran as quickly as I could after him. He was heading for some trees along a creek still flowing. I kept him in my sight. He had my secret now; I wanted to share more of it with him.

When I reached the trees he was in the water. There was enough to run over his long brown body as he lay in its path, elbows supporting his shoulders, his head back to catch the sun, long hair dipping into the stream. As I ran up, panting, he raised his head and stared at my cock, which tossed from side to side as I ran.

"You are large, Hokolesqua. Would you like to fuck me first?"

I could not think of anything I had ever wanted to do more. I nodded yes. He rose from the creek, water streaming down and around the long muscles of his body. I could not believe he was giving me this gift.

He waited for me to come to him. I was hesitant but knew I must be the man. I had been with Strong Heart. I remembered how.

With quick strides I brought myself next to him, his wet skin touching my dry. I put my arms around him and kissed his face and neck and chest, paying careful attention to his nipples on my way to his cock. Strong Heart had always liked this.

I held his cock in my left hand while I licked down his abdomen. I looked up to see Kakouhthe's face, his eyes closed, lips parted just enough. But to do these things under the open sky was embarrassing for me. I looked for a place in the trees, out of sight. I saw a good one.

He followed me without hesitation or sound as I led him by the hand through the brush to the spot, under the largest of the small trees. I began to kiss his body, jerking his cock even more alive with my right hand. His grunts made me know he was enjoying himself and I became more confident, more aggressive in my lovemaking. I fed myself into his mouth and fucked it as I stood above him. The only sounds now were my groans and the slap of my balls against his chin.

I felt close to coming and pulled out before I could. I knew what a man did, where a man came. I made him turn onto his stomach and raise himself up under me. I felt the collision of his skin against mine like lightening striking the earth. He raised his ass to me, and I kissed his broad back in thanks. I found his asshole with my cock.

When I slid into Kakouhthe, I felt the wind rush in my ears and around my body. I felt drawn up into the sky, as if we were flying, as if we were whirling in some ancient sacred dance, the two of us joined by my cock. The wind whirled faster and faster as I pushed myself into and out of Kakouhthe. I heard shouts and moans and long groans in the wind as I pounded into him faster and faster. When I came, the sky blackened and I could no longer see or feel. I only heard the wind and our screaming. Kakouhthe was coming too.

When our panting lessened and the world around us returned, my cock softened inside Kakouhthe and dropped out.

"I am sorry," I said, ashamed.

"It's my turn anyway," he said, still on all fours under me, turning his head to laugh. "But first a bath in the stream." He scuttled out from under me and stood up, hands on his hips, eyes sparkling like sun on water. I took his offered hand and stood up next to him. He held me close, our groins touching, eyes watching eyes.

"Maybe not," he said without a smile, feeling our cocks harden against each other. He took me in a rush, without preliminaries, pushing me down on all fours, fucking me like a dog. I howled like one as the wind swirled around us again, lifting us up in a dream, his legs and hands alongside mine. We came and fell to earth again like a thud in my heart. Kakouhthe stayed on top of me, still hard, then just as suddenly as he had taken me, withdrew and stood up. I tried to stand as well but found my legs would not support me yet. I heard him chuckle.

"Stay in that position then, beautiful man. I like to see your ass ready for me." I got up to my knees and he laughed. "That is a good position, too!" He pulled me up into an embrace. "I must go, pretty one, but I will return for you. Tell your people you have met me but do not say what we have done." He winked and chuckled again. "It is enough that we know." He began to run off, faster than before. Over his shoulder he yelled into the wind, "Save yourself for me!"

I thought about this as I gathered my clothing. I walked to the stream to clean our seed off my body; Kakouhthe's was leaking from my ass. I washed mine off only. I decided to wear his under my pants and shirt.

In the council of the elders, I asked permission to speak for the first time. I did as Kakouhthe had instructed; I told them of my encounter with Cyclone Man. Everyone listened, even the wisest and oldest and most brave. When I was silent again, there were murmurs. I could hear what they said, disbelieving and disapproving, but then Nawahtahtha, our peace chief, spoke above the noise.

"We have all heard of Cyclone Man. The old stories talk of his power and of his benevolence. He said he would come again?" I nodded yes. "We must be ready to receive him."

Under the Council's orders, everyone began strengthening their houses with fresh lumber, repairing faults in their roofs, adding shutters to their windows if they had none. Every floor was swept clean each day. Everyone mended and washed their best clothes.

As the days passed, many of the people asked me questions. The men asked how strong he was, the women how he looked. I answered truthfully but hoped my feelings didn't show on my face or in my pants.

One day the air was strangely quiet. No birds chirped in the trees around our village; they seemed to have vanished. Even our chickens, who usually roamed everywhere in the streets, refused to come out of their small houses. Our dogs seemed anxious, as if a visitor were coming.

My family was working our fields. In the stillness I heard my name called, my given name, the name people never spoke. The voice belonged to Tahlonteeskee, our doctor.

"Weyapiersenwah," he repeated. "Cyclone Man is coming. You must go out to greet him. He will expect it." He looked at me, in my breechcloth, sweating and dirty. "Prepare yourself."

My father gave his assent and I ran off, eager to be with Kahouhthe again. I washed quickly and put on my best clothing, a necklace and several arm bands. My mother added her most elaborate necklace to mine, looping it over my head. As she settled it onto my chest, she looked at me approvingly but sadly too. There was no time to ask why.

My father placed his ceremonial headdress on my hair and held my shoulders, smiling. I felt a strange feeling come over me, as if I were a bride being prepared for her wedding. Perhaps I was.

All the people followed me out onto the prairie towards where I had met Kakouhthe, but after a few yards Tahlonteeskee spoke to Nawahtahtha and he in turn shouted to the families.

"Stop! Weyapiersenwah must be the first to greet Cyclone Man. Go ahead, Weyapiersenwah. Give him our greetings."

I had turned to hear Nawahtahtha's words. I smiled at my family and at all the people lined in an arc around me. They would see how handsome Kakouhthe was and how good.

I set my feet towards the plains again. In the distance I saw him coming, the wind stirred by his racing feet creating a cyclone dark against the cloudless sky, so huge above the small earth. I ran to meet him.

He ran more quickly than I of course. As we neared each other, Kakouhthe grew taller and wider and much darker in the sky, larger, far larger than the first time we met. I thought this must mean that he was eager to be with me again and was running harder, stirring up more dust in his hurry. I felt my cock rising and my nipples tightening. I would be ready when he arrived.

At last I felt the edges of him, the first hint of wind between my legs and into my shirt, across my chest and around my back. I spread my legs and opened my arms to make it easier for him.

The wind pushed harder at me now. I leaned my head back to accept it and felt its caresses on my neck, its kisses on my lips and face. Kakouhthe was with me, lifting me up into himself in front of all the people, tearing my clothing from me with the fierceness of his fingers. I felt myself naked and entered, Kakouhthe's cock inside me and pushing so eagerly that I rose even higher in the sky, whirling, whirling up, held by his strong arms and impaled by his member.

I felt myself coming and screamed into the winds. I screamed and screamed until the world was gone and so were we. There was no more Cornstalk and no more Cyclone Man. We were one in the wind. The sacrifice had been made.

# HUNTING

The boys of the manhood ceremony came with us on the hunt. Around the first campfire, they asked me to tell how Kayode and I had founded Ilobu. No matter how many times they hear the story, they want to hear it again.

I wondered if I should tell them the truth this time. Shouldn't someone else know before I die? Kayode of course knew the secret part, but he has been with the ancestors for years now.

Back then, in Oyo town, when I was a new man like these boys, I was proud and certain of my place in the world. My father was the oba, and I would be king after him. I would marry several wives, father many children and live my life in Oyo. But that was before Erinle came to me.

It was on a hot and humid day. We new men had been hunting together. We had found meat and sent a runner back to town. Women came to cut up the meat and carry it to Oyo. Our work, the man's work, was done. I suggested we go to the waterfall to cleanse ourselves and relax. I started trotting. I knew they would follow.

This waterfall was the happy result of an unimportant stream plunging over a sudden escarpment. It became the pool we loved to swim in. When we reached the grassy bank above the pool, we shed our loincloths and scrambled down the rocks. As usual, I tried not to look at the naked bodies of my friends too closely. My cock rose so quickly in those days.

Kayode was especially difficult for my eyes to avoid. He had been a pretty boy but thin. Now his skinny body had broadened and stretched. Although not so tall as I, he was deeper of chest and thicker in his legs. His ass was like ripe bara melons, hard skinned but sweet within. I saw it bobble as he trotted ahead of me, and I ran faster for the water.

The eight of us swam and splashed each other for quite some time. I hoped my cock would go down but it was stubborn. It insisted I take care of it so I climbed out of the water and ran towards the dense growth of trees and bushes past the grassy bank.

"Where are you going, Laarosin?" my friends yelled after me.

Without stopping or turning around, I yelled back, "To take a pee!" They laughed and continued to splash and shout insults at one another.

The grove was cool but did nothing to remove the heat of sex from my body. I looked around to make sure there was no one to watch and began to stroke myself. It would not take long and then I could rejoin my friends. My eyes closed with the pleasure.

"*Ya oju*," I heard. "Open your eyes, Laarosin," a deep voice commanded. I did, startled that I was not alone. A few feet from me I saw an older man dressed in fabulous woven fabrics, cotton and silks. He was handsome and well built.

"Lord Erinle!" I shouted and dropped to my knees. I was in the presence of the god of hunting.

"Shh," the god said. "You do not want to bring your friends, do you?" He walked quickly towards me. "Here, this will keep you quiet." I felt the tip of his cock press against my lips and opened my mouth in surprise. He quickly slid inside me but pulled himself nearly out again, then in, then out. I had wondered what a man's cock would feel like but this was a god, not a man.

"Now, do this for me," Erinle instructed. I stood immediately, at first eager but then shy. How could I insert my *oko* into the mouth of a god? Erinle solved my dilemma by kneeling and taking me into his mouth on his own.

It felt so good, too good. I knew I would erupt soon. I tried to pull away. Erinle looked up at me, let me go and laughed.

"What? So soon, Laarosin? I will have to instruct you in the art of waiting. It increases the pleasure, I assure you." He stood then and removed his robes entirely. His body was more beautiful than that of any human. Mine ached for it.

Erinle lay back on the accumulated leaves under the alawefon trees and held his hands up to me. "Lie on top of me, Laarosin. *Eko re bere.* Your lessons begin."

I hesitated a moment but the god insisted so I settled myself carefully onto him. My body began to smolder wherever it touched his, but when he moved my hands to his chest I could not do as he told me.

"I am man and woman, Laarosin, depending on my partner. With you now, I am woman. Play with my chest like you would a woman's."

I did as he commanded and felt relieved to see him smile and sigh at my touch. When he turned onto his stomach and rose to all fours, I knew what was next but waited to be told.

"Enter me, Laarosin." The expected, and hoped for, words seemed like an incantation. I rushed to obey. Erinle winced and said, "*Laiyara, omo!* Slowly, boy! You do not want to injure your partner."

I made a note and slowed the progress of my cock into the god, listening as well as feeling. When I was full inside, I held myself in place, not daring to move.

"Fuck me, Laarosin!" the god said sharply, looking over his shoulder. "You do know how to fuck, don't you?" I did. I had seen animals fucking and once a man and woman in the bush. I began to move inside Erinle, my first time inside anyone, man or woman. Or god.

I could not stop smiling as I pushed and pulled myself into and out of Erinle's ass. I could have come within seconds but Erinle made me take my time, to increase my pleasure and let him find his. When we were panting, he put his cock in my hand to bring him close. When we were groaning, his insides clenched around my cock and there was wet in my hand. He had come! The idea and the feeling made me lose control, and I pounded my seed into the ass of the god again and again.

"*O seun.* Thank you, Lord Erinle," I gasped out, my body collapsing on top of his.

"*O kaabo.* You are welcome, young prince. You did very well. Now, look over your shoulder at your friend."

My head jerked around. Kayode was not ten feet from us, eyes changing from intent to alarmed. I pulled myself out of Erinle and stood, wanting to run, but Erinle stood with me and held me fast with his strong right hand and arm.

"Don't be afraid, friend of Laarosin. Come," Erinle said to Kayode and beckoned him with his free hand. I could see Kayode also wanted to run, but no one refuses a god and lives. He started slow steps towards us. His cock was hard. It was short and thick, like him. The god placed my hand in my friend's. "This man is yours," he told me. "Do with him as you have done with me."

Kayode hung his head, denying what his cock told us. I hesitated, because of this and because it was one thing to fuck a god and quite another to fuck a man.

Erinle's voice grew stern. "It is your wish and my command. *Se o ye?* Do you understand?" I nodded and looked at Kayode. I did want him, so much. Erinle pressed us closer until our outstretched cocks touched. We continued into an embrace. "Good," Erinle said and disappeared into the day.

Kayode's muscled shoulders felt like granite beneath my hands. I whispered to him, "Is this your wish?"

"Yes," he whispered back. I brought his chest against mine, my long arms reaching around him, hardly believing the gift I was being given. I began to knead the tense muscles of his back and then his bulging ass, the feeling of it better than any imagining. With that, our bodies took over and I did with Kayode what I had done with the god.

It is blasphemy to say, I know, but sex with Kayode was even better than with the god. We came once on all fours, then side to side, then Kayode on top of me. He let me take and take.

When at last we could stop, I noticed the sun was low through the trees. I listened for but didn't hear the voices of our friends. Carefully, keeping Kayode's hand in mine, I crept through the brush and looked through to the waterfall and pool. No one was there.

"*Nwon ni osi.* They are gone," I told Kayode.

"I'm not surprised," he said and we both laughed. I released his hand and ran towards the pool, Kayode close behind me. We dove together into the cleansing waters, splashed at one another like boys and then struggled onto the bank. When we were dressed again, we ran to Oyo town. We knew how late we were.

Through the months ahead, we hid our love from everyone but Erinle, who returned to us from time to time with more instructions and commands. One was to marry and father children. "You have a responsibility to your people," Erinle told us.

Another was that Kayode would become a doctor. Erinle was the god of healing as well as hunting. Kayode obeyed the god, learning everything he could from our own doctors before my father sent him to Lagos to learn from theirs. He did not return for two years. I had messages from him and sent him mine, but what are slow words across long miles? My body felt like half of itself without him.

I also obeyed the god. In Kayode's absence I married and fathered two sons, one each year of my marriage. My father was proud of my potency and my mother was happy with her first grandchildren.

I could have had another man, taken another lover in Kayode's absence, but I did not want to. I wanted Kayode so I waited and hoped he would return.

On another hot summer day when the humidity and heat had driven everyone inside at midday, I heard a terrible ruckus and rushed outside with my weapons. People were running from their dwellings towards the entrance to our town, yelling greetings at the top of their voices, with trills and songs, dancing on the way. Someone important was arriving. I ran to see who.

When the crowd reached the main road, I saw Kayode floating in the sky on the shoulders of two strong men. I wanted to be one of those men, the only man. I rushed to them and pulled Kayode onto my shoulders, looping one of his legs over my head so that he rode me like a master rides his beast. I knew he still cared for me. I felt the proof of it solid against my neck.

When we reached the town square, I was afraid to set him down, both because I didn't want to expose his erection in front of all the people and because I didn't want to lose the touch of him again so soon.

But Kayode struggled so I bent my back and he slid to his feet. I looked at his groin. He was wearing loose Arab clothing; there was no sign of an erection. I wondered if I had dreamt it. I had had so many dreams of him.

He grinned broadly and waved the crowd silent. He thanked them for their welcome and said he was glad to be home. He added that he had learned a great deal and would take good care of the people.

My father came to us, the people parting in respect. On behalf of all of us, he welcomed Kayode back but chastised him for not sending word.

"We would have had a house prepared."

"My old house with my parents is fine." Everyone murmured their approval of his modesty. I could not take my eyes off him. He wore a beard now, also Arab style. His skin had lightened from his indoor work. I wanted to stroke it with my darker hands.

"Tell us about all you have seen and studied," someone cried out, startling me awake from my idle daydream. I heard others agree.

My father silenced the shouts. "Our son is tired. He has come so far, out of loyalty, to be with us again. *Je ki i ni isimi.* Let him rest."

"Not just out of loyalty," Kayode said so quietly I am sure I was the only one to hear him. He looked at the ground as he said it. Kayode had never taken a wife, no matter what the god had said. He looked up at me and smiled. It took everything not to pull him to me in front of all the people.

My father led Kayode and his parents to their house. His mother and sisters brought water for cleansing and then food and drink. I sat with him, watching him refresh his face and hands, eating and drinking with him for a few minutes before Father commanded me to leave. I went back to my own house, a place Kayode had never been. I saw my wife working in her garden, carrying the baby, my older boy at play beside her. I thought of Kayode and myself while I watched them. My wife's body suddenly disgusted me. I ran away from her, into the country.

My run took me up the hills, following the path to the waterfall. I came to the pool and sat, disconsolate, listening to the falling water strike the still. After a time I felt a presence behind me and turned happily. "Kayode!" I exclaimed.

But on this day of all days, Erinle was in the clearing, not Kayode.

"*E, odo oluwa.* Greetings, young lord," he said, raising his spear. "Your friend has returned?" I nodded. "Why are you here then?" I said nothing. I felt sullen. I had no wish to speak with a god when I so badly wanted a man, a certain man.

He removed his garments and came to me. I turned away.

"What?" Erinle said, his voice not really sounding surprised. "You do not want my body?"

I dared to say, "I want only Kayode's."

Erinle gave a wicked smile. "*Tio, asiwere awon okurin.* Oh, foolish men. Look! He comes." I followed the length and point of his arm. It was true. Kayode was walking towards us, no longer in his fine Arab garments but clad only in a loincloth, just like me. His body was more magnificent than ever. Every muscle seemed to have grown in our time apart. I stood, immediately erect and hoping.

Erinle remained beside me. When Kayode reached us, Erinle took his hand. "I gave you this man," he said, placing Kayode's willing hand in mind. "I give him to you again." I closed my fingers around Kayode's and looked at him longingly. Erinle laughed and pushed us together. "*Ni ibalopo,*" he said, still laughing. "Have sex."

We began before he left. I could not wait for privacy. My hands rushed all across Kayode's body; my cock entered him quickly. In seconds I exploded with the pressure of the many months we had been apart. Kayode writhed beneath me, his ass clenching and unclenching around my cock. The god was gone when we were done.

Kayode and I cleansed ourselves in the pool and sat together after our swim, one of my arms around his shoulders, one of his hands upon my knee. "What happens next?" he asked.

*"Emi ko mo.* I don't know," I admitted. I stood up and we returned to Oyo.

Weeks passed. Kayode took his place as a doctor for the people; my life continued as it had been. I slept with my wife and gave her pleasure. I taught my boys. I went hunting with the men. But I lay with Kayode when I could, which was not often or at least not often enough.

Late one hot afternoon, we hunters walked back to town, singing our songs. It had been a good day, but I did not feel good. I saw the trail to the waterfall ahead of us. We were men now; we never went there after hunting.

"I am going to the falls," I said impulsively.

"We will go with you," Olabisi said.

"No."

The men looked at each other.

*"Mo gbodo ro.* I must think," I explained.

They looked at each other with worry now. Thinking was strange in a man who hunted. I ignored them and turned onto the trail. I looked back once to make sure I was alone.

On the grassy bank I prostrated myself and prayed to Erinle. "What should I do?" I asked. The god would know what I meant. A rush of cool air told me Erinle was with me. I looked over my shoulder and saw him disrobing. When I felt him unknot my loincloth, I raised my ass to him and let him enter me. He pulled me up onto all fours.

"You will found a new city," he whispered in my right ear as he fucked me. "You will dedicate it to me," he panted in my left. "You shall call it Ilobu!" he shouted as he came inside me. I moaned yes to each command and came with him as he spurted into my ass.

When I returned to Oyo, I went to Kayode immediately. He was busy with patients, but my impatience made him look concerned. He finished quickly. I pulled him after me to a private place.

"*A fi,*" I said in a low urgent voice. We are leaving.

"*A fi?*" he echoed.

"Yes. Erinle has told me to found a new town. You are coming with me."

"We can't just leave, Laaroisin. We have responsibilities. We aren't boys anymore."

The words stung me with their truth. I looked at his handsome face and imagined the beautiful body under his long robes. I looked down my own man's body. I felt renewed resolve. "No, we are not boys. But the god commands us. We will live together in this new place.

"Laaroisin, you can't abandon your wife and children!"

"I'm not. They will come with us." I knew what his next question would be; I put a hand over his mouth. I didn't know how it would work. I didn't care. "We will look for Ilobu before we move. We will tell everyone we are going on a long hunting trip."

"Ilobu?"

"That will be the name of our new home."

We took little but our weapons and some small amount of food and water to last until we found meat and new streams. It was still the first dry season. We would need no shelter beyond each other's bodies.

I led Kayode generally east, towards where the sun rose. We would come to a place and I would ask Erinle, "*Se eyi ni ibi?* Is this the place?" There was never an answer. At last, 10 days from Oyo we arrived at a river with sloping banks and sweet water. The god appeared at once.

"How do you like your new home?" he asked, smiling lasciviously. "Down!" he commanded. Kayode and I dropped to all fours. We heard the god disrobing and felt him removing our loincloths. I jumped as Kayode yelped beside me but relaxed when his moans began and I heard the slap of Erinle's groin against his ass. I didn't know what I was supposed to do, but doubt ended when Erinle's cock entered me. He took turns fucking us until Kayode and I shot onto the ground. The ceremony was complete when Erinle pulled out of me and his seed joined ours on the brown earth.

He allowed us to rise. "We will wash ourselves in the river," he announced.

"What is its name, lord?" I asked as we splashed water on our bodies and rubbed the earth and seed off them.

"You will name it after me," he decided, standing knee deep in his namesake. "Each year, you will celebrate this day on its banks. Feed me pounded yam and sekete wine. Sacrifice a fine ram to me, but," he admonished, "Do not cut its throat. Give it to me whole, in my river." He took our hands and joined us again. "Have no more doubts about the future. *Mi ni yi ife*. This is my will."

After the god left us, Kayode and I faced one another. A future that had seemed impossible was here. We embraced for the first of a lifetime of long moments in our new home, then retrieved our packs and began the journey from our future home to our home that was.

There would be explaining. There would be talk. I no longer cared. I was following Erinle's will and my own. *Je ki ojo iwaju sele*. Let the future happen. And that is what we did.

This is what I want to tell the boys. Perhaps I shall.

# Shen Lung and the Old Farmer

I remember that it was a good day. The sky looked like rain at last. I hurried out of the house early in the morning with my cup of tea still in hand. I set it on the porch.

"Plow," I told myself. "If it rains, it rains." I knew I was speaking out loud but, since my wife had died, there was no one to hear and no one to worry. My son had gone back to his home after we finished harvesting the wheat, and my sister wouldn't be by today to clean.

I opened the shed and started my tractor. I always began with the farthest field. Every day it took less time to get to work and somehow that made each day seem easier. The work was hard. Anything that made it less hard was good, even if it was only my imagination.

By the time I reached the field, the sky was very dark. "Maybe I shouldn't have tried to plow today," I told myself. When I felt the first drops of rain, I turned the tractor around and headed back to the shed. There was lightning and thunder and the sky opened. Rain pummeled me. The damn tractor stalled and I got off the seat to see what I could do. Part of me wanted to run for the house, but it wouldn't be good for the tractor to sit in a downpour. The rain was warm anyway.

While I tinkered under the hood, the sky seemed to get steadily darker and strong wind gusts began to blow. Oddly, they came straight down. I heard the wind screech wildly and looked up.

A huge blue dragon filled the sky above me, hovering. Steam came from its enormous nostrils; its large yellow eyes focused unswervingly on me. Wings feathered in sky blue beat the air. Its scaly azure body undulated over me, casting a spell. I woke from it though when the dragon screeched again, sapphire tongue showing in its wide indigo mouth.

I screamed and ran but talons caught me. One set of yellowed nails gripped my shoulder; the second tore at my clothing. A heavy body, cold and slick, pushed me onto all fours on the muddy ground. I felt legs between mine, pushing them apart but soon felt something much worse. The tip of a cock was searching my ass. It found the hole and pushed in, stretching me so wide and so suddenly I thought I would die from the pain. Hands held my shoulders now. I turned. It was not a dragon who was fucking me but a man. He was young, very plain and azure blue.

The blue man's cock pounded into me, accompanied by his groans and my continued screams. I had never had anal sex before. It hurt like knives.

"Relax," a deep voice commanded. "Relax, old man. It will be easier. Relax."

"How can I relax?" I thought to myself.

"You can," the blue man answered. I must have spoken out loud. That's what comes of talking to yourself. You don't know when you're thinking and when you're talking.

"How? It hurts."

"Breathe deeply," the blue man explained. "Let patience settle on you."

"Just stop. Leave me alone. Why me anyway? I'm old and ugly."

"No, old man. You are beautiful. Beautiful shoulders, beautiful back." He rubbed his hands across them. "I saw you in the field and wanted you. Shen Lung takes what he wants." He slapped my ass.

"Shen Lung? Is that your name?"

He was pounding away at my ass again and ignored my question. Since he showed no sign of stopping or of coming soon and withdrawing, I followed his advice and took deep breaths. I felt my sphincter relax. The fucking still didn't feel good, but at least it didn't hurt so much.

Shen Lung's grunts and thrusts increased. He wrapped his arms around my body, hands on my chest, fingers playing my nipples like they would a woman's. I used to do that for my wife, but no one had ever done it for me. I began to moan with the pleasure.

"That is good, old man. Enjoy it. Enjoy," Shen Lung whispered in my ear. But I did not want to enjoy. I grit my teeth and made myself stop moaning.

At that, one of Shen Lung's hands was on my cock. "I will make you enjoy it!" he spat out. The thing grew hard against my will. I began to pant. The fucking did not feel good, and I could pretend his playing with my chest did not either, but jerking me off was an inescapable pleasure. I heard him chuckle. He slowed his thrusts into my ass and increased his masturbation of my cock.

"Stop, please! I'm going to come!"

"Good," he said and began to fuck me as furiously as he was jerking me off. I did come, yelling, and soon after felt him spurt inside me, a strange feeling, warm and wet. Was this how it felt when I came inside my wife?

We stayed on all fours, catching our breath, the rain softly falling on us now, the sky a soothing grey. I felt ashamed.

"At least we're done," I thought.

"No, old man, we are not. You are very handsome, even for an old man. I want more of you." And so Shen Lung began again.

He did not let me up until we finished the third time. My ass ached worse after he withdrew than when he fucked me. I kept my head down in resurfaced shame. He lifted my chin with a blue hand and smiled. "You are a good fuck, old man. What is your name?"

"Xin Qiji," I muttered.

He squeezed my chin. "Xin Qiji? A name like poetry. Now, Xin Qiji, how about some tea?"

I could not believe the man who had just raped me was asking for tea. Well, at least it wasn't beer or a cigarette. I turned towards the house.

"Wait!" Shen Lung yelled. "Should you leave your tractor in this weather?"

"It won't start," I yelled back.

"Try it now," Shen Lung told me.

I put the hood back in place and climbed up. "Ouch!" I yelped and Shen Lung laughed. I eased my ass more gently onto the metal seating and turned the starter. The engine caught fire immediately. Shen Lung hopped on the back, holding onto my shoulders as I drove. It reminded me of his hands on my shoulders while he fucked me. It was not a good memory.

When we reached the house, I cleaned myself off on the porch with rainwater collected in the barrel. Shen Lung demanded I wash him as well. I found clean towels inside and dried him off thoroughly and then myself. When I was done, Shen Lung walked into the house uninvited.

"You live very simply," he said, looking around the front room.

"I am a poor farmer."

"Not as poor as some and, in any case, you won't be poor any longer." He didn't explain, just walked into the kitchen as if he owned it. Indeed, he acted like a lord and I began to treat him that way. I hurried about heating the water and making the tea. We sat at my small table with the stained oilcloth while it brewed, Shen Lung calmly looking all around us and at me, ownership in his eyes then too.

I was conscious that we were both still naked. I offered him my best shirt and pants but he declined. When I said I would get dressed and rose to go, he said, "You will not. Looking at you gives me pleasure. Your muscles swell and flow like rolling hills or the deepest ocean." He reached out to flick a nipple with the fingers of one hand.

My nipples still ached from his play but they tightened at his touch. He noticed. My cock rose. He noticed that as well. "You are hard again, Xin Qiji. Good. But first we will have this tea." I poured for us, self-conscious about my bobbing cock, but Shen Lung drank his tea serenely, smiling at me and talking of his plans.

"I like you. I will visit every year at the first rain. I will make you rich. My seed in you will be like the seeds of your wheat and cotton in the ground. They will grow in strength and beauty and so will you. They will mature each year and be cut down in harvest, but each year you will grow younger. You please me now but I will be more pleased not to see so many wrinkles." He traced the deep lines across my forehead with a long thin finger.

"But my lord," I said quietly while the finger curved along my jaw. "I am not a man who goes with men."

"Good," Shen Lung said firmly, tapping my nose. "I am not a man. And I do not want you to, as you put it, go with other men. You will save yourself for me. Once a year, that is not so bad or so much, is it? In return, you will grow rich and young. Millions of men would beg me to fuck them for such rewards.

But, among all these men," he said, suddenly imperious, "I have chosen you."

"Why?" I asked, bewildered.

Shen Lung swatted away my question like it was a fly. "I was passing. Your face and form caught my eye. An impulse but I enjoyed it. Did you?" He looked at me with threats in his eyes.

I didn't want to say. "Tell me the truth," he roared. Almost imperceptibly, I shook my head no and hung my head. He lifted my chin again. "I will teach you better then. You will look forward to the first rain." And with that he stood and pulled me up after him. His cock was erect, as was mine. I could not believe my body wanted more of him.

Shen Lung embraced me, standing close, running his long fingers down my back, cupping both hands around the mounds of my ass. He began to kiss my neck and shoulders. I tried to pull away but his strong hands kept me against him. "I will teach you," he whispered as his lips reached my earlobes and stopped to suck. I shivered in spite of myself. "Good," he said. "The lessons begin. Take me to your bed."

The sex was different there. I wanted to think it wasn't because of his promises. I hoped I didn't submit because the more he fucked me, the richer and younger I would be. I tried to believe I was not his whore.

The dragon man spent much time on my body before he entered me again. He kissed my lips, face, neck, shoulders, arms, hands, stomach and chest. His lips were soft and moist against me. When his mouth reached my nipples, he sucked them gently and licked. That aroused me and made me ashamed again.

"Do not worry so much, Xin Qiji. There is nothing to be ashamed of." Shen Lung said this while his hands began to stroke my body, blue fingers massaging me. I resisted relaxing but found I could not. His touch was too gentle now, his voice too soft and seductive.

When he raised my legs onto his shoulders, fear froze me again but it was his tongue that found my asshole, licking it, prodding, making me squirm. I worried that I was unclean, but Shen Lung didn't seem concerned. As he probed and licked and chewed, it became exciting. My mouth opened in unwanted ecstasy and the dragon noticed.

"Good, Qiji. Good," he said before his mouth found my cock. I had never been sucked before. I had wanted it but my wife had gently refused in our early days and I never asked again. I murmured now in happiness. Shen Lung whispered, "Good, Qiji. Good," releasing my cock for the words before he took me again, suddenly full length, into his mouth. I thrust my groin up into his face, shouting.

He sucked me fast, then slowly, agonizingly slowly. I thought I would burst into his mouth but his face pulled away and his yellow eyes looked up my body, catching mine. "Now, you," he said and got onto all fours above me.

His cock found my mouth and entered it. I sucked him inexpertly and without real interest. He must have noticed because he began to push himself into and out of my mouth. I let him. What else could I do?

After a short while, he stopped. I knew he was going to fuck me again but I didn't resist. I was strong but Shen Lung was stronger, much stronger. I braced myself.

To my surprise, he entered me gently from the front, blue thighs spreading my legs and holding them all the way back, like I was a woman. When I didn't fight, he commanded me to wrap my legs around the small of his back. That gave his hands room to play with my chest and I moaned in immediate response. When his lips pressed against mine, mine pressed back. When his tongue entered my mouth, mine let it play.

"Take your cock," he told me and I obeyed, unsure whether it was willingly or not.

I knew by now he would want me to come with him so I watched and listened carefully, masturbating myself while he fucked me. When he increased his pounding, I increased my pulling. When he began to lunge, I arched myself up to meet him. He yelled unintelligible words as we both came. When his spurting inside me stopped, I knew I was full of his cum. I was truly his concubine now.

Shen Lung held himself above me. "That was delicious. You are a quick study, Qiji." I wasn't glad to hear that but I cannot deny that some of what we did excited me. I hadn't had sex with anyone since my wife died. Skin against mine felt good, even if that skin was blue and belonged to a man. But then Shen Lung, as he said, was not a man. Fucked by a dragon, I thought. No one will believe me.

He stayed the rest of that day and through the night. I made us simple meals but he didn't seem to mind. We had sex whenever Shen Lung wanted it, which was frequently. I remember falling asleep at last with his arms around me in the dark. He felt like Wang Na, my wife. Her arms had been strong too, from working in the fields beside me.

In the morning I woke to sunrise and an empty bed. It was cold where Shen Lung had lain. I thought perhaps I had dreamed it all, but the marks on my body and the tingling in my ass told me the truth.

A new work shirt and trousers were hanging from the coat hook. I put them on and made my breakfast. It was a clear day. I took the tractor out and began plowing, looking up at the sky frequently.

When my sister visited to clean and cook a special meal for me on Saturday, I told her nothing about Shen Lung. When my son arrived to help pick the cotton, I hoped he didn't see that my wrinkles were fewer. A neighbor had already noticed and asked me for my secret. I handed her one of my wife's creams. I hadn't been able to get rid of anything that was Na's.

The cotton crop was our best ever, and of course I wondered if it was in truth the effect of Shen Lung's seed. I felt my ass, remembering how much the fucking had hurt, and kept busy planting wheat. When we harvested it that new spring, my son Ban said what I was thinking. There was more of it than ever.

As the next rainy season neared, I began to worry. The dragon had said he would be back. I was glad for better crops but did not look forward to more sex with him. Perhaps Shen Lung had changed his mind. Perhaps he had forgotten me. Perhaps he had found another man, or woman.

The first rainstorm came one night in June. I was on my bed, worrying, when I heard a knock on the door. Outside was Shen Lung as a man, dripping wet streams onto my porch. "Come in, come in!" I told him, pulling him indoors before I could think, wondering why he had knocked. I raced to get a towel. When I returned he was fully erect. Looking at him I became hard too. He looked better somehow.

Shen Lung took the towel from me and asked how the crops were. I told him and he smiled. "You are more handsome than ever, Qiji," he said, drying himself quickly. Dropping the towel, he leaned in to kiss me, one hand reaching for my cock and the other for my chest. I gasped but did not object when he guided us into the bedroom.

I lay on my mat of my own accord and when he lifted my legs I did not flinch. I had expected his cock for a year of long days and nights. When he entered me, it felt familiar and the pain was less. I gave myself to him. My crops had been good; payment had to be made.

I was surprised how good the fucking felt that second year. Shen Lung's body excited mine in every position and with every brush of skin, not only through the deliberate touch of hands and lips and cock.

He spent the night and most of the next day. I could tell when he was wanting to leave but held him at the door. "Once more?" I asked and he smiled like sunrise.

"Here?"

"Here," I agreed and leaned my arms against the door to keep it shut. He dropped to his knees to prepare my ass, then rose, sliding inside me so slowly I thought I would melt beneath him. When his hands reached around for me, I cried out in happiness, just like a woman. What we did together felt good, without measure or judgment.

After Shen Lung left, I felt regret and, already, impatience for the year to end. I didn't care anymore that he fucked me or, rather, I cared very much. But impatience vanished with the work of daily life through busy weeks and months. I thought of Shen Lung often throughout the year, daydreaming of him when I masturbated, waking from night dreams wet and panting.

Our crops were even better than the previous year, and everyone said I looked much younger. I knew that was true from the man I saw in the mirror. I was grateful for the crops and increased money but truthfully didn't care about the youth.

However, Shen Lung did care. When he returned for his third visit, he held me at arm's length and smiled in satisfaction. "You are more beautiful than ever, Qiji."

I blushed like a maiden. "Why do you call me beautiful?"

"Would you rather I call you handsome?" he asked, understanding. "It is just a word."

"No," I answered, letting his blue arms pull me close, my man's body against his. "It doesn't matter."

In my thoughts I wondered if that were true. A woman is beautiful, not a man. Was I a woman to Shen Lung? I didn't feel like a woman but, when he fucked me, I didn't feel like a man either.

He stayed that day and night and into a second day. As another night came, I kept expecting him to leave, worrying that he would, foolishly hoping he would not. When it was dusk, I asked, "Will you stay another night with me?"

We were in bed, holding one another under the blanket. He traced down my nose to my lips. "Are you getting greedy? More of my seed, more riches?"

"I don't care about the riches. Or the youth," I said, taking his finger in my mouth and sucking it.

He turned me onto my back and lay on top of me, hands on my shoulders, yellow eyes locked with mine. "I believe you are telling the truth, Qiji. But then, if you do not care about money or youth, tell me why you want me to stay."

I could not say the word.

"Is it love?" he guessed.

"Yes," I agreed forthrightly, not looking away. He would soon be gone. I wanted him to know. I wanted him to remember in the long, long months ahead. I wanted him to come back.

"Good," Shen Lung said. "It is love for me too." The love we made then transported us. We were drifting slowly in the air, flying on a gentle breeze, the earth arrayed below us.

But the next morning he was still gone and I was still alone. I felt for his body across my mat; I smelled his scent on my skin. I didn't want to leave the bed. I didn't want to start another year without him. But, as the sun rose in the sky, I knew I had to. I was a farmer. The crops needed tending. The chickens needed feeding. So, I got to my feet against my will and padded into the kitchen. I would wear nothing but him until I had to.

And there he was, sitting at the table, drinking tea. I rushed to him and dropped to my knees before him, resting my chest on his thighs, my cheek on his cock.

"What is this?" he asked, as if he were tut tutting.

"I'm so glad you're still here."

"But I will be leaving soon."

"I know." The sadness overwhelmed my happiness.

He raised my face to look at him, cupping my head in both hands. He was smiling gently and looked so handsome. How could I ever have thought him plain? "Would you like to accompany me?" he asked. Before I answered he added, "There would be no coming back."

I thought about this, about my son and sister, about my farm. "Will this be dying?" I asked.

"Something like but something not like it at all. You will live forever. You will be with me forever."

"Then I will go!"

He looked away, thinking. I worried he would change his mind but then he spoke. "Consider it a year. When I come back next rainy season, tell me what you have decided."

"I don't want to be here alone another year!"

"Forever is a long time, Qiji. A year is nothing. Consider and decide." And then he rose and left my house. He leapt into the sky and became the dragon once again. I watched him fly away until I could see nothing. I went back into the house to have my tea, dress and begin a new year without Shen Lung.

At first I didn't think. I was determined and angry. Why was he making me wait a year? He knew my heart; he knew my thoughts. It was cruel. I shook my fist at the sky on dark days and nights when it rained, yelling for him to come back. "Shen Lung! Shen Lung!" I shouted over and over. If my neighbors heard, they must have thought me crazy, calling for the holy dragon.

And then the rainy season ended and I stopped shaking my fist and shouting at the sky. I planted the cotton, the cotton grew and we harvested it, just like every year. I planted wheat and my son and I harvested that. I bought more land, for my son, not for me. I gave rich presents to my sister. I made my will and prepared for the rain.

When it came I was in the fields again. I stopped the tractor and watched the sky. Shen Lung appeared first as a dark dot far in the heavens, becoming blue as he approached. In seconds I could distinguish the length of his body and his wings, then his legs, his eyes. The wind swirled around me, almost flattening me onto my back. The rain fell like pellets into my eyes but I didn't close them. I wanted to see him, this strange being that was my lover. He landed as a dragon, his serpentine body curling and thrashing, but as he walked towards me he coalesced into the man's body I made love to, into the man I loved. I ran towards him and, like a boy, jumped into his strong blue arms. He laughed and kissed me again and again.

"You look so young, Qiji. Like a boy."

"No!"

"Well, like a young man at least. A very, very handsome young man. And powerfully attractive," he added. He started to carry me towards the house.

"No," I shouted over the thunder. "Let's fuck right here."

"Here? In the mud? It is raining too hard."

I struggled out of his arms and onto my feet. "Here!" I said, kicking off my boots and ripping off my clothes. Shen Lung looked at my body with eager eyes.

"All right then," he agreed. "Here."

I got down on all fours and he fucked me in the mud and rain. I didn't care where we were. I didn't care if anyone saw us. I wanted to be one with him. When he reached under me for my cock, I shouted "Yes!" with great joy. When I came, I felt a greater joy, knowing he would soon be coming inside me and, when he did, I shouted his name into the wind over and over.

We stayed on all fours for the longest time but not long enough. He didn't soften but withdrew anyway. "Let us get the tractor into the shed," he said, rising, slapping my ass playfully. "And us into the house."

When the tractor was safe, we ran like boys across the yard onto the porch. I cleaned the muck off Shen Lung. He insisted on cleaning it off me.

"No, Lord, I will do it."

He looked at me with his yellow eyes. "No, Qiji. Love makes us equals now. I will wash my lover." And he did, slowly, letting each chilly cupful slide from my head and shoulders down my body, rubbing me with the cloth, careful with each curve and length of my skin, as if it he was revering me.

"You are beautiful, Qiji."

"It's just a body, Lord. Inside I am the same."

Shen Lung nodded. "It is true for me as well, Qiji. Dragon or man, I am myself. Shall we go into your house?"

"Why? I'm ready to leave now!" I stood tall, my cock erect, every feeling in me erect and ready.

Shen Lung looked at me as if he were evaluating. Then he spoke. "Have you thought this over carefully? Remember, there is no return." I nodded. "Have you said your farewells?" I considered that.

"What will they find?" My sister would be first. She would tell my son.

"They will find the body of an old man lying on his bed."

"Then no goodbye is necessary. They know I am prepared for death. They will know I'm grateful for all they've done for me."

"Then we will go," Shen Lung said decisively and led me by the hand into the center of the yard. "Climb onto my back." I hesitated, worrying I might hurt him. He repeated, "Climb onto my back, Xin Qiji." I did as he commanded, wrapping my arms around his neck and my legs around his waist. "Now!" he yelled and leapt into the air.

The change came quickly. Wings rather than arms, scales rather than skin, a long serpent's body, a dragon's head. I lurched away in fear.

"Hold on, Qiji!" Shen Lung roared, flames shooting from his mouth and smoke from his nostrils. I did as he commanded. I was determined to hold on forever. We flew into the rain clouds, grey surrounding us completely. I no longer felt the rain.

# LEPRECHAUN IN NEW YORK

He was a man hard to miss, even across a crowded room, with his skin like pink alabaster and hair like a torch. I had seen him many times before, in this gay bar or that. He never went home with anyone, just drank and left. Tonight, I decided, I wouldn't give up.

When I reached his corner though, he was gone and someone else had already appropriated his stool. I spun and caught sight of red hair moving towards the door. He was shorter than I thought. If he hadn't been ginger, I would have lost him.

I set out again through the mass of gay men celebrating St. Patrick's Day in the Hit and Run. When I finally made it to the door and outside, I just managed to see him turn the corner towards East 12th. I almost ran the block to catch up.

On 12th, I saw neither hair nor skin of him but, in the one a.m. silence, I could hear the slap and splash of his boots as they hit puddles left by an earlier rain. I followed the sounds until he was back in sight, a half block ahead of me. Iridescent oils made rainbows in the puddles where his boots had been.

The straightaway gave me time to ask questions, like what was I doing trailing a stranger? Had he noticed me? If yes, why was he walking away? But my decision stood. I sped up, keeping him in sight while keeping my distance.

We walked in sync, a quarter block between us, before he turned into another bar, an Irish one I hadn't been in, since it was straight. I pushed through the door a minute after him.

The Dubliner was even more crowded than the Hit and Run, full of women as well as men, celebrating St. Pat's in the traditional Irish-American way of laughter and shouts and too much alcohol. It was a part of my ancestry I didn't usually honor.

At first I couldn't see him because of the dark, but then his head leaned across the bar into the light like a light itself. I squeezed my way through to him and made myself say hey. His pale eyes widened. They were blue or grey—I couldn't tell—but I could see he was beautiful: the red hair short but curling across his head and down its sides, the body better up close, much better. My fingers twitched in longing.

I extended them to him. "My name's Jack," I said.

After a moment's hesitation, he took my hand. "Aed," he answered.

"Ed?"

He frowned. "No, Aed," he emphasized, dropping my hand. "It means fire." I looked at his hair. He looked away in some sort of disgust.

"Let me buy you a beer," I said to his hair. He turned back with a smile.

"I'll take a Guinness and thank you."

I indicated to the bartender that I'd like two pulls of the dark stuff and tried to think of subjects to cover while they drained into their mugs.

"How long have you been in New York?"

"Oh, all my life," Aed answered in his deep brogue. "Nah," he laughed. "Just three years. And you?"

"Oh, all my life," I repeated, telling the truth. "My grandfather came over after the war."

"Married a local lass?" I nodded. "Irish?" I nodded again. "We're both 100% then," he said, with a look I couldn't interpret in the dark of the bar. Thankfully, then the beer arrived, sooner than expected but gratefully received.

"Slainte," I said, clinking his pint against mine. "Happy St. Pat's."

"Happy St. Pat's," he agreed, looking sardonic. The slanted grin looked good on him.

He took a long drink, too long. It drained nearly half the glass. He was ready for another when the bartender came back by with one in his hand. He set it down in front of Aed. "They know me here," he explained. The sound of his brogue sent shivers up my back.

He drank more slowly this time, maybe because I was watching him so intently. I didn't care. I was memorizing.

Aed was short, no more than 5'2", but he was well and solidly built. He seemed to be assessing me as well. I hoped he liked 5'9, dark hair and a beard. We drank our drinks and continued our evaluations.

When I asked him home, he gave me an excuse, drained the last of his third pint and said good night. I was left alone in the loud and happy crowd, wondering why. I thought about it 15 seconds. He was too handsome to let go, even if I wasn't his type. I chugged my third beer and became his stalker.

He had another lead, and I let him keep it. I didn't want him to turn around. He didn't walk far, just past Tompkins Square to a basement apartment on Avenue A. He opened his door and closed it behind him, leaving me on my own again. Now what, I asked myself. Oh well. At least I knew where he lived.

All through the week I thought about this Aed with hair the color of fire. On the weekend I walked by his building, hoping to see him. I did not.

The next week, I took a day off and tried again, arriving early. At 7:30 a.m. he hurried up the basement steps and trotted west. I trotted after, wishing I jogged more or at least used the treadmills at the gym. I hoped Aed wouldn't hear my labored breathing.

Between 1st and 2nd Avenues, he stopped in front of a shoe repair store and unlocked the door. He was a cobbler then. Didn't I have some shoes that needed mending? The next day I brought them to him.

"Well, hello!" I said as if I were surprised. "Didn't know you worked here."

"Three years," was his only reply. Daylight showed his eyes were pale green, almost translucent. He took the shoes, careful not to touch my hands, looked at them all and asked, "New heels?" When I agreed he wrote the receipts, put my shoes on a shelf and turned back to his work, sitting at a counter, not looking at me, not looking up at all. I knew I should go but somehow I couldn't.

For too many minutes, I watched him remove old heels and soles and apply new on other people's shoes. I concentrated on the ginger curls of his bent head. He looked up once and smiled and I felt encouraged, even if it was just the slightest of slight. When another customer entered the shop, I realized I was late for work. I ran for the subway, thinking ahead. We would meet again and we would speak and who knew what might happen?

On Friday, fifteen minutes before the shop closed, I arrived with my proofs of purchase. "Just made it!" I said, too loudly, my voice breaking in a squawk.

"Indeed," he acknowledged, looking up at the clock before turning to take up my two pairs of shoes from a rack nearby.

He set them on the counter. "That'll be forty and six," he said confidentially, hands gripping the counter, torso leaning towards me, his chest apparent under the leather apron and v-necked tee.

"You remembered my shoes."

"I remembered you," he said, with a smile broader than the last. Was he flirting? I leaned towards him, as if for a kiss. He didn't pull away but just then an even later arrival entered his shop and he reached for a pair of tan high heels, which she paid for with her card and quickly carried out. So much for remembering me, I thought and took out my own credit card, ready to pay and leave and maybe give up, but then Aed came round the counter, locked the door and turned the sign to closed. My heart thumpety-thumped.

"Forty and six," he repeated when he came up close.

"Can I buy you dinner?" I blurted.

He smiled with lovely small teeth. "Surely but first the forty and six." I gave him my card, and he let our fingers touch. I watched him ring up the sale.

"Where shall we go?" I asked while he removed his apron, my eyes focused on the bulge in the crotch of his jeans.

"McNally's might be the place," he answered as he hung the apron on a peg, giving me an excellent view of his tidy posterior. I knew where that was, an Irish pub not too far. I settled in to wait, and his look became suspicious. "I've got to make a deposit. I'll see you there, say at 7:45?" Any dreams about sex among the shoes dissipated like smoke.

"All right then," I replied. He opened the door for me and I brushed past on purpose, giving him something to remember me by for a couple of hours.

I arrived at McNally's at 7:15, wearing tight black clothing, my Queer color of choice. 7:30 came, then eight o'clock. I assumed Aed was standing me up. Maybe his interest had been imagination; maybe he was just trying to get rid of me. I swallowed the remains of my second beer. I'd have dinner at home before trying for another man at yet another bar.

Just then Aed came in the door and his pale eyes caught mine immediately. He didn't look very happy.

"What are you having?" I asked after he'd maneuvered his way to me, my lips hoping for a kiss or at least an explanation.

"Guinness please."

I ordered two and was silent, waiting for the apology.

"What happened?" I asked at last.

"What do you mean?" Again, his look was suspicious.

"You were late."

He sighed and looked away. "I almost didn't come. But then I figured you'd be after me if I didn't." I laughed, and he frowned. We didn't say another word while our two Guinnesses slowly filled their pints.

When they arrived we clinked glasses. "Slainte," we said simultaneously. We drank, Aed peering over his glass at me. I tried to start a conversation.

The hostess appeared before I got very far. "Your table's still ready, sir," she said to me in her own Irish brogue. "Hello, Aed." She looked at his nearly empty glass. "Ready for another?"

"I am that, Patricia," he answered, with a smile for her.

"I'll bring it to you then, once you're settled."

They pushed through the crowd and I followed as best I could, holding my glass. I had waited forty-five minutes. I could wait a few more.

We ordered, ate and talked. Aed's eyes barely blinked as he asked questions and listened. After his third pint, he seemed to reach a decision. His knees found mine under the table and didn't move away.

I realized over my fourth beer that I was drunk. Aed was too, after six. Through the fog I grasped that I'd better make my move while we both were still conscious.

"Would you like to go to my place?"

Aed immediately called for the bill, so abruptly I almost laughed but the intensity of his look and sudden set of his jaw made me stifle anything but a serious return of his staring.

After I paid he pulled me up and after him, holding my hand firmly as he threaded our way out of the bar but dropping it as soon as we were on the street. We walked side by side to my apartment, hands in our pockets against the cold and against touching again, but he did slide a small hand into my back pocket as I inserted the key into my door.

Inside, I turned up the heat and took his jacket. He looked perfect in his red checked shirt.

"You look good in red."

"Thanks. It's my favorite color." The brogue was stronger now, after the beer. I smiled to hear it. Aed smiled back and led me to the couch as if it were his home, not mine. He pulled me onto it, small hands going round my shoulders, soft lips onto my mouth. His kisses were many and urgent, down my neck and onto my chest. He unbuttoned my shirt and nuzzled my plentiful chest hair, then removed the shirt entirely and tossed it aside. He almost tore his getting it off.

His chest was a marvel: tight pecs lightly brushed with redder hair and tipped by large pink nipples, large for a man at least.

"Beautiful," I said and began to press him back onto the couch.

His hands stopped me at 60 degrees, propelled me up to 90 and then flattened me at 180 on the couch. It wasn't my usual position but I warmed to his touch. I was moaning and twisting when he stopped abruptly, eyes asking one more question. I rubbed the ginger hair of his forearms, trying to answer.

He must have understood the yes because he lunged back into action, rapidly unbuckling my belt and unzipping my pants, pulling them down in a frantic rush to my boots, which he removed and observed with a professional eye before setting them carefully onto the carpet.

He stood up fast, balancing himself on one leg and then the other, taking his own boots off. They were beautifully made. He hopped out of his jeans and lowered himself back onto me, his full weight pressing mine into the cushions. I had time to think a quick surprise I was still on the bottom before his mouth prevented me from protesting, "But I'm a top."

He reached to remove my briefs, and I unwillingly arched my groin. I tugged at his out of fairness though, and he was out of them like a shot. His head bent over my cock. I ran my fingers through his curly hair as much as I wanted while his head bobbed vigorously over it. Each time he looked up, his eyes seemed greener and shinier. I cupped his face in my hands, wondering at the emerald color they became.

"I have condoms," I whispered.

"So do I," he whispered back, reaching down for his pants. Condom in hand he sat up, spreading my legs like a fan before him, blowing into the condom like it was a balloon. He lubricated us both with spit before he slid it on and in. I winced and yelped.

"Just relax," he said in a low throaty voice. I did my best.

It didn't take more than a minute or two. He came and pulled out, slumping against the couch, chest heaving with the record-setting effort.

"Ah, but it's been a long time," he said, with what sounded like regret. He took another deep breath and looked at me strangely. "I guess you'll be wanting your three wishes now."

I blinked. "What did you say?"

"Nothing," he muttered. "How about another go?"

"All right," I said. "But not here." I led us to the bedroom.

His second "go" was much less rushed and the third came deliriously, deliciously slowly. Afterwards, he rolled onto his back, panting.

"You'll be making me weak at the knees, boyo. How about a cuppa?"

Over naked tea he asked if I'd been to Ireland.

"Yes, twice."

"Do you know much about the fairy stories?"

"Some," I said, remembering books my mother had read to me. "What should I know?"

"Nothing," he answered and swallowed his tea. "Well, I'd better be going," he said, standing up in a lurch.

Dazed by the transition, I followed him into the bedroom and watched him cover his body again with clothes. I gave him my phone number and hoped for an email address or at least a kiss. There was neither in his goodbye, just the word.

All the next day and night, I hoped Aed would call or text me. I waited the week, saying no to invitations from friends, keeping my schedule open.

The second week I went by his shop with more shoes, but his hello was curt and my attempts at conversation were rebuffed. When I collected my mended soles and heels late on Friday, he said no to drinks and dinner.

Still, I waited the Saturday, hoping he'd call. When he didn't but friends did, I grabbed my coat and walked out into the night before I could think.

Don and Dave were loud and comforting. They asked how I was, and I said I was fine. They heard the lie in that and bought me drinks and told me funny gossip to cheer me up. Over the rim of the second pint, I saw Aed come through the door. I apologized to my friends and went to intercept him. My hand took his shoulder, caressing it more than I meant to.

"Jack," he said, without turning to look.

"Can we talk?

"Jack…" he began, with a deep sigh.

"Please, Aed. Give me a chance."

He looked at me intently then, and something seemed to let go in his chest.

"What's wrong?"

He sighed again and took my hand, his touch an appreciated blessing. "It's complicated, boyo. We should go to my place." My thoughts and face brightened. Aed smiled up at me and chucked my chin. "Sure and you're a handsome lad. Come on then."

I waved goodbye to my friends as Aed led me to the door.

We walked along without further words, the thump of his boots and slap of my sneakers loud in the night quiet around us. He looked at my feet.

"You're not wearing your boots. And after all my hard work." He chuckled, but I didn't. "Ah now, my treasure," he said, taking my hand. "Don't be that way."

We held hands until we came to his basement apartment. I waited a step above him as he opened the door and flipped on the lights. The room was unremarkably masculine. Tan walls and plush darker carpeting, expensive looking brown leather chairs, a chocolate covered sofa in more matte finish leather, photos across the walls.

"Do you want a beer?" he asked.

"No."

"How about some whiskey then? I have Jameson's."

"I don't need a drink."

"I do," he said, looking nervous.

"All right then. I'll join you."

After he left the living room, I looked at the photos. They were all by famous photographers: Diane Arbeson, Annie Liebovitz, Jay Maisel. There was even an Alfred Stieglitz. The newer ones all seemed to be signed.

"Do you like photography?" he asked behind my back. Without waiting for an answer, he handed me a pint and tapped it with his. "*Firinne*," he said.

"What does that mean?"

"Truth."

He sat on the couch and so did I, although not too close. The word *truth* bothered me. He took a long gulp of his beer and then another. I put mine on a coaster.

"What did you want to say?" I asked. Bad news is better heard sober and quickly. But how bad could it be if we were in his apartment?

He took another long pull on his beer and sucked in a deep breath.

"I'm a leprechaun, Jack, and I'm really really old," he said, all in a rush.

"What the hell?" I yelled, jumping up off the couch. "Do you think that's funny?" He tried to pull me back down. I resisted but he won and I fell on top of him. I had forgotten how strong his arms were.

He held me close. "Do you believe me?" he asked up into my face, looking as if he didn't expect me to.

"Oh, of course," I replied sarcastically. His green eyes looked at me too long. Their radiance was blinding. "All right," I said, to make him blink. "You're a leprechaun. Why tell me? Isn't that dangerous?"

"It can be but I saw inside you."

Visions of lungs and other body organs came to mind. I was in the apartment of a crazy person and a strong one at that. My face must have said my thoughts. The glow in his eyes faded, and his head dropped. His hair was so lovely.

Against my better judgment, I asked, "What makes you think you're a leprechaun?" I remembered a list of delusions from college Psych 101 but "thinks he's a leprechaun" wasn't on it.

"I'm short, with red hair, and pink skin."

I nodded.

"My favorite color is red…"

"Wait a minute! Isn't it supposed to be green?

He tried to chuckle. "Anyway, I live underground. I work as a cobbler. I have a...." I stopped him before he could finish.

"Check, check, check. But why does all of that make you a leprechaun?"

He looked at me like he couldn't tell if I was putting him on. "Come with me," he said, yanking me after him down a hall into his bedroom.

I noticed it immediately, a rainbow painted in an arc across the wall behind his wide bed. He pointed it out anyway.

"So?" I said.

"Good God, man, are you truly Irish?" He dropped my hand and walked to the wall, removed a large photo of Ireland and revealed the door to a safe.

"Aed, you don't have to...." I stopped myself. I had no idea what he was doing so how could I tell him to not do it? He twirled the dial right and left and right and left, stopping at numbers along the way, then used a key to open the small square door. I saw papers and a bag inside. Aed removed the bag and rained its contents onto the bed. Gold coins, lots of them.

I stared at the pile and then at him.

"Well?" he asked, with tight lips and waiting eyes.

"Isn't it supposed to be in a pot?"

He grabbed at me, laughing for real now, and tumbled us onto the bed, his kisses overpopulating my face, his hands busy at my clothes and his until they were piles on the floor. We rolled naked across his coins. I felt them pressing into me, hard and cold, until he pushed my legs apart. I forgot the hoard.

"This is crazy," I said when we were done and panting. He looked disappointed. "I mean, making love on all your money."

His eyes twinkled again. "Oh, this isn't all of it, not by half. Most of it's in stocks and bonds. And this building."

I sat up. "You own this building?"

"Surely."

"Then why do you live in the basement?"

"I told you. I'm a leprechaun. Leprechauns live underground."

The explanation still did not compute. Handsome wealthy man lives in the basement of the building he owns, rather than the penthouse. Thinks he's an elderly leprechaun. I looked at Aed's young face and fine body. So what if he was a little crazy? I told myself not to be picky. A leprechaun isn't so bad–Aed wasn't green or anything–and, however old he was, he was very *very* well preserved. Besides, being in love with a leprechaun could hold all kinds of advantages.

"Now, about those wishes…," I began.

"You only have three," he reminded me.

"No worries. I only need one."

# My Mother's Head

I was born when Perseus decapitated my mother and took her head, the snakes still writhing. She was pregnant by Poseidon, who started all our troubles. My brother Pegasus came first. Perseus claimed him. I followed, full grown, gigantic and unnoticed as Pegasus galloped into the sky, Perseus upon his back, urging him upward.

I was left below with my mother's body and blood. I burned her on a pyre, saying all the prayers necessary to speed her soul to Hades, but it was not to be. That night I dreamed of her, headless, standing at the edge of a river.

"My son!" she cried from within her breasts, wringing her hands. "I cannot cross the Styx to Hades; I have no eye coins for Charon. Bring me my head, Chrysaor! Bring my head, my son, I beg you, or I will be lost forever on this unfriendly shore!"

I woke crying and promising my mother that I would make her whole. I would place Charon's coins on her eyes myself.

First, I had to find Perseus. I had had a glimpse of him before he jumped onto my brother's back and disappeared into the clouds. He was handsome, like the stories say, but then so am I. Did you know that? No, I'll wager. I am just a minor character in the stories of Greece, almost forgotten, but I too have a story to tell.

In body, I was well formed but huge, four and a half cubits tall and nearly four talents in weight. My skin was dark, darker than my mother's, but my hair was hers–hers before Athena's curse. Long black curls sprang from my scalp. I wore a golden suit of armor and carried a golden shield and sword.

In mind I was a formless child. People thought me an idiot. I was a monster to them and cast out, but my father, great Poseidon, saved me. It was he who showed me how to build the pyre and arrange my mother's body on it. It was he who made the fire. My father stood close beside me and told my mother's story while her headless body burned.

I hated him then; his rape was her ruin. But in time my feelings changed. He was kind to me and taught me well. My mind expanded to match my body, thanks to him. But he would not let me leave him. I spent years within the sea, learning and growing even stronger. One day, I kept repeating to my mother. One day.

On my 16th birthday, my father arranged a marriage for me and I assumed a throne in Atlantic Iberia. My bride was Callirrhoe, daughter of endless Oceanus. She was a Titan like her father and as large as I in body. We coupled but produced no children, which was no matter to me. I neither wanted to marry nor to lay with her. I dreamed of men, of feeling a muscular, hairy body holding me down. I always woke before consummation and sometimes turned to my wife for release. She rode me like Perseus rode my brother.

My mother came to me again in dreams. She told me where Perseus was and how to reach him, across the inland sea. I had a ship built large enough for the journey. We would sail down the coast to the Gates of Hercules and through, across the Mediterranean to far-away Thessaly, where Perseus lived in exile. He had killed his father after he killed my mother. A fine hero. He deserved exile–and worse. On the prow of the ship I had the builders fit an image of my mother's head, to remind me of the goal. I named the ship Mendekua–revenge, in our Iberian language.

My father saw to it that our voyage of so many leagues went well. We had fair wind, calm seas and friendly ports of call along the way. When our ship rode into the Gulf of Pagasae, a well protected bay, I felt my mother urging me on.

We docked inside the harbor, and a large crowd formed on the pier. I'm sure they were drawn by the exotic look of our ship and the oddity of its name.

When I proceeded down the ramp to the dock, the crowd coalesced around me. They were like children, all a cubit or more shorter than I. I held my arms above them and announced my name and intentions in their tongue. I had come from Iberia to establish trade between their land and mine. I would travel to their capital Larissa to speak with their king.

"Tagus," someone corrected. "We call him tagus. We elect him." The crowd nodded its heads in agreement. Strange, I thought. Their king and our river share a name. I took this as a good omen.

Ready for the road, I hired fine Thessalonian horses on which to ride north along the Larissa road. I thought of my brother Pegasus but, brushing weakness aside, I left men to keep watch over our ship and set out with my entourage. I had the gifts for this Aleuadaen king, this tagus–and for Perseus– carefully stowed on the finest horse of all. That horse remained riderless, representing to me my mother's headless state.

More crowds gathered along the way, passing word of our progress on to Larissa. Emissaries greeted us outside the town and escorted us the remaining distance to the palace of their tagus, whose name was Jason. Perseus and an earlier Jason were both been men of Argos. This, I believed, was another omen I would succeed.

At the palace I left all but one of my men to tend our horses and to rest. I asked for a bath, and my clean hair curled black and tight. I put on fresh clothes, not the ceremonial garb of an Iberian king but the gold I had been born with. I would make this Perseus remember.

When I was ready, Abilio and I were led to the audience chamber of the king. At the far end of the unprepossessing room was, I guessed, Jason, seated on the highest chair. Beneath him, on a lesser level, a woman sat to his right and a man on his left. I supposed one his queen and recognized the man as Perseus, even though he was much older. Perseus spoke to the tagus as we entered and the king inclined his cheek close to the murderer's mouth. I wondered whether asylum was the only favor this tagus bestowed upon his guest.

"Welcome, King Chrysoar!" Jason said, rising and walking towards me in a friendly manner. We met halfway to his throne. "Welcome to Thessaly. You look well." His eyes confirmed his sexual inclination. I stored this information with the rest. "Let me introduce you to my queen and to Prince Perseus." My blood roared in my ears to hear his name. I wanted to lunge forward and kill him immediately with my hands but I resisted. I would need his help.

The queen and Perseus rose and also descended the throne to me. Perseus was a little taller than the king but still stood palms less than I. He was handsome for an old man, wrinkled to be sure but not much. His face was broad and long. He had fine dark eyes, a prominent nose and full lips. I could see why my mother loved him and was tricked to her death. I too felt an urge to kiss those thick lips and be held in those heavily muscled arms.

I suppressed all my urges and greeted Jason's queen with a smile and bow. Then, I turned to Perseus and waited for him to bend to me and, slowly, he did. Still, it was a pretty bow and gave me knowledge of his full head of salt and pepper hair. He righted himself and smiled charmingly into my face. He seemed to have no idea who I was, other than some foreign king. I spoke to him.

"Prince Perseus, I have heard of you, of course."

"My thanks, your majesty. To be spoken of so far away is a great honor." He bowed again slightly. I didn't tell him what I'd heard and he didn't ask.

The tagus was in no hurry to begin trade negotiations, nor was I. What, really, did we have to exchange? Thessaly didn't need our beef and wine. I had seen plenty of cattle and vine-yards on my ride to Larissa. Oh, well. I would think of something.

We spoke about my journey and my impressions of Thessaly, drank sweet red wine and ate delicious figs. It was all very pleasant. When I asked to be released to see to the comfort of my men, they bowed me out of the room.

I found my men, like the good and faithful troops they were, practicing with their weapons, pretending it was just ex-ercise. There would be, I expected, little need for them to protect me and, as for Perseus, I intended to kill him myself, when the time came.

I listened to my captain's report and joked with my men a while. It was a comfort to speak our own language and see true Iberian faces. Being a stranger in a strange land, I had found, was exhausting.

After that spiritual refreshment, I walked around the pleas-ure gardens before returning to the palace. There was still some time before dinner and I did not feel like resting in my rooms so I asked a servant where the library was and followed him down long halls to a room full of scrolls, dust and silence. It was a large room but dark for reading. The servant went for torches. I began a survey, to learn its organization. I first found philosophy, the invention of the Greeks, but the scrolls were in an older form of their language which I could not read. I returned them regretfully to their shelf and went in search of easier literature.

Finding poetry, I settled on a lounging couch near a small window. After a few minutes, a polite knock came at the door and, assuming it was the servant returning, I said "come in" and continued reading. I felt the heat of the torches approach and could see the Eustachus poem more plainly. I thought the man would insert the torches in their sconces and depart, but he cleared his throat and I looked up. It was Prince Perseus himself who held the torches. I rose to my feet with a start.

"The servant said you needed these."

"Yes," I agreed, thanking him. I took a torch and walked to the nearest sconce. Perseus placed the second in the next closest. When I returned to the couch, he joined me there, sitting near me. He picked up the scroll.

"Poetry? I think I heard this Eustachus recite once in Athens."

If my mission were successful, we would both be in Athens soon. I moved closer beside him, the hairs of our thighs brushing each other.

"Really?" I said to keep him talking. "And how was it?" My gambit worked. Perseus began a review of the reading and supplied anecdotes about the great people he had seen in the audience. But then he stopped.

"You are very much like your mother."

I tried not to be flustered. "My mother? How do you know her, sir?"

"Come now, King Chrysaor. The masthead of your ship? But I would have known in any case. Your hair, your looks. I do see her in you." His look turned grim. "Why have you come here? What do you want? Contrition? An apology? I have neither for you."

I stood and shouted down at him. "My mother comes to me in dreams. She cannot cross the Styx to Hades. You know she was innocent. She was praying to the goddess when the god attacked her."

"Your father," he interjected. I nodded in reluctant agreement. "Then, we are alike in some ways, both the sons of a god." His eyes appraised me. "You are wise not to name names though." He reclined on his elbows against the couch, his body moving under his tunic, his manhood close enough for me to grasp.

"Sad boy," he said. "Your father a rapist, your mother a monster. Some call you a monster yourself."

"Don't mock me! And as for my monstrosity...." I straightened to my full height and flexed my muscles for him to see. It was a foolish moment. He extended a leg and tripped me with it. I fell on top of him.

His mouth came close to mine. He breathed lightly against my face and frowned. "I ask you again what you want from me." I spoke before he could overwhelm me. My cock and his were growing.

"I want you to help me regain my mother's head."

He started to laugh, cruel and hard. "And why would I do that, boy?" He covered my ass with his hands. "What would be my reward?"

I tried to ignore his fingers clutching at my ass. "I will give you half my kingdom and any treasure you require."

He looked at me, calculating. "Any?" he asked. I nodded in agreement, and he squeezed my ass rudely. "Then give me yourself. Half your kingdom and all of you, that is what I want."

I did not believe him. Oh, I could believe he wanted me but I did not believe he would help me. I would test him. I put both hands against his chest to stay him, feeling the mounds and nipples there. I made myself concentrate. "After I have my mother's head, you will have me for a night or forever, whatever you wish. But," I could not keep from saying, "Is that really all you want?"

He squeezed my ass again and chuckled. "Is that not enough? Do you value yourself so little?" He pulled my tunic up my thighs and rested one wide hand on my now bare ass, fingers inside the crack. "Shall we not have a sample of the prize now, my young and strapping king?"

I stood up abruptly. My cock pointed perpendicular, in acknowledgment of its interest but my mind battled it for my decision and at last won. "No," I said as firmly as my cock. "Think it over. I stay here three more days."

"And if I say no?" I just looked at him. "You will not succeed without me," he said, finger pointing for emphasis. "The goddess will not listen to your prayer."

"If she does not, she does not," I replied, with a nonchalance I did not feel.

He looked at me shrewdly. "You might be able to steal what you seek but she and her acolytes would chase you back to Iberia and kill you there, if not before. Ah, but you would have the protection of your father," he said, thinking. "On the sea at least," he concluded. He pushed himself off the couch and stood beside me. "I will think it over," he told me, bending my head down to kiss. "Sweet lips," he said before strolling out of the room.

I was left wishing I had given him his sample and wondering what he would decide. I had my answer after dinner.

We ate and drank with our hosts until late. By the time the evening ended, I was very drunk but then everyone was. The tagus' guests walked on wobbly legs towards our rooms, our torches clasped in shaky hands. One by one, the others found their spaces. I found myself walking alone with Perseus. He lurched against me and took my hand.

"I do not want to wait."

"That is just the wine talking," I dared to say.

"Perhaps. But I do not want to wait." We were at the door to his room. "Come in," he commanded. I tried to walk on. He insisted. "Come in or my answer is no, drunk or sober."

With that I entered his room but stayed near the door, alert and undecided. He turned to me with bleary eyes and pointed, grinning. "You need more wine." He staggered towards a goblet and a jug on a table near his bed. He drank from the jug and spat it out. "Bah! Water!" He looked at me, his head wavering. "Come here," he coaxed, beckoning me with a weaving arm. I stayed near the door. "Closer!" he bellowed. I lurched forward. "That's better." He reached up for my shoulders. I could tell he wasn't used to being with men bigger than himself. He pressed up against me, our cocks mashing each other. "Why do you say wait when your cock says now?" He loosened my tunic, and it dropped to the floor. Both scarred hands clamped my chest. "Beautiful. As beautiful as your mother's." The rest of me became as stiff as my cock. "Sorry," he mumbled, fumbling out of his own tunic.

We were naked now except for my sandals and his. He embraced me clumsily and started suckling at my left nipple, then the right. "You like that?" he asked, eyes looking up at me while he sucked. I said nothing. "Bah!" he said again, pushing me away. "I'm not a rapist. Unlike your father," he added, dropping to a sitting position on the bed.

He patted the place beside him but I remained standing. "Sit!" he commanded in the voice I knew must motivate men to die for him. I sat. He fell back against the bed.

"I'm so tired," he told the ceiling, closing his eyes. I stood to leave but a long arm and strong hand pulled me down. "Don't go. We won't have sex if you are against it but don't go." I doubted he would just rest with me the night but thought the tussle might at least answer who was the stronger so I complied.

"Lie with me," he wheedled, like a child. I lay next to him.

He thanked me and snuggled close, his body aligning with mine. Within seconds, his snores told me he was asleep. I could have pulled away, I could have left; he might not have noticed until the morning. But I stayed. I felt the length of him, this man my mother had loved and, for her love, had died. But then everything she loved died, turned to stone by her look. Perhaps death was a blessing for her, a release from her curse. Would she tell me in my dreams tonight?

I looked at her murderer beside me. Perseus snorted in his sleep and said some words I didn't understand, tensing then relaxing. He threw an arm across me and then a leg. Both were massive. I felt the heat of his skin seep into me. I felt the comfort of a man's body on my own. I felt desire. After that I do not remember.

The next morning a knock on the door woke me but not Perseus. We were under bedclothes, naked, lying parallel with the bed, not perpendicular. Perseus was on top of me, still snoring. We had moved; what else had we done? My ass didn't ache. At least he hadn't fucked me.

I shook him awake. "Someone's knocking."

"My servant," he mumbled. "Go away! Come back in another shadow." I heard the slap of sandals retreating and remembered my own. Hadn't we fallen asleep with them on? I felt Perseus' foot with my own. Neither of us was wearing sandals now. I saw them later on the floor, his nestling on top of mine.

Perseus raised his head and rubbed his face awake. It was a very handsome face, even more handsome close than far. "Good morning," he said with a sleepy leer. "Did I get my sample?" He braced his hands on my shoulders and raised himself, looking down our bodies.

I lay inert, arms splayed. "I don't know. I don't remember."

"Me either," he said. "If I did get it, it doesn't count." He rolled off me, landing at my side. His fingers found mine and we both stared at the ceiling, two large men on a rather small bed.

"Did you sleep well?" he asked.

"I don't remember that either."

He laughed. "I feel very well rested. We either had sex or you made me much at ease. It's rare I wake so refreshed." He then was Hippocrates to me. "How about you? Any headache?" When I replied that I was fine he said, "Good," and squeezed my fingers with his, like old friends. I wanted to move away, to get up, to leave before he did anything more. But I didn't. I realized I wanted him to do more. I stayed beside him, waiting.

He looked at me, less groggy now. "You're still here."

"Yes," I agreed and let him mount me without another word.

He was expert in lovemaking. Well, perhaps that is not a fair assessment. I after all had never been with a man except in dreams. But he seemed expert to me.

He began by playing with my hair, his fingers deep among my curls. Then he held them while he kissed my face and lips. A hand went to my chest and squeezed the muscles there. Fingers found a nipple and played it like a flute. His other hand traced down my abdomen, along my stomach to my cock. Perseus jerked me slowly to moaning.

That made him frantic. He ground his pelvis into me, smashing our cocks together in some wild dance. When he lifted my legs I was ready. This was what I'd wanted from life. I moaned again when he entered me, first with one finger, then two and then his cock. His cock! It thrust into me like a sword, like the sword he used to kill my mother.

I worried that the servant would return too soon, but he just shushed me and kept fucking, moving me to my side and onto my stomach, on all fours and then to my back again until I was begging for release. He grinned and began to pound me furiously, with grimaces and growls, threats and entreaties until I yelled and felt semen shoot from my cock onto my chest in several sizable spurts. He roared then and I felt his cock press as far inside me as it could, shooting hot liquid deep within me again and again. I was full of the seed of my mother's murderer and was glad of it.

He kissed me once more and withdrew, landing on his back, reaching up with a hairy arm to wipe the sweat from his face.

"By the gods," he said, still breathing heavily. "That was good. Do you always come like that when a man fucks you? Without a hand, I mean."

"I don't know. You are the first man to try."

"Really?" He leaned over, kissed me again and then smiled crookedly. I didn't know what the smile meant and didn't ask. I was catching my own breath and thinking my own thoughts.

One thought was that now this Perseus would renege on his promise. He had had his sample. I was also thinking how pleasurable sex with him had been. I wondered if any other man would be as good and, if they weren't, what would that mean for the rest of my life.

I felt him looking at me and turned. His eyes were soft and brown. The skin around them crinkled in a smile to match that on his lips. Then his face turned serious. "What is your plan?" he asked. I could not believe my ears but calmed myself. Asking was not necessarily helping.

"I will go to Athens, to the goddess's temple, pray to her and ask her for my mother's head. I will tell her why. My mother is dead. She can be no rival now."

"I have a better one," Perseus said, propping himself up on one thick arm. For a second I remembered what those arms and hands and fingers could do with my body but he regained my attention. "We do not need to travel so far. Athena is also the patron of Larissa."

"Then, there is a temple for her here?" I asked hesitantly.

"Of course," he said emphatically, as if I were an idiot. I bristled at that and tried to stand.

His strong arm kept me with him. "Do you think I did it willingly? I was under her orders."

"Orders?" I asked. That was not the story I had heard.

He looked at me askance. "You think I killed your mother of my own volition?" Yes, I thought but no, I said. He kissed me again and fondled my chest. "Good. I would not want to be that much of a monster in your eyes." His fingers diddling my nipple made my cock stir. He noticed and commented. "You are an eager boy. You will wear me out. Ah, but then it may be worth it." His hand masturbated my cock as his lips kissed mine. I was ready to give him another sample, but he pushed himself off me with an effort.

"No, we must think this through." The we again. My hopes rose as high as my cock. "We will go to the temple here and call to her."

"Will she come?"

He scoffed and arched an eyebrow. "Will she come? I wager she will. We will pray at her temple tomorrow. Now, my love, kiss me."

I did so distractedly, wondering to myself why not *this* day but wondering more at the words "my love." I had never felt love, not even from my mother. Did men fall in love so fast? Did that mean the antithesis would prove true as well? I had to hope his love–or whatever it was–would last long enough for me to get what I wanted. After that, we would see.

We made love often throughout the night. I felt amazement that he made me stay with him after he had had his sample. Did half my kingdom matter so much?

The next morning we bathed and ate and set out at an early hour for Athena's temple. I had not really seen anything yet in Larissa town, between Jason's entertainments and Perseus' lovemaking. There was, I found, not much to see. Even the temple was less than I would have expected. In Iberia, we had magnificent structures for our strange gods. My wife honored them regularly but I went with her even less often than we had sex.

Perseus and I climbed the steps side by side and passed through the colonnade directly in the naos, which was not very large. I wanted to hurry into the cella and call the goddess, but Perseus whispered we should be more deliberate. After so many years, I found it difficult to wait minutes rather than seconds but I took deep breaths and slowed my steps through the pronaos to the door of the goddess's sanctuary. I could see her massive statue through the portal. The builders must have been devout; they spent more of their money on the statue than its enclosure.

I knew the gods lived but I never saw life in their statuary, no matter how elaborately carved and painted. Athena's likeness was no different. It was just a pretty thing. But then Perseus called to the goddess, begging her to come to us, and the statue became flesh and cloth, sword and shield and helmeted Athena was before us. My mother's head was in agony frozen on the shield.

"Why have you called me, Perseus? And why are you with *her* son?" she further asked, turning to me with a glare and a raising of her sword.

"I can easily answer the second question, goddess," he said, taking my hand and smiling at me. "As for the first...." And with that he turned to me. I faced the goddess. I was as tall as she but had no weapon. Still, my hands wanted to encircle her neck and choke the divine life from within her onto the temple floor. She smiled sardonically, as if she knew.

"What is it you want, monster spawn of monsters?"

Perseus held my arm, and I held my tongue. "Great Athena," I said, the words bile in my mouth. "I have come to ask for my mother's head." Her eyes flashed and her lips parted. I rushed to close them. "Please hear me, please. I beg you as a son. My mother has called to me nightly since her death. Headless, she cannot cross the Styx to Elysium…"

"To Hades, you mean!"

I let the venomous words pass. "She must have eyes for me to place the passage coins upon. Please let her rest. She can be of no further irritation to you. Or threat," I thought it wise to add.

Her glare continued after I finished. She turned to my companion. "Perseus, you always did think too often with your heart and not your head. Or perhaps it is with some other organ. In any case, tell me, if I grant this wish, what will you do?" I started to answer. The goddess shouted at me. "I am asking the Argonian."

Perseus grasped my hand again. "I will go with him, wherever that might be."

"Iberia?" Athena sneered.

"If that is where Chrysoar is going."

Athena looked grim. "You assure me that Medusa cannot be raised from the dead?" Before we answered she waved her question away. "I am asking for assurance from mortals?" She thought for several moments, then sighed and I knew that we had won. I also knew the victory belonged to Perseus, not to me. I kissed him in full view of the scowling goddess.

Her grey eyes were stony. "Here," she said, removing my mother's head from her shield. "Take it and go." She handed it to Perseus. "And never expect another favor. I do not know why it is I grant this one." And then she smiled alarmingly. "Perhaps I have been too frequently with my half sister in recent days."

I gave a silent prayer of thanks to Aphrodite and opened the bag of woven gold I had brought from Iberia. Perseus placed my mother's head inside and we bowed our way out, not turning our backs until we were well within the pronaos. Perseus took the bag and my hand and we began our return to the castle of the Thessalonian tagus. I wondered if it really were the beginning of another journey to another Tagus.

We walked a stadion in silence. I could not think what to say. At last, I stopped and faced my mother's killer and savior. "Thank you," I told him. "The words are too small and not enough for what you have done. But I thank you and am ready to give you half my kingdom. " I lowered my eyes to my feet. "You needn't come to Iberia. I will send you an accounting and the profits as often as you ordain."

Perseus lifted my chin with calloused fingers. "Ah, but then how would I claim my second fee?" I looked down at him, un-believing, until he turned us to walk again. I suggested we inspect my ship, since the port was not far off. Perseus agreed.

He admired the masthead and asked, "What does the name mean?"

"Revenge," I answered as I led him up the gangplank, pre-paring my sword.

# Song of Sambandar

I heard Sambandar singing and decided to visit. Appearing before him I realized we were at the lake in Tamil Nadu where we first had met. The lake was the same but he was not. He had changed from boy to man, a very handsome one. When he was young, I had enjoyed his songs to me. Now, as a man, I thought I might enjoy something else of him.

His song, as much as his body, gave me the idea. Its notes stirred my passion; I felt the urge to dance. The hands of my four arms began to make the *mudras*, the sacred motions, and my two feet the *chari*. Sambandar's face shone with joy as if his fondest dream had been realized.

"My Lord Shiva! Welcome!"

"Sambandar, thank you. Please, keep singing."

With that invitation he continued, weaving notes and words like silk into the sky. I could see the fabric of his song floating above us, disappearing into the golden morning air. Sambandar stood dark against the glow, tall for his people and well built. His chest swelled with muscles, and his waist narrowed provocatively. He danced in place, his thighs flexing while he sang.

I had last seen him as a chubby boy, smiling and singing for me. I inspired him to create hymns to the gods, to me if he wished. Today, he was still smiling and singing for me but, with the movements of our dance, his manhood shifted seductively inside his tight white lungi. My eyes focused on the protrusion there.

I watched his hands insert feelings into the song, his fingers turning just so, then curling back. I was entranced. I felt my own manhood grow. He reminded me of Agni and our times together. I had not been with a male since but this Sambandar stirred me even more than the flame-haired one.

I danced closer to him while he sang. Our groins came close and moved in parallel motions, side to side. The musk of him rose. I breathed it in, like a delicious perfume.

When his song and our dance were done, I commanded him to sit with me. He smiled broadly, his teeth stark white in the dark brown of his face, and sat at my feet. My legs assumed the lotus position. My multiple hands folded together in my lap. I felt my manhood rising higher.

"A beautiful song, my boy," I told him, one hand leaving its fellows to caress his cheek.

"Thank you, lord. I wrote it just now. For you. I hoped you would hear it and come." He was so artless. Still, I am suspicious of humankind, always begging for favors, so I was direct in my response.

"Is there something you need from me?" I asked, looking at him sternly. He became shy and ducked his head against his lovely chest. I watched it rise and fall before I spoke again.

"Here. Sit by me." I patted the place beside me on the higher bank. Sambandar complied, rising gracefully, and sat close. I leaned against him. The skin of our bodies clung together only a moment before he pulled discreetly away.

"Do not be shy. I understand." I pulled him back.

He did not look at me but sat tall and proud, presenting his body. Two more of my hands went to his chest, found the nipples and began to play them slowly. When his mouth opened in a gasp, mine met it, hurrying my tongue inside. He leaned his head back ecstatically. To be kissed and touched by a god. I can only imagine what that must feel like to a human.

I held him in place with another hand against the small of his back while the fingers of the other two flicked and pinched, rubbed and pulled. He loved this as much as a woman and I enjoyed giving him this pleasure, but we both knew a god is not satisfied with foreplay.

My fourth hand reached into his longhi and found his manhood risen, hard and thick. I pulled on it slowly as I played with his chest, seeing his eyelids close and his mouth open for new kisses, kisses I did not give.

"Is there a place we can be together?" I asked, not wanting to take him like an animal in the mud by the lake. He tried to stand. Two hands held his broad shoulders down, not wanting to let him escape, not now. He would be mine before I left the lake this day.

"There is a boat house that way." His head nodded to the east.

"Is it far?" I did not want to wait too long.

"No, lord sir. Do you see? Just there." I followed the pointing of his long muscled arm and slender finger. It was indeed not far. I stood, one hand taking one of his as I rose, another sliding around his shoulders, a third returning to his chest. The heat of his skin against mine excited me further. I hurried us to the long building, which inside was almost empty.

"The men are fishing," Sambandar explained. "They won't be back for hours." As if I worried about the arrival of men. What fears would Lord Shiva have of them? I would blind these fishermen if they saw, make them mute if they told.

Sambandar unrolled reed mats for us and spread them on the packed dirt floor. "I am sorry," he said, eyes downcast in shame at such a primitive reception for a god. I raised his blunt chin with a finger of one hand while the fingers of the others stroked and petted him.

"Don't be," I said softly, wanting him ready again, receptive to my seed. I untied my garment and let it drop to show myself to him. His eyes widened and his mouth opened in surprise. He knelt before me with hands clasped in homage and bowed his head in submission.

"Open, Sambandar," I commanded and he obeyed, his thick delicious lips forming the required o for my cock. I slid into him slowly, letting him ingest its great length without choking, until my coarse pubic hairs flattened against his face. My cock seemed to swell even more inside his mouth.

"You please me," I assured him, as he slowly licked up to the head of my cock and back down to its hilt. Talking ceased as he swirled his tongue around my cock, then inserted it inside my foreskin and navigated its inner circumference.

I reached for his nipples with two hands, the other two holding him in place by the shoulders. As I pinched and pulled, his sucking became more vigorous, more exciting. I began to fuck his mouth, slowly at first, then faster and faster, slamming against him with my groin, hearing his moans and cries, seeing his body squirm in delight. He was ripening.

His hands stayed assiduously at his sides. I brought them up to my ass to feel what would happen next. A look of rapture flowed across his face as he dared to hold the buttocks of his lord. He grew brave enough to massage in light circles around the mounds of them.

"That is good, Sambandar," I whispered and his fingers became more dexterous in their motion, kneading the muscles as they pushed and pulled out of his moist and clinging mouth. I held his head close, my fingers entwined in his curling hair, mixing it with the curling mass around my cock. His chin was flush against my semen sacs. I rotated inside his mouth and felt the beginning of his throat, knowing I could release my semen there and it would flow down his gullet, be digested and become part of him. I could impregnate him if I wished and he would bear my child. It would be beautiful and strong. But I made myself wait. I pulled out of him and gently brought him to his feet, watching his wondering face as I untied his lungi, both of us watching as it fell to the mats beneath us.

His cock reached upward, straight and true. It was of course much smaller than mine but perfectly formed and as beautiful as the rest of him. I pressed the greater length of mine against it and rubbed up and down to let the young man know my intentions and to excite him further. I held his ass with two of my hands, cupping the bulbous mounds of men when they are young. My lips and tongue bent to his chest, knowing now how much he enjoyed this. He moaned while I sucked, yelped when I bit and sighed as I licked. Fingers slipped into the cleavage between his ass cheeks and separated them, a third hand found his pleasure hole, opening it for one finger, then two, then three. He cried out each time, the first from fear or anticipation I could not be sure. The second told me he was a virgin, which was good. The third said he was willing.

I whispered to him as I licked and bit his ear lobe, "Don't be alarmed, Sambandar. I know you have not been with a man. It will hurt, yes, at first but then the fucking will feel more wonderful than anything you have felt before."

I watched his eyes show me hope, as well as fear. It was time.

I lowered him quickly onto the mats. It was time for me too. For a moment I stood above his tense figure, with legs apart and hands on my hips, to show him his lord in all his glory. He spread his legs for me and held up his hands for my embrace. I smiled my approval and lowered my body onto his, pushing his thighs wider and back with mine, finding his hole immediately with the tip of my cock. He stifled another cry as I pushed just the head inside him.

"Boy, that is barely a *dismil*. I have ten more for you!" His god would not be stopped from his pleasure now. But I felt sympathy for him. One of my hands manipulated his cock and two more pulled at his nipples. The fourth caressed his cheek. He relaxed and I eased in a *dismil* more but stopped when his body stiffened again in fear. I could have taken him without hesitation, without scruple, but I remembered his song and our dance and decided I would be gracious. I held the additional *dismils* of my cock outside him while I manipulated his body, giving him his time. He relaxed at last completely, his face finally smiling. I kissed it and slid further inside him, watching his smile broaden. He no longer seemed afraid. I pushed all of myself in.

"I am all the way within you, my beauty," I said quietly, kissing him softly once, twice, and then third time more vigorously as I began to fuck him with both my tongue and cock. Two hands squeezed the muscles of his ample chest, as large as many females', and plucked the small nipples more rapidly now. The other two pushed his legs further back and held them there. I pressed my groin against his. He closed his eyes, joy blooming across his face. I pulled partly out, exposing my shaft, watching my cock stab back into him. He moaned and rolled from side to side.

"My Lord Shiva!" he gasped.

"I know, my beauty. I know." I held his head up to see my cock, as well as feel it, as it plunged into and out of him. Another hand jerked his cock in time to my fucking, coordinating our pleasure. I accelerated the pumping of my hand and cock. He yelped each time I sheathed myself inside him. I had found the place that would make his liquid flow and pounded it with vigor and speed, slapping against the thick muscles of his ass, feeling the receptive softness of him against the invasive hard of me. I watched his eyes glaze in approaching ecstasy and knew that he was close. I began to grind inside his ass, as well as penetrate it.

Sambandar writhed beneath me, moaning so deliciously. This excited me to a wildness I rarely felt. When he began to yell my name, I knew. His ass gripped my cock and my seed shot into him as his spurted onto his slender stomach. We both yelled then, incoherently, as our bodies crashed and held, crashed and held against each other.

I thought again of giving him a child. I could have if I had willed it, but I decided again not yet. I would have him many more times like this before I disfigured his body with the swelling of a child. I would take him with me when the child was conceived. He would give birth to our children in the *char bagh* of the gods and he would be honored by humans.

I finished expelling myself into him, knowing I was now a part of him, knowing he would realize this after I had left and be glad. He would not be lonely, knowing I was still inside him.

But I would not be leaving soon. I stayed with him for hours and we came and came again together on those simple mats in that unextraordinary room. I held the fishers back until we were upright and dressed again, standing arm in arm beside each other on the shore, seeing them as they arrived at last near sundown. Their catch was mighty. I had filled their boats with fish while I filled my Sambandar with seed.

When I slipped away at last, I left him with a message on the evening wind. "I will return for you, my beauty. I will return for you."

Through the days which followed, I heard Sambandar's prayers for my return and his songs. They all pleased me but I had other pleasures and other duties. It was therefore some time before I made good my promise.

I found him walking in the forest near his home and took him there against a tree, then on all fours and a third time lying on soft boughs he cut for us. I lingered after, while he sang new songs for me and we danced together. It was with something like regret when I finally left him, disconsolate, among the karevelum trees of the sacred grove.

In the two years following, Sambandar and I met and conjoined many times. At one meeting, after we had lain together and I had filled him once again with godly semen, Sambandar told me he was to marry.

"My parents insist on it."

"It is good for humans to marry," I said in a neutral tone. "You will produce beautiful children if your wife is handsome."

He looked at me intently. "Then you think I should marry?"

"Of course," I said, smiling at his intensity. He could marry and I could still have him any time I wanted. There would be no change for me. After he had lain with his bride, I would lay with mine if I so chose.

"All right," he said with a new, stubborn look: chin out, jaw set. This surprised and did not please me. He looked less the bride and more the groom. I softened his look with hands on his chest, tongue among his teeth, and my cock up his ass. I left him dreaming.

He sang fewer songs for me after that visit and I came less often. I watched him transform into a man, which was unfortunate. Sambandar was not really made for manly ways.

His fiancée was indeed lovely and of a very fine family. They would have many beautiful children and be rich, but I knew Sambandar was not happy. This bothered me more than I wanted it to. He had his duty to his parents. He must fulfill his responsibilities. My irritation may have been peevishness; I did miss his songs—and his body. I knew his heart though. I knew he was still mine, underneath the anger and disregard.

On the day of the wedding, with Sambander's bride beautiful in a flowing red sari of the finest silk and Sambandar himself handsome in his spotless *longhi* and *sattai*, everyone

was happy but the groom. He stood on the edge of the festivi-
ties, his arms folded, face stern, smiling when approached with
congratulations but relaxing into frowns when left alone.

I watched all of this, very saddened. Perhaps I should have
given other advice. Perhaps I should have been more selfish
and demanded he save his body and seed for me, his lord god.
Perhaps I should have made good on my plan to impregnate
him and take him to my home on Mt. Kailasa in the Himalayas.
I still could but I saw the happiness of all but one around me
and hesitated.

The wedding vows started. The priest began his incanta-
tions. My bride and his faced each other. It was then I heard
Sambandar's prayer rise from his heart.

"Save me, Lord Shiva. Save me from this. Take me now. Let
me be with you forever." He repeated this over and over, in his
head and then out loud, shouting it into the air like thunder.
He was still mine! I sent lightening in response, in answer to
his prayers. Fire caught on his clothing, singeing then burning
the beautiful cloth. It leapt to his head, making it darker than
dark. He fell, consumed into ash. His bride fell with him. Her
parents, his parents, her family, his family, all their friends
were burnt into ash and then reborn as their deeds and
thoughts required. Only Sambandar did I bring to me in
*moksha*, free from *samsara* forever.

As I enclosed him in my arms, I thought my thoughts and
his. We would be together always. He would have my children. We would start the impregnating soon but not just then.

I held him, glad that he was mine and no other's, man or
woman, and would be mine through time and time again. I
kissed his eager face and opened his sattai. My fingers found
his nipples and played music on them for his songs. I removed
his longhi and spread his legs, entering him with no additional
preliminary. Only then did I realize how much I had missed his

body. I began to fuck. His song grew louder. My voice joined his. We would sing together through forever.

# Science Fiction

INHUMAN BEINGS

# Cat Man

"Hey!" I said to a large black cat sprawled across the speed bump in Elizabeth alley. "You nearly tripped me." He gave a friendly meow. I bent down to pet his sleek black fur, and he stretched to sniff my crotch.

"You must be a gay cat," I said out loud, laughing at my own joke. He meowed again like we were having a conversation and rolled onto his back, inviting me to rub his stomach. I could see he hadn't been neutered. When I obliged he closed his olive eyes and began to purr. After giving his belly a final rub, I rose to finish my run. He was staring after me both times I looked around.

Back home on 26th Street, I forgot the cat and went on with my day. I took a leisurely shower and made a second cup of coffee before wandering to my desk in a sleeveless shirt and baggy sweat shorts. I didn't envy my neighbors having to take vehicles to work downtown or down the Peninsula. My commute lasted 10 seconds.

Coffee at hand I began writing my next blog post. I'd started the blog because my editor said, "All authors should have a blog," which was the same argument my agent had used to get me to set up a website. After an hour on the blog and 30 minutes updating the website, I spent the rest of the day editing the proof of my next novel. It had to be finished before the book tour for my current one started on the 27<sup>th</sup>. Once I'd finished the tour, I'd start writing the new novel. I really couldn't juggle three projects at once, like my agent and editor wanted me to.

The day passed productively and the evening was spent with friends for drinks and dinner. Writing is solitary and I'm social so most of my evenings are booked. I don't date much though. After Dan left I'd thought I'd take a break from men.

I staggered home and fell asleep more quickly than usual, but sometime in the night a persistent noise woke me. I looked at the clock and then at the noise. The black cat with the olive eyes was scratching at my second story window. When he saw me, he stood on his hind legs, displaying his cock and balls a second time for me.

"All right, all right," I mumbled, still mostly asleep, throwing back the covers.

I raised the window and let him in, leaving it open enough so he could leave when he was ready. I got back under the covers, and the cat snuggled next to me. I fell back asleep to his loud purring.

I had a weird dream that night. The visiting cat became a man, as black as the cat and just as sleek. He said his name was Abayomi and that it meant bringer of happiness. He was tall and slender, with skin the color of aubergine. The cat man fucked me twice, changed back into a cat and left through the open window before dawn.

In the morning the bed was rumpled, the blanket was half off me and the cat was gone. "What a dream!" I thought, struggling upright. My body felt all tingly, like I'd had an excellent massage. I scratched my ass, pulled on my jogging shorts and stumbled zombie-like to the kitchen.

I allowed myself one cup of coffee before heading out for a run. While the water boiled, I noticed the scratch marks across my chest. Where had they come from?

After coffee, I finished dressing and headed up Church Street and back down Elizabeth. The black cat was not in sight when I reached the speed bump but I heard a meow nearby. Still no cat but there was an attractive man raking leaves in the small yard across from the bump. He wore baggy sweats, a tight t-shirt and thick black framed glasses. His skin was the color of Japanese eggplant.

"Good morning," he called, smiling broadly. I smiled back.

"Good morning."

He held out his hand and I stepped to take it across the picket fence. "Jack," I told him.

"Case," he said and then repeated it for me. He had a strong, warm grip. "I just moved into the neighborhood." I heard an accent in his voice.

"Where from?"

"New York." His accent didn't sound New York to me. He must have seen the doubt in my eyes. "I'm Jamaican," he said quickly and let go of my hand. I regretted that. His touch had reminded me of how good a man can feel.

We chatted a few minutes more before I asked about the cat. "Have you seen him, a big black one? Really friendly."

He looked at me with an odd smile. "That's Aba." I tried not to show my surprise. "It's an African name, short for Abayomi. It means…."

"Bringer of happiness," I finished for him.

"Yes," Case agreed, with a grin. "You know Yoruba?" I noticed his almond shaped eyes were green behind the glasses.

"Not really." There didn't seem to be a good way to explain so I didn't. "Is he your cat?" I asked.

"In a way."

"Huh?"

"Well, you know. Cats think they own *us*." We both laughed.

"He came to visit me last night," I said and wished I hadn't. "At least I think he did. I may have dreaming." I didn't tell him about the dream I *knew* I'd had.

"Probably," Case agreed. "He does like to wander after dark." He began to rake leaves again in a very determined way. I looked at my watch.

"Well, I better get going." I didn't really want to.

"Okay. Enjoy your run," he said, looking up to smile me off. I looked back once and caught him looking. He waved. I waved back and thought about him for the rest of my run, wondering whether he were gay. He was really good-looking and very friendly. I wondered what he did, how old he was, whether he liked sushi. I spent the day thinking about Case whatshisname and didn't get much work done.

That night I went to a movie with my sister and talked too much about Case and Aba. "Ask him out," she whispered over popcorn, tired of shushing me during the movie.

"I don't even know him."

Alix gave me one of those infuriating looks women have and poured the last of the popcorn down her throat.

At home, after I went to bed, the black cat was back outside my windowsill and the black man reappeared in my dreams. This time, he looked just like Case but without the glasses and without the clothes. The cat man made love to me slowly and thoroughly. After our consecutive climaxes, he collapsed on top of me. Our sweat mingled comfortably.

I woke up suddenly, expecting the man still to be there, but of course he wasn't since he never had been. Neither was the cat. I threw back the covers and noticed I had come in my sleep. What was I, 15 again? Also, my ass hurt. What had I eaten? A trip to the bathroom produced no information, except I had more scratches across my body.

Wednesday morning I was back on Elizabeth, hoping to see Case and follow my sister's advice. He wasn't in his yard but I did see Aba perched on his speed bump. As I slowed to pet him, he stood up and looked at my crotch. I bent down to let him take a whiff, thinking how freaky that was. He leaned in and nuzzled my privates. I stood up abruptly, scaring the cat.

He ran into Case's yard and around the side of his house. I looked down at myself, wondering what to do with my erection, especially when I heard a door open. Case was leaving his house, dressed in a pale grey business suit. It outlined his body perfectly. I put my hands over my crotch.

"Good morning!" he called. His eyes went to my hands. He opened his gate still staring at them.

"How are you?" I asked, embarrassed but not wanting to leave.

"I'm fine. You're looking good," he said to my groin. "Out running again?"

"Every morning," I mumbled, staring dreamy eyed at his high cheekbones and perfect skin.

"Maybe we should run together."

I could think of other things I'd rather do with him but managed not to bring them up. "Okay," I told him, in a lame sounding voice.

"When do you run?"

"Every morning," I repeated.

He laughed. "I meant, what time?"

"6:30?" I said, hoping it wasn't too late or too early.

He glanced at his watch. "I had better go. Tomorrow at 6:30 then." I nodded and he left, walking in the direction of the J train. He looked back once and waved before he rounded the corner. Sighing too audibly I went to Case's gate and shut it for him. Aba was nowhere to be seen. After several moments spent hoping one of them would return, I sighed and resumed my run.

That night, Aba and Case came to me a third time. Case and I seemed to fuck all night. In the morning I overslept as if we really had, leaving myself no time for coffee and only 10 minutes to get to Case's house. I jumped into yesterday's jogging clothes, wet my hair down to a lower level of disorder and ran flat out to Elizabeth.

"Sorry I'm late," I huffed as I skidded to a stop in front of him. He was waiting outside his house, leaning against the fence, arms folded across his chest, hips thrust out. Oh man, so hot.

He straightened up when he saw me. "You didn't have to run, Jack. I'm Jamaican after all," he joked. "No worries, mon." He reached for my shoulder and gave it a squeeze, which felt comforting and exciting at the same time. It also felt familiar.

Out on the street, I followed his ass for a while and then he followed mine. Eventually, we ran side by side, chatting easily. Case told me he worked in marketing for a national pet supply company. I confessed I was a writer, and he asked what I'd written. My answer was way too long. By the time I'd finished, we were tired, sweaty and running down 24th Street.

"Want a cuppa?" he asked in a lilting voice as we neared Martha's, a local coffee hangout. I remembered I hadn't had caffeine yet.

"Please!" I wheezed out. Case ran at a faster pace than I normally did.

He looked amazing, walking out of the shop with my coffee and his tea, all six foot two of him. Heads turned. I was proud when he sat down next to me in the parklet outside Martha's. We settled back into red metal chairs and conventional conversation, like neighbors over a fence.

"I ran track at Sen Jen's," he said in between sips when we got around to talking about college.

"Is that a school in Jamaica?"

He laughed. "Oh, sorry. St. John's. In New York. Sometimes the Jamaica in me does come out. Did you run track too?"

"In high school. What was your event?"

"Hurdles," he said. "And 100 meters." That explained the thighs.

"How about you?"

"The mile and 1500."

"I'm impressed."

"Don't be. I didn't say I was any good."

"I bet you were." He looked at me over his tea until I answered.

"First place senior year in regionals, fourth at state in the mile. Seventh place in the 1500."

Case nodded his head approvingly, as if I'd told him the truth he already knew. "You have a lot of stamina."

"Yes," I agreed, not sure where to go with that. I took another sip of my breve latte and asked, "So, why did you move to San Francisco?"

"Oh, you know, the gay thing."

I choked and dribbled coffee down my chin. Case quickly and thoroughly wiped it off with a square brown paper napkin imprinted with Martha's logo, as if I dribbled every day in front of him.

"Thanks," I mumbled, trying not to look at the local eyes around us. I had enough of a literary name for them to notice. I'd hate for friends to forward a photo of me in mid dribble.

"No problem."

I noticed his coffee cup was empty. Mine was half full and cold. "Oh, I'm sorry. I don't want to make you late for work."

"Finish your coffee," he said and reached up for my arm to hold me in place. I sat back down, wishing he wouldn't let go, but he did of course. I gulped my latte, trying not to look at him too much.

We trotted back to his house, my coffee sloshing inside me. Outside his gate I lingered a while, hoping for an invitation to shower and maybe more. Case looked like he might be considering it, but then a decisive look came over his face. "I have to get ready."

"I know. Same time tomorrow?"

He agreed, seemed to bend towards me, but pulled himself back from an almost kiss. "Tomorrow," he repeated, like it was a different kind of promise.

The following morning, after another nocturnal visit from black cat and man, instead of heading to Martha's, Case led us back to his house after we finished our run. We thudded to a stop in front of his gate, chests heaving, shirts drenched in sweat, like we'd already had sex. He looked up and down the street, then put both hands on my shoulders and leaned towards me into a kiss. His lips felt so good, so soft and moist and strong. I opened my mouth for his tongue, and it played with mine like it did in my daydreams.

He pulled away and took a deep breath. "I'll be late for work."

I couldn't decide between saying "so, be late" and "okay, I'll go". He leaned in for another kiss and pressed his erection against mine.

"Damn," he said when he pulled away a second time. He shook his head ruefully. "See you tomorrow?"

"Okay." I was disappointed though. I hadn't had sex in months, except for dreams and they didn't count. He probably hadn't had that problem.

I watched Case close the door to his house and felt the loneliness I tried to avoid after Dan. Damn, I said to myself and turned to run home. A loud meow brought me back to Case's gate. Aba bounded towards me, leapt over the fence and landed in my arms. I held him close, grateful for his touch, and gave him a kiss on the head, which he didn't seem to mind. After I set him down on the speed bump, he stretched up my thigh on his hind legs, holding on with one paw and batting at my erection with the other. I pushed him down; I wasn't that horny.

"If you were human, Aba, I'd be on you in a minute." He meowed indignantly and ran off, inside Case's yard and around the back of the house.

Saturday morning, Case and I didn't go to Martha's either. When he turned off Sanchez onto Elizabeth, I tried not to yell hurrah. By the time we ran the half block to his house, I was hard.

We stopped at the gate. Oh no. Not another goodbye.

"See you tomorrow," he said quickly, giving me a quicker kiss, then walked into his house. I waited. Maybe at least the cat would come see me but no such luck. I trudged off to my place, tired of running and even more tired of men.

I wasn't surprised to receive a text canceling our Sunday run. Case lied that he had to fly suddenly to Dallas on business and wouldn't be back for a few days. I would be on my own again. After spending time with Case every day, that was a depressing realization. Oh well. At least I'd have Cat Man during the night. No such luck. No Case and no Cat Man. I had to jerk off all by myself.

Monday morning, Aba wasn't waiting for me and didn't come to greet me. On impulse, I snuck around to the backyard. No cat there either. I admired Case's gardening skills for a few minutes before deciding to head out. I didn't want the neighbors to call the police and report me as a suspicious character. That would look good on Huffington Post.

I didn't run down Elizabeth Tuesday or Wednesday. Case wouldn't be there and Aba seemed to have moved on in his affections, the way cats do. Even Cat Man had deserted me. I was alone in my dreams all three nights Case was gone. I missed all of them, for different reasons.

I thought maybe Case would call or text me while he was in Dallas but no. I said it was okay but didn't believe myself one bit. By Wednesday night, I was really expecting a call. I mean, were we running Thursday or not? But no messages were received, whether voice mail, text or telepathic. I tried to be philosophical. We had just met. Maybe he wasn't into white guys. Thoughts like that kept me from getting much writing done, at least anything I wouldn't want to delete the next day.

At least Cat Man came back to me Wednesday night. We fucked like we hadn't seen each other in 20 years.

I assumed no Thursday run and no further possibility of romance between me and Case but I was wrong, about the run at least. He called at 6 a.m.

"Is it too early?"

"No," I mumbled, rubbing my eyes. I hadn't climbed out of bed yet. Why should I? It wasn't like I was meeting anyone.

"Good. Sorry I didn't call last night. I had a late flight." Before I could comment, he went on to ask if I wanted to take a run. Against my better angel, I agreed.

We met, we ran and we wound up in front of his place again.

"Would you like to come in?" he asked, olive eyes staring.

"Sure," I said, trying to be casual. Case opened the gate for me and squeezed my ass as I passed by him. I would have done it in the front yard I was so hot for him.

Inside, once the doors were closed, our hands were all over each other, tearing off clothes, pawing skin. We were kissing like we were starved for it. His hands did everything I liked without me asking. When he pushed me down on all fours I didn't argue. I pressed my ass against his cock and arched.

"Wait, baby," he whispered. I heard him stand and walk away. I turned my head around. He was opening a condom package, for which I felt grateful. I would have done something stupid.

He hurried back, jerking his cock inside its protective sheathing. I felt the head as he guided it inside me.

"Ohhhh!" I yelled, glad there were no neighbors with contiguous walls.

"Mmmm," Case purred. He leaned down to kiss my back. When he bit my neck, I screeched in surprise. He seemed to like that because he bit me again. His hands reached under me, holding me tight, and his groin began to pound insistently against my ass. When I reached for my cock, he growled his approval. He came inside me, yowling into my ear and scratching at my chest. I felt as if I were dreaming, except my dreams had never been this good, not even with Cat Man.

Case rested his head against my back, his hands rubbing my chest where he'd scratched. He kissed my neck where he'd bitten.

"That was so good, baby."

I leaned my mouth around to meet his.

We both got hard again. Case pulled out and stood up. "Come take a shower with me," he offered as a consolation prize.

"Okay but no funny stuff."

He gave me a quick smooch. "Well…"

"Uh uh uh," I said, wagging my finger. He bit it, waggling it back at me in his teeth.

When we said goodbye at the door, him in his suit, me back in my sweaty running togs, he asked me to spend the night with him. I agreed but worried about it all day. What if Cat Man came again in my dreams?

I woke the next morning from a dreamless sleep in Case's bed. He was curled against me, a real man, not an imaginary feline version of one. When I stroked his shoulder and sleek arm, he started purring. I reached around for his cock and he turned to face me and give me kisses.

"You still horny, baby?" he said in a sleepy voice, patting my head.

"Always," I replied, my hands stroking his back like I'd learned he liked.

He stretched, eyes closed, mouth open. "Ooh, that feels good." When I stopped petting, his head lowered and his eyes opened. "How did you sleep?"

"Great!"

"No bad dreams?"

"No dreams at all."

He smiled enigmatically at me, solemn olive eyes blinking once.

We got our run in, had our shower and said our goodbyes. I jogged back home, hopeful and happy with a real ache in my ass from Case's real cock. It was a reminder of him all day as I sat at my desk.

Our morning runs and nightly sex continued for weeks. Cat Man didn't reappear in my dreams, and I almost forgot about him. I also didn't see Aba much anymore. Case said he had taken to wandering. He didn't seem very worried. I made the mistake of pressing the point.

"Maybe he's hurt. We should offer a reward, put up posters."

"We?" His eyes narrowed.

"I mean, you," I amended hurriedly.

"No," he said simply and returned to reading his book.

"Why not? Don't you care about him?"

"Look, he's my cat."

"Yes, but...."

"There is no yes but," Case said with a finality I didn't understand until later.

The next day, he called me from work. Another quick trip to Dallas. I said I'd miss him and asked him to call.

He didn't.

I sent messages, tried emails and posts, tweeted, everything. Nothing but silence from him.

I felt depressed and didn't run while he was gone. I didn't even leave the house. Thursday morning though I suited up and ran down Elizabeth to see if he was home. There was a for sale sign in the yard. I knocked on the door, but there was no answer. I thought about waiting until he left for work but didn't want to be that guy. I called his office number after nine. They had to go get him.

"I can't talk right now."

"You're moving."

"I'm being transferred. Look, I'm in a meeting."

"You just moved here."

He took a deep breath. "Let's talk about it tonight."

"No, there isn't going to be any 'tonight.' You're moving and you didn't tell me. When did you find out?"

"Okay, okay. I'm in the hall now. I found out a couple of days ago. In Dallas. I'm sorry. I should have told you. It was sudden. Let's talk tonight. I'll stop by after work."

"Don't."

I hung up and slumped back in my chair, fuming. Oh, what the hell. I went off for another run. I tore up hills, trying to get rid of the anger and hurt. It didn't work. I called up a gay masseur, got a rub down and had sex. I'd never done that before. I'd never done a lot of things before. I might try them all now. Men were rats. I might get a cat, a big one, to keep them away.

During the day I ignored Case's calls. When Aba showed up at my window around lunch, I called a friend to meet me at The Cove in the Castro and left the house. I watched a double feature at the Castro Theater and went to a bar. It was late when I got home. Aba was at the building door but I kicked him away. He was leaving too after all.

I took my clothes off and lay down alone in bed. As I was drifting off, I heard the window open. Case was putting one leg in and then the other. He was naked.

"What the hell? How did you get up to the second storey? Damn, dude! You're naked."

He closed the window after him and stood next to the drape. "I climbed down from the roof."

"The roof? How'd you get on the roof?"

"It's easy, for a cat."

"A cat? What the hell do you mean?"

The next moment Case began to change. Within a few moments more he had become a cat. He had become Abayomi. Aba looked at me with Case's eyes and leapt in one swift move on top of me. I watched and felt as he became Case again.

"I sure hope I'm dreaming."

"Is that supposed to be funny?" Case asked hopefully.

"Not yet," I answered. "Get off me." He rolled away. "Why?"

"I wanted to meet you. I'd seen you run past my house."

"I mean, why as a cat?"

He looked me in the eye. "Some white people take better to a black cat than a black man." We both thought about that a few moments.

"Okay, I'll go with this," I said, sitting up against the wall. "When did you start changing into a cat? Or were you originally a cat and changed into a man?"

Case sat up next to me, inches away. "It started when I was a kid. I wanted to be a cat and then I was. I thought it was cool. Eventually, I could change anytime I wanted. But sometimes it just happens."

He looked so forlorn I reached over to stroke his arm but, when he closed his eyes and began to purr, I jerked my hand back. His eyes widened in surprise. We stared at each other, neither of us blinking.

"So you raped me," I said finally.

Case's eyes turned angry. "No, I didn't. I did not rape you. You invited me into your bed."

"But not into my room. You took advantage of me. I thought it was a dream." I folded my arms across my chest.

"What difference does that make? You still invited me."

I refused to say anything more. Case got up.

"I'll go. This is why I'm moving. I knew this would happen. It always does."

"It wouldn't if you were honest."

"Honest? Like this? Hey, mon, sometimes I'm a cat and, brudder, I'm always black. You okay wid dat?" We stared each other down again, and then I got up too.

"You'll need some clothes." I pulled a tee shirt and shorts out of a drawer and held them out to him. He took them, smelled both and sighed.

He handed them back. "I'll just change." And then he did, leapt onto the windowsill and disappeared.

I didn't get much sleep that night.

When it was light, I got into my running shorts, shirt, socks and shoes and headed to Elizabeth Street. I knocked on Case's door and called his phone but he didn't answer either of them. He had to be home. I went around the house to the back, where his bedroom was. A window was open a few inches to let fresh air in. I raised it higher.

"Who's there?" he yelled from inside, sounding alarmed.

"Just the cat," I replied and put one leg over the windowsill. "Just the cat."

# Exchange of Fluids

He found me in the ruins where the wild dogs went. I didn't ask what he wanted. Men only visited dogs for one reason. I turned for him so he could decide, hoping he would pick me and not keep looking. When he began to take off his clothes, my mouth filled with saliva. I would drink today!

He bent me over and down, forcing my hands and knees onto the rubble of the ruined building. I couldn't help wagging my ass, although we no longer have tails. After Destruction, we lost them and our dog's ears and noses. We still have body hair, which is good since the Outsiders won't let us wear clothing against the cold. Tails or not, we are still dogs in their minds–and in ours.

I prepared myself for hurt but he stopped just inside me, letting me get used to him. When he did slide further in, it was slowly, not the hard quick push that would make me yelp. Men like the yelping; it reminds them of what we are.

This man was different though. He took his time. I was the one who felt impatient. Just let me drink, I wanted to say but didn't. Men don't like talking dogs.

The man inside me delayed, wrapping his arms around my body and hugging his to mine, kissing my neck and back. I was so thirsty I began to fuck myself. I pushed into him and pulled away, pushed and pulled. Finally, he began on his own. He was slow, so slow it almost felt good.

I listened to his panting. He began to grunt and pound against my ass, like all the rest of them. When the yelling began, I was glad. The feeling of wet was inside me. I was drinking. I might not die that day.

The man's breathing returned to normal but he stayed on top of me. Maybe he would give me a second drink. Most men pulled out and left without a word. They had fucked the dog; time to go. I squirmed against his groin to let him know I was willing.

"No," he said, pulling away. It was strange to hear his voice. Men didn't talk much to dogs. If they did, they barked orders like they were the dogs, not us, or said sex words when they got excited.

My man that day brought me back to standing, two legged again, and held me at arm's length, looking at me. I looked too. I could see now he was an Insider. He was clean and his body had meat on it. He ate often. I envied him.

The Insider gently urged me down to my knees. His cock rose into my face. I clamped my lips around it to make sure no fluids escaped and began to suck. He reached down for my nipples and tugged at them gently. I felt nothing from it but let him play. If it made him happy, maybe he would return and give me more drinks. It did happen. Men had a favorite dog. Sometimes men even took dogs home with them, giving them drinks every day. At least I think they did. We had never seen those dogs again, except for one.

My man took over now, sliding his cock in and out of me. It was a good cock, not too short, too long or too wide. Some men hurt me with their size but didn't mean to; some men enjoyed the hurting. I didn't care much, as long as I got to drink. I only fought when a man tried to leave without giving me his fluid. Then, I bit and scratched. If they didn't want to lose their fluid, they shouldn't come to where the wild dogs live. I made sure they remembered that.

I was thinking of those men when the Insider began to yell and spurt fluid into my mouth, shooting it so far inside me most of it drained directly into my throat. I was sorry for that. I liked the feel of moist in my mouth.

The Insider patted my head. "Do you want to come too, boy?" I shook my head, wanting him to leave. My stomach was growling. There would be no food if I didn't hurry.

"I'll come again," he said in a kind voice. I had learned not to trust kind voices. They were the men with clubs. I never drank from them but some dogs did, the desperate ones. I hoped I never became one of them.

The Insider did another strange thing then. He pulled me up and pressed his lips against mine. Some men wanted to do this before but never after. But this man held his lips against mine for a several clicks. The feeling was strange but exciting. His arms went to my shoulders and then around my back. Our cocks landed against each other. He was hard again too.

"I'm sorry," he said over my back. I had never heard that word before. "I have to go." I understood *go*. "I'll come again," he said, sounding sincere. I wagged my ass.

As soon as the man left, I ran out of the ruins towards the nearest Keep. Many other dogs were already there, pawing through the garbage the Insiders had thrown over the walls. There was nothing left for me. I would be hungry this day unless the late one was late again.

I went to where she always threw her leavings over. Other dogs were there too. When she came into view over the rampart, we jostled for position. When the debris fell onto us, I clutched at it frantically. Any food would do. I caught something that felt edible and chewed it quickly, swallowing before one of the other dogs could force the food out of my mouth into his.

I licked my face to make sure of any crumbs or bits stuck to the dirt on me and looked up in case there might be more. The Insider who had given me two drinks that day was looking over the rampart at me. I felt ashamed and slunk away, back to the ruins.

I found our pack there and, after sniffing everyone and letting them sniff me, I exercised to keep myself looking good for men. After that I tried to sleep. Big Dog wanted sex with me, but then he always did. I was his favorite bitch. I let him fuck me, and he let me suck him. It was that way among us dogs, an exchange of fluids. Dogs that didn't follow the Rule were cast out of the pack. If they learned and were lucky, another pack took them in. If not, they were excluded, alone and doomed.

Our pack was all males. In the mother pack, if we wanted sex with other males, we left it for one like I was in now. I saw my mother now and then but she was always busy with new pups. After a while I stopped trying to make her see me.

Big Dog protected us. He was strong and fierce and very popular with men. They vied for him and brought him gifts. One time, he said, an Insider took him into a Keep, which was dangerous for the Insider and Big Dog both. Dogs are not allowed Inside. The man wanted Big Dog to stay, to wash, to work in the Keep, to live like the Insiders. But Big Dog didn't like Inside and he left. He told us stories though. I daydreamed sometimes about being Inside. If a man took me there, I would stay.

The Keeps were all built around a fluid source. They were big enough for gardens and a few small meat animals. The one near us was larger than most. Our pack roamed from Keep to Keep during the day but always came back to the ruins at night. It was our place. We were the wild dogs of the ruins.

The next morning I was back in my spot, hoping again a man would choose me. Men had already come for Big Dog, and he had made his choice. I could hear the man fucking him through the chinks in the wall between us, the man grunting and Big Dog howling already. He was always noisy in sex. I got hard listening to them.

Footsteps said another man was approaching so I stood to display myself. It was good to be hard when they inspected you.

When the man rounded the corner, I could see it was the Insider from yesterday. I smiled—men like smiling dogs—and he smiled back, coming to me without stopping to evaluate. I felt glad. He wanted to give me another drink.

He got me onto all fours again, where dogs should be anyway, and lowered himself on top of me. His cock was hard and rubbed up and down my crack. Some men spilled their fluids that way but I knew how to stop them. I had learned a lot in three years.

When I reached around for the man's cock, he let me take it. I found my hole and put his cock inside it. He slid in right away and held himself against me. That was good. I would get all the fluids, including the beginning drops.

His cock twisted slowly inside me. Big Dog did this, and I liked it. I began to pant. The Insider reached around for my nipples and jerked at them as he fucked me harder. He pinched, and I yipped. That made him fuck faster, which was good. Then one of his hands grasped my cock.

"No," I said, pushing it away. He seemed surprised. He could have beaten me for saying no, but I didn't want to lose any fluid. It was one thing with Big Dog–he was our alpha–but with a man I would risk a beating to keep my fluids.

"Okay," the Insider said, letting my cock swing free. He kept his arms close around me though, resting his chin on my shoulder.

He licked my ear, his fucking regular now. He was in the middle stages. When he bit my earlobe, I yelped and he bit again. I felt strange. My body was tingling. Usually, I only got excited with Big Dog or another bitch, never with men. I even began to moan. The Insider liked my moaning and started grunting into my ear, fucking really fast and hard. When he came he spurted several times, more than the previous day. I felt refreshed, not just inside but all over.

Our panting merged and slowed. I waited for him to leave but he surprised me again, turning me onto my back. Men never had sex with male dogs that way, although Big Dog says they do with real bitches and women. I was curious.

At first, the Insider just looked down at me, smiling again. I smiled back. He was good looking–for a human–nothing like Big Dog but still pleasant to see. The hair on his head was clean and combed. He had as much body hair as I did across his chest and stomach and down his arms and legs but it was blond.

His body bothered me because it was so clean and mine was so dirty. I hadn't thought much about my dirt before; dogs and Outsiders were all dirty. I heard there were Outsiders and dogs by the Great Sea who were clean but I didn't believe it.

This man was the first Insider I had seen up close. Crinkles appeared beside his eyes when he smiled. He was still smiling when he held our cocks together. I started to say "No" again but he made a calming sound and let them go, bending over to kiss my lips and then my nipples. He played with my body for a long time, making me squirm beneath him. He liked that, I could see. It was different, looking up into the eyes of a man. They were blue, like Big Dog's.

When the man kissed down my belly, I got nervous again but he didn't take my cock in his mouth so I relaxed. He licked down the length of it and back up, which I enjoyed. When he lifted my legs and pushed them back, I thought he was ready to fuck but he began to lick my ass instead.

"I'm…dirty," I stammered out, feeling ashamed.

He looked up from his licking. "Then I will make you clean."

Clean! No part of me had ever been clean. I felt a new kind of happiness and put my hands on his head, feeling his curly pale hair, which dogs should never do. I jerked my hands away and prepared for blows, but he only smiled up from his licking and said, "Keep doing that. I like it," so I threaded my fingers back into his waves.

When he inserted his tongue in my ass, I knew what the cleaning was for and held my legs further back for his pleasure. But it was pleasure for me too. I moaned and squirmed, wagging my ass against the dirt. The Insider eased onto his knees and moistened his cock, which was thoughtful. I held myself open for him as he slid inside me, as slowly as yesterday. I felt something and said a word without thinking, only one but still a word.

"What did you say?" the man asked, holding himself still inside me.

I looked away, frightened. "I…I said…good."

He grinned like dogs do before they attack. I tried to roll away but his hands pushed my shoulders down and his arms pressed my legs further back, tight against my chest. His cock was farther inside me than any man's or dog's had ever been. My own cock hardened again while he fucked me, and against all my will my own fluid erupted from me as the man came inside my ass. His head was thrown back in ecstasy, but when he looked down he saw my distress.

"What's wrong?"

I was crying, which was not good either. "My fluid." I looked down between us. The man followed my eyes.

"I'm sorry," he told me for the second time and explained what the word meant. He sat up, his cock still inside me, and scooped my fluid up with a finger and fed me every drop he could. I barked my gratitude but he didn't understand.

"Thanks," I interpreted.

"You're welcome. I didn't mean to make you do that. Tomorrow, just in case, I'll bring you a bottle of water." I heard the human word for fluid. Water. It had a magical sound.

I didn't believe the man of course but, the next day, there he was with his clean clothes and clean body, a small bottle in hand. "Here," he said, holding it out to me. I looked around furtively. We would have to hide. Water would make the other dogs go mad. I took the Insider farther inside the ruins.

I wasn't sure what clean water would taste like. The man unscrewed the cap and held it to my lips. I took a very small sip. Clean water was thin and cool and melted across my tongue and mouth. It moistened me more completely than any man's fluids. I wanted more but was afraid. Maybe it was just this one sip he wanted me to have, but he put the bottle back against my mouth and so I drank a second time and then a third.

I pushed it away finally. "No," I whispered. "Too much."

"Save the rest for later then."

I hung my head. "I cannot. The other dogs. The Outsiders."

"Would they hurt you for it?"

I nodded my yes. "And maybe you too."

"I better hide it then," he said, inserting the bottle into a deep recess in the wall. He turned to me after the water was safe, and I knew it was time to make the exchange equal. He began to remove his clothing. Oddly, he arranged his pants and shirt in a pattern on the floor. I sat in the dirt on my haunches to watch him but he pulled me back up.

"Lie down on my clothing," he told me. I couldn't believe he meant it. "We should have a blanket, I know, but it's the best I have today. Lie down." When I still didn't, he looked puzzled. I thought he might be angry and prepared to dodge but his voice was smiling when he spoke again. "What's your name?'

I hung my head. "Red Dog," I mumbled.

"What?" he asked, coming closer.

"Red Dog," I whispered.

He lifted my chin with a gentle hand. "Red Dog? Red is a good name for you," he said, looking at my matted hair. "My name is Erack." I mouthed the word after him.

"Lie down, Red," the man Erack commanded again. I watched his lips sound the first word of my name without the second.

"Red Dog," I said in a small voice, amazed I dared correct him.

"Lie down please, Red," he repeated, with another new word I had to learn.

I settled myself uncomfortably onto his clothes on all fours, but he turned me onto my back. From that day on, we always started with my front to his.

When we had finished, he shook out his clothes and put them back on his body. He looked down at me as most men do, observing the thing I am, but his voice was kind. "I can bring you clothes."

I shook my head.

He repeated his offer.

A very long sentence fell out of my mouth. "They would take them from me."

"They?"

"The Outsiders."

"Outsiders?" he asked. "Oh, you mean the Others. That's what we call them." I wondered what Insiders called us dogs but didn't ask.

The next day Erack came with a bundle on his back. I hoped it wasn't clothes. We went to the place farther inside the ruins. I waited for him to remove his clothing but instead he began to clean my face with water from new bottle he pulled out of his bundle. The feelings of touch and water were so delicious I got hard immediately. Erack took my cock in his hand but I wasn't afraid. It felt good there. I decided I would let him make me lose my fluid if he wanted, but he let my cock go and poured the rest of the water over my head. It was amazing to feel so wet without the rain.

He dried the hair on my head with a cloth from the bundle and combed it back from my face with his fingers. "Beautiful," he said before he kissed me on my right cheek and then my left. He continued his kisses over all parts of my face, holding my clean head in his strong hands. When he stopped, I wanted to ask for more but was afraid to of course.

Erack turned again to his bundle and pulled something else out, a much larger piece of cloth, the largest I had ever seen. "Blanket," he called it. He commanded me to lie down on this blanket and I did. I would do anything for him. I knew that. When he removed his clothing, I felt our difference more than ever. I was miserable in my filthiness.

"I'm dirty," I said.

He ignored me and started making sex to me in his slow way. It made my body feel so good, I forgot my misery. I even forgot to worry that I would lose my own fluid or to be upset when I did. Erack came into my ass soon after I came. I could tell he liked it when I lost my fluid. It made him happy. And anyway, it made the exchange of fluids equal since he brought me water.

After our first fuck, Erack returned my fluid to me like always and then retrieved the bottle of water from the wall. He took another bottle from his bundle. I wanted to tell him he was wasting it on me but I knew he wouldn't like that so I kept quiet, watching him use the cloth to clean my cock and pubic hair. He looked up, grinning. "Fire crotch!" I did not know what he meant. I sat up quickly, ready to jump away from danger.

"Shhh now, lie back. I didn't mean to frighten you, Red. It's just that you are rare. Do you understand that word?" I shook my head no.

It took some time for him to explain and by then he was hard again and so was I. He had me sit on his cock and fuck myself with it. I came again but didn't care because Erack's fluids were shooting into me and it felt so good to be coming at the same time. He gave me water to drink and licked my nipples clean and sucked them dry. I lost fluid for the third time that day.

When Erack left, with his blanket folded and back in his bag with the empty water bottles and filthy cloths, he looked around and waved. He said as always that he would return. I believed him now. When I was alone, I rolled in the dirt to make myself filthy again. It would not be safe for Erack or for the dog he called Red to be seen by Outsiders or other dogs as clean.

I looked up at a noise. Big Dog was standing in the broken doorway. "Your Insider came again?" he asked.

"Yes," I answered, sitting on my haunches, my front paws on the ground between my legs, my head down in obeisance.

I could hear Big Dog's feet shurshing through the dirt to me. When he was near, I raised my head and opened my mouth. He stuck his cock in, and I began to suck. His paws went to my hair. I tried not to wince. Would he suspect or know that I had been clean? But no blows came. He just played with my hair, which he had never done before, and began to fuck my face. After his fluid had drained down my throat and he had had his drink from me, he stood and held me close, which he also had never done.

"I will miss you, Red Dog," he growled into my ear. My eyes stared at the jagged walls over his shoulder. He pushed me back so our eyes met. "But if the Insider asks you to go with him, you must go." I tried to shake my head no but he grabbed it with both paws and did something else he had never done to me. His lips hit mine hard and we kissed. In moments, his paws were all across my body and his teeth were biting at my neck. He pushed me onto the ground and fucked me fast. When he had finished, he left without making the exchange an even one. I stayed on my hands and knees, panting, feeling his fluid deep inside me and wondering what it all had meant.

The next morning I hoped the Insider would not return. Big Dog had kept me with him all night, waking me to fuck or suck several times. My body was filled with his fluids—he had even given me his piss—and my mind was full of hopeful thoughts. I knew I was his favorite bitch but thought maybe now I might be something more, his mate.

I had plenty of fluid to last me for the new day but Big Dog went to his place to wait for men and said I must go to mine. I fell asleep in a sitting position against the farthest wall inside the farthest room.

A paw shook me awake. I jumped at the touch but relaxed quickly. The Insider had returned.

It was as Big Dog had guessed. Erack made his proposal before we fucked, even before he had removed his clothes. Over his shoulder I saw Big Dog enter our room, coming near. I leapt to my hind legs and so did Erack, putting himself between me and Big Dog.

My alpha leaned his face very close to Erack's. "Do you want this dog?" he asked, pointing at me with his right paw.

"Yes," Erack said in a strong voice.

"Do you mean to take him Inside and have him live as a human?"

"Yes," Erack repeated. I squeezed in between them, to take the bites and blows I thought sure would come then, but Big Dog just gave me a deep sweet kiss and leaned over my shoulder to speak again to the Insider.

"Good. Then I give him to you. He is a good bitch," he said, his voice softer than I had ever heard it, his eyes kind. But he pushed me aside and confronted Erack again with the stubby forefinger of his paw. "Listen well though. If I hear you have mistreated or dishonored him, I will track you down and kill you, inside your Keep or not. Do you understand?"

I was terrified for Erack. Big Dog's teeth were bared and his eyes burned red, but my human only returned his glare calmly and said, "I do. Don't worry. I will be kind."

"You will love?" Big Dog persisted.

"I will love him," Erack confirmed. "I do love him." My paw went to my mouth.

"Good," Big Dog said. "Let us clean him."

Big Dog used his tongue and Erack his water and cloth. It took some time. When they stopped and looked at me with appreciation, I gazed down my body in wonder. My skin was pink.

Erack produced clothes for me to wear. I hesitated but Big Dog thundered. "Stupid bitch! Put them on! You can't go Inside naked like a dog." So I slipped my legs and arms into unfamiliar territory and learned how to fasten and zip. I put one sock on and then the other. Erack tied the strings of the boots for me into bows.

When I was no longer naked, Erack and Big Dog looked at me with satisfaction. "You will make a good Insider," Big Dog said, front paws crossed on his black hairy chest.

"He is very handsome," Erack said, and Big Dog nodded at the word. I didn't dare ask what it meant.

Erack folded the blanket and put away the bottles and cloths. He shouldered the bundle and took my hand. My heart raced. We were leaving. Suddenly, I didn't want to and tried to pull away, but Erack's strong hand kept my paw tight inside it.

Big Dog said, "It will be all right, Red Dog." He looked sad, something I had never seen him look.

I leaned my mouth close to my alpha's ear. "I will be back to give you fluid." He shook his head sternly no. I smiled and nodded my head yes. I was human now. Big Dog lowered his head. I patted it twice and left.

When we reached the door of his Keep, the Insider used something he called a key. He said he would have one made for me so I could come and go. I thanked him. I intended to keep my promise to Big Dog. And then Erack opened the door and I went Inside to begin my life as a human, as a man.

# I Can't Live Without You

"Virion dead ahead."

A small planet about the size of Mars grew closer out the window, its surface mainly landmasses, its color mainly brown. It looked peaceful, as if it contained all things good. I knew it did not.

The Orion eased into the Virion Interplanetary Air Station, slowing alongside a ramp. Other star trains were entering or leaving. As ours hissed to a stop, I took up my travel kit and shuffled out the compartment door along with the rest of the first class passengers. The ramp began to move, taking us to the main hall.

"Edmund de Vasselin" the sign read. I smiled at the driver, another Terran. We chatted as we waited for my baggage and during the vacuum pull. I asked about the virus.

"Nothing's happened yet, sir," he answered into the viewer. "Of course, we've only been here a few weeks."

"All the reports say it isn't aggressive."

His image in the viewer half smiled. I wished my fears weren't so apparent. "They aren't, sir," he said.

Viktor dropped me off at the embassy entrance and wished me well. The building was pure post-Gehry. I looked from it into the pale green sky. Which direction was Terra? I straightened my shoulders and went inside, walking with a spring in my step I didn't feel. Gravity on Virion was less insistent than Terra's.

A guard directed me to the charge d'affaires office. I waited 30 minutes, listening to last year's music on the ear-set provided. Finally, I was admitted.

"Welcome, de Vasselin," the official said in a gruff voice, rising from her desk to shake my hand in a fleeting exchange of palms. She was an attractive but aging veteran of the diplomatic corps. Junior staff were not allowed on Terra's first mission to Virion. Even the driver had been in his 30's.

Guillory welcomed me briefly, gave me my schedule for the first day, then transferred my video packet and sent me off to "settle in" before my afternoon of meetings. Nothing was said about lunch.

I found my quarters on my own. My luggage had been unpacked and stowed. That was always mildly disturbing, but I understood the need. What we could bring into and take out of other worlds was prescribed and proscribed. I had been through the drill many times.

I ate something from the automat, rinsed myself and changed my clothes. I was glad I wasn't required to wear the uniform. Allowed, Guillory and her kind would have said. I glanced at the aging man in one of several mirrors before leaving.

"You look well," a vice consul named Guy told me in the conference room after introducing himself. He was chatty, informing me that he had taken a temporary demotion to get this posting. He assured me that many of the staff had. "Even our driver was a 3Q," he boasted.

I had taken no demotion. The Ministry of Mines said go, and I packed my bags. Most of my colleagues envied me. Virion was a new venture and potentially lethal. When they asked their questions, I just shrugged. Even in engineering it's best not to show your weaknesses.

Guy began my briefing. The first two hours were about Virion, in case I'd forgotten anything from my studies. When allowed questions, I asked about the virus.

"Surely you've received a briefing about them," Guillory answered. "Anyway, there's a summary of everything we know in your video packet."

"Yes but...."

Her hand forestalled me. "We don't know any more than that, de Vasselin. Our onsite experience is preliminary, as you doubtless can realize. Just limit your contact as much as possible." I knew what kind of contact she meant. As long as you weren't fucked by a Virioni, you were safe. If you were, you'd be dead within months of leaving their atmosphere. Of course, it was a little more complicated than that. Not all Virioni were viruses.

We had the espresso break at mid-afternoon and more of the staff joined us. Everyone wanted news from home so I gave them what I could in 20 minutes. I was sure they had frequent transmissions from Terra but, with unification, there was even less reason to trust the media than before.

The post-espresso session was on mining. After it finished, Guy was looking at me expectantly. He was certainly attractive and undoubtedly horny, given the situation, but it had been a long transit for me and I wanted to rest up for the obligatory first night reception so I shrugged at him apologetically and left for my rooms. There was a knock on my door but I ignored it.

I wore my best unisuit to the reception. My last partner always said that blue brought out the color of my eyes. Jacques wasn't around anymore but blue was still my default color when shopping.

I drank my first cocktail and observed my first Virioni. They lived up to their reputation, being without exception tall, slender and beautiful. They did indeed smile a lot, but they seemed genuinely happy.

A hand caressed my shoulder, reminding me for a second time of Jacques.

"Shall we dance?" someone asked, not in Jacques' voice. Of course it was Guy. I held up my arms since his were already in the I'll-lead position. As we danced I asked about problems of living on Virion, which was perhaps not the conversational direction he wanted to take.

"It's fine. In most ways," he added, his mouth nearing my ear. I didn't resist when he pulled me close enough for our crotches to meet. If it had been a long time for him, it was going to be even longer for me. I'd be out in the field, surrounded by gorgeous Virioni, for months. Maybe I should make an effort with Guy.

In the middle of my wondering and Guy's increasing urgency, another voice said, "Pardon," and I was transferred into the arms of a Virioni a few inches taller than I. He held me further apart, for which I was grateful. I knew transmission was only by fucking but I still felt apprehensive. The Virioni started us off.

I learned during the dance that his name was Negarth, he was in the military and was only sixty-seven. I am also in my sixties but on Earth that's middle aged. On Virion you still have three quarters of your life ahead of you.

Negarth was probably assigned to obtain information from me, but he was the most handsome man in the room so I danced two more dances with him and accepted another drink. If Negarth thought he could get me drunk, he would be surprised. I *am* from Marseille after all.

I was enjoying the third drink and Negarth's conversation when a Virioni somewhat older than both of us approached. He was the tallest person in the room, nearly three meters. On Earth, at 2.2 meters, I'm considered tall but here it was nothing.

Negarth reflexively snapped to attention, introduced us, then moved away quick step, leaving me looking up at Manget Seri, the minister of mining for Virion. I felt bad for Negarth if he had so obviously failed in his mission that his superior's superior needed to step in. I could have told them that beauty was not necessary to win my heart and ineffective in loosening my tongue.

The minister and I talked for a few minutes about mining and my career, in what felt like a formal review of my c.v. His background had been thoroughly covered in my briefings on Earth. Still, I asked polite questions. We were both pretending, but isn't that part of diplomacy?

The music changed to an unfamiliar rhythm, and Seri began to sway in place. "Ah," he said, "My favorite song. You are a very good dancer, monsieur. Would you care to?" He took me in his arms without waiting for a reply and, in seconds, I was following one of the most powerful men in Virion around the dance floor. He held me close but there was no chemistry.

After our dance the minister returned me to Negarth. The rest of the evening, thanks to Negarth and Guy and some other Terrans and Virioni, I was never alone. When I wasn't dancing, I was drinking or chatting with some extraordinarily handsome person or another. Guy was as good looking as most of them.

At the end of the evening, the charge d'affaires came up to whisper, "That was a success. Everyone said how charming you are—and how handsome." She pulled away to look, did not seem impressed and leaned close again. "You made a good impression, de Vasselin, especially on the mining minister. I had wondered if Seri were gay."

"I don't think he is," I told her, leaving her mystified.

The rest of the week there were more briefings and meetings and social events. I wished I'd brought more unisuits but knew my social activities would be over by Sunday, at least the ones at which unisuits would be required. On Monday, I'd be off for the mines of Abersalant.

Abersal was why we Terrans and the rest of the universe were here. It was a non-radioactive substitute for uranium and, as such, finally made nuclear power completely safe. Abersal was found only on Virion, and Abersalant was where the principal deposits were. Terra needed abersal badly. We were far behind in nuclear technology, not a good fact in the dangerous sector we lived in. The skirmish with the Mektons had shown us that.

The briefing on Abersalant showed a visually desolate area, the brown I'd seen from the star train. Close-up shots showed little more of interest. There were few geological features and no plants or animals. The images depressed me so much that, when Guy knocked that night, I let him in.

Thereafter, he was with me every briefing, every social event and every night the rest of my stay in the capital. I began to think that he had also been assigned to me, rather than interested on his own. That took the romance out of our nightly ardor but not the sex. Unless there were compliant off-worlders in Abersalant, it would be a long two years of celibacy for me, even if the years were Virioni, not Terran. I had no intention of taking my pleasures with the natives.

Monday morning, Guy kissed me goodbye and made me promise to spend my leave with him. I saw Guillory watching us from her office window, wearing an unpleasant smile. I made a noncommittal response to him and an ambiguous gesture to her and let Viktor fold me into a more utilitarian vacucar, which took me directly to the mining camp.

In front of a small administrative center, Viktor offloaded my bags, wished me luck and reset the vacuum. In seconds, I was alone. An odd feeling swept over me, which I analyzed as terror. Before I could do something foolish—like use my transponder to call for help, someone exited the admin center and greeted me in French. He was shorter than I, good looking in a rough way but by far the least attractive Virioni I had met so far.

"Ricain Marbustra, head engineer here," his rather high voice said. "Please call me Ric." He looked very young, no more than 60 at the most.

"Edmund de Vasselin," I said, taking his proffered hand.

I felt an immediate and nearly overpowering jolt. An electrical current flowed between us and my host's face was transformed by an emotion I could only call joy. When I extricated my fingers, his face fell into disappointment. I wanted to say I was sorry but didn't know for what.

"Not a problem, Edmund," he said aloud, making me flinch. Could the Virioni read your thoughts? That hadn't been part of my briefings.

"Did you have a comfortable trip?" Marbustra asked, folding his hands behind his back in a formal military stance. My shields rose. This Ricain Marbustra could be a military officer as well as an engineer. The Virioni might not be in the abersal business for economic gain alone.

"I did," I answered, beginning an inconsequential chat while my luggage was loaded onto a kind of hovercraft nearby. It gave me time to observe my host more closely. He was very tan but almost unwrinkled, with dark hair on his head, arms and legs. A sleeveless shirt and shorts proved the appendages were well muscled. When he turned he displayed a spectacular shelf of an ass.

"The boat is ready," he said, a hairy arm indicating the hovercraft. Strange, I thought, they call them boats in the desert. Maybe I misunderstood; his French was very bad.

"Are you tired?" he asked in halting words when we were on our way. I told him no. "You must be hungry. We will have…" he paused over the French word. "Lunch," he concluded. We both then turned our attention to the back of the driver's head for the remainder of our brief trip.

"Your new home," Marbustra announced as we stopped outside one of several low buildings. He handed me down the hovercraft steps like I was a nineteenth century female. The electrical current flowed mightily again.

Another young Virioni, taller and far prettier than Marbustra, picked up my bags and followed me silently to my room. He looked interested but I ushered him out and changed into short sleeves and shorts to match my host's informality. Even the prettiest Virioni was not going to tempt me.

When Marbustra and I met as arranged in the main hall, he looked at my new outfit with interest. "Good," he told me. "You will be more comfortable now." His words seemed to say something else as well. I felt embarrassed, as if I were naked.

We sat with a number of other Virioni, all male, young and—with the exception of their commander—uniformly gorgeous. There were no other off-worlders. Our talk was about Terra and mining. We began in French but switched quickly to Vironese. I was careful with my disclosures.

After lunch Marbustra stayed with me. "Please don't let me take you from your duties," I said, hoping he would leave me with a subordinate. Every time he touched me, I felt a power surge and was left breathless.

"Not a problem," he replied in his strange accent. "Would you like to rest or take a tour?"

"A tour please." I wanted to make sure he didn't think me a weakling.

He nodded and led us back to the hover jeep. This time there was no driver; he got behind the controls himself. I tried not to let my Adam's apple spasm when I realized we would be alone.

The nearest mine was some kilometers off. We spent the drive time chatting about this and that, both of us cautious, although we did eventually veer into the personal.

"I grew up in Nourin," he said. I knew that was another large city, in the colder, northern hemisphere of the populated zone. That explained the different accent.

"It's very cold there, I understand."

"Very," he said with a shudder. "Most Nourini do not come to Abersalant. Too hot. I prefer it." His smile was quite disarming. I wondered if all Nourini looked like him.

"I am not typical of Nourin," he said, making me flinch again. I would definitely have to report this telepathic ability.

"Is it cold in Marseille?"

He had to repeat the question. I had been absorbed in studying his thick red lips and wondering what they might feel like against mine. I blinked but recovered well I think.

"Sometimes. At least, it seems cold to us." He laughed when I told him the average Celsius.

During the ensuing silence, he watched my mouth intently. I was glad when we reached the mines in the Terran concession zone and were again with other humanoids. Marbustra halted the vehicle and settled it onto the ground outside a tall building beside a huge mound of rocks. I marveled at the sameness all around us, flat to the horizon, punctuated only by rock piles at regular intervals. More mines, I assumed.

A local supervisor hatched out of the building, greeted us, shook our hands and led us off for our inspection. I was thankful there was no electrical transmission between the supervisor and myself and no answers to unasked questions, but wondered even more so why there were both with Marbustra.

I forced myself to turn my attention to the facilities. I could see the mine was safely built and carefully maintained. The extraction processes were familiar and efficient. I began to wonder what I would have to do here if all the mines were like this first one. I might have to ask the embassy to transmit more abooks and nonfic packs to me.

After the inspection, back at the main camp, Marbustra excused himself. I felt both relieved and bereft.

I returned to my quarters, showered and lay down, naked, on the sleeping platform. I looked around the room. It was Spartan, which agreed with my own inclination. I played with myself, trying not to think of Ricain, but when I came it was into his hand and it was under his body.

I dozed then, until a loud buzz woke me. The commo screen indicated an incoming from the man himself. I looked for a robe, found none, and so rewrapped my towel around me and clicked accept.

"I'm sorry. I was…"

"Taking a shower. So I see. Sorry to disturb you." He examined me at will.

"You didn't actually," I said, glad he hadn't contacted me a few moments before.

"Good. Could you join us in an hour? I will come by your room."

I didn't know if I liked the idea of that, or rather thought I liked the idea too much, but I agreed and clicked close conversation. My mind started its what if's. I made it hush and myself dress.

I couldn't decide what to wear. Usually, clothing decisions are not so traumatic for me. At last, I put on a light yellow cotton tunic and loose blue pants. Ricain arrived at my door in the same outfit he'd worn on our inspection tour. He looked at me appreciatively.

"You look very attractive, Edmund. Very," he underlined, resting a hand on my shoulder. The electricity flowed. Ricain seemed to want it and didn't drop his hand as quickly as I wished. Why does this happen I asked myself but, if he heard me, Ricain didn't answer.

Over drinks, I saw some of the same men I had met at lunch and some I had not. There were women too, from another mine in the area.

"You will be with us two years?" one of the women asked. I sipped the musky clear cocktail we all had been given.

"Yes. That's the standard length of our assignments."

"On Terra," she said as if she were correcting a student. "Ours are much longer." Ric looked at her, and she closed her mouth.

"Have you been to many other planets?" someone else asked. A discussion of other worlds ensued. None of them had been off Virion. My shields came back up. Perhaps they were all viruses or carried the virus and couldn't leave.

Ric drank slowly and silently but whenever I looked at him he looked back with that disturbing focus he had. "I would like to travel," he said at last, giving the words more meaning than the dictionary would have. "But I never will."

"Why not?" I asked. Our companions all looked at one another.

"I'm an engineer. Such travel is reserved for diplomats and the military."

"I'm an engineer," I reminded him.

He gave a rueful smile. I decided it was time for another drink.

By the end of the evening, I had successfully avoided any more electrifying physical encounters with Ric and had met everyone in the room. The lounge had gradually emptied. Men and men, women and women, women and men exited together, in couples and small groups. However, Ric left alone and no one followed him.

I turned to Lucen, who was still with me and perhaps hopeful we would depart together. "He has no partner?" I asked.

Lucen looked at me curiously. "No," he said slowly. "He is *asergii*." I didn't know the word. "Unattached virus," he explained. "No one has needed him."

"Needed?'

"For sex."

*Asergii* had not been in my briefings either. "Why?" I asked. Lucen looked at me like he had just gathered new information for *his* report. "I mean, he's intelligent, well formed and in command." I clamped my mouth shut before I could disclose anything else for Lucen's report.

"Yes but he is also *asergii*. There must be the attraction. And, unfortunately, our commander is not very attractive. To us at least," he added, waiting for any change in my expression.

"Still, chemistry happens," I suggested.

"More like electricity," he said, clinking my glass, now clearly ready for us to leave. I finished my drink and said good night, not waiting to see if Lucen was disappointed. My mind was too full of Ricain Marbustra and electrical attraction.

"One more thing," Lucen said, a bit acerbically. "If Ricain remains *asergii*, he dies." I turned back to him. He seemed glad to have caught my attention. "Yes," he continued. "Unless two Virioni need him to produce a child or he mates with a woman…or man," he said pointedly, "He will die young. Very sad," he said in a voice anything but sad. "But that is all viruses are meant for anyway."

I wanted to punch him in the mouth but merely repeated my good night and left the salon as quickly as possible.

In my room I undressed and lay on my sleeping platform. My mind drifted before sleep. Men and women, humans and viruses, *asergii*. I pictured Ric's body beneath his clothes, imagining him naked, but turned the images off and went to sleep. He was a virus and must be avoided.

The next morning I woke to twin suns shining through my windows and the sounds of other beings getting ready for the day. I showered, dressed and went to the dining hall. I saw everyone but Ric. I wanted to ask after him but also wanted to avoid betraying any further interest. I returned to my room for my pads and sunglasses. There was a message on the screen. I clicked hear and laughed at my disappointment. It was only my driver, ready to whisk me off to another mine.

This daily activity repeated itself for weeks until I had finished my inspections. Thereafter, I reported each day to the Earth main concession. I found I had more work to do than I expected.

At first I went to the lounge or activities room every evening, but the nightly pairing off made me horny. As my sexual frustration grew, I began to take walks in the absolute dark surrounding the tiny outpost. Men and women offered to accompany me, but I managed to decline gracefully. However, when Ric offered, I felt I could not say no and, truthfully, I didn't want to.

We became frequent companions in the desert after dark. I could barely see him but I could sense him—his pleasant male smell, his weighty presence. We walked with hands behind our backs and avoided lurching into one another. We talked, especially about ourselves. Finally, one night, I asked the questions I wanted to know.

"Uh, this may be far too personal but I feel we've gotten to know each other…"

"We are beginning to," he said. I could feel him smiling.

"Yes. Well, and maybe it's even part of my job…"

"Oh, then ask," he said, with all the icy irony my sentence deserved.

I was silent.

"I am sorry, Edmund. You can ask me anything." His voice was soft when he said this, softer than I had ever heard it. It made me lean towards him. Our bodies bumped and electricity jolted into kinetic energy and flowed between us. I didn't move away until I felt Ric becoming part of me. I had to catch my breath and slow my heartbeat.

"How is it?" I continued, after our mutual silence. "I mean, I don't understand. Human and virus. How does it work?" I felt embarrassed, like I was asking who is the man and who is the woman. "I'm sorry," I apologized. "That was stupid."

"Not stupid," he said. "A little clumsy perhaps but not stupid." He started us walking again. "Virioni humans must mate with a virus to have children. Virioni viruses must mate with humans to live."

"I know that."

He hesitated. "Then you are asking…"

"Yes."

We walked silently again for several strides.

"I am a plural," Ric said at last. I had heard of plurals but never met one, even with all the worlds I'd lived on.

"By plural you mean…"

"I can have sex with anyone in any way. I can be the man, the woman, something of both. It depends."

"On what?"

"The specific attraction," he explained.

I wanted to take his hand but was terrified of what might happen next.

"It's all right, Edmund," he said, reaching for mine. The electricity flowed again between us, strong and urgent, compelling and connective.

"I'm afraid," I said, my body stiffening.

"You have reason to be, from what I hear," he said flatly, releasing my hand from his. I grabbed it back, and he gasped. I held on, waiting. With no negative from me, Ric pulled me closer and I found out what his lips felt like against mine.

Our hands explored the fabric across our bodies. It was as if all the weights of fear and wanting had been shed. As long as we don't fuck, I told myself. I reached to undo his shorts.

"Not here," he said, breaking away.

"No, not here," I agreed. We walked, then ran back to my room, where I locked the door and turned on the lights. We watched each other disrobe. His body was beautiful, far more beautiful than mine. Mounds of thick muscle covered his shoulders, arms, chest and legs. Dark hair grew abundantly across the muscles. We held each other for elongating moments, skin to skin, being to being.

We did what we could in bed. He was the top, and I was the bottom. I assumed he want the one thing both of us understood would kill me and let him live. We avoided it very deliberately.

This unsatisfactory routine continued for weeks until one night he asked if I wanted to fuck him. "I can try," I answered. He knew what I meant.

"It's all right, Edmund. It probably wouldn't work for me anyway. My gameon levels are too high. Virioni visuses have several glands whose secretions determine and regulate what aspect of plural they are in any given attraction." That made me think too much but, when Ric began to kiss me again, my thoughts turned to other things.

Our nights together continued over more weeks and months. We became a couple without coupling. The Virioni recognized our connection and made their assumptions. When Lucen told me he was glad Ric was safe now I didn't respond. I loved Ric but did not want to die. I loved him and did not want *him* to die.

I had been at Abersalant nearly two years when I felt I had to make a decision. I told Ric I was going to take a trek in the desert.

"Just one night."

"I'll come with you."

"No, I need to do this alone."

He rose, leaning across his desk, thick arms akimbo. "Is something wrong?"

"I need time to…think." Decide, I almost said. He took my hand, understanding.

"You have your gioti?" Ric asked the morning of my departure, fussing.

"Yes," I assured him for the third time.

"Your transponder?"

"Yes."

He looked forlorn. I held and assured him, "I will see you tomorrow." I walked away from his eyes' longing and mind's hoping.

I tried to concentrate on walking, to slip into mindfulness, to let answers come unfiltered, but my mind battled between love and fear throughout the day. No messages were received or conclusions reached.

The debate continued after dark, after I ate, after I inched into my pod, after I tried to sleep and couldn't. It was only when I ran out of thoughts that the decision appeared. It might have been a dream but I doubt it. My eyes were wide open. I saw the stars of the universe and imagined all the planets orbiting those stars. I thought of Terra so far away and Ric so near.

The next morning I retraced my steps, surprisingly free from second thoughts. After kilometers I forgot to count, I saw the buildings reappear and then a figure moving towards me, becoming definite, becoming Ric. I began running, eager to tell him. He stopped moving, watching me run. I collided into his open arms.

"I love you."

"I love you, too," he replied, accepting my kisses, but love was not new information. He waited for more.

"I want you to fuck me."

He pulled away as if stung. "You'll die!"

"Not if I don't leave."

His mouth tightened. "You still have time to think about it."

"No, tonight. I want you to fuck me tonight." He pulled away. I pulled him back. "I can't live without you," I said.

"You are determined?"

"Yes."

He stared into me, searching for any reluctance. There was none to find.

"Tonight then," he agreed, taking my hand and turning us towards Abersalant. I felt the electricity flowing between us. I stopped resisting, and we became each other. Everything else, I knew for the first time in my life, was beside the point. I smiled at Ric, finally knowing who I was. He smiled back, sending more electricity between us. I welcomed it all.

# In the Closet

I was finally going to a gay bar. I wasn't sure what to wear but went with black. There are lots of black outfits in my closet.

Outside the bar, an overweight tattooed bouncer gave me a thumbs up and a leer before demanding ten dollars and stamping my hand with an unidentifiable blotch.

"Lookin' good, dude."

"Thanks. I wasn't sure what to wear."

"Don't worry. With a body like that, you ain't gonna be wearing much for long anyway." He waved me in. I hoped he was right. It had been a while.

From outside, the bar had looked like a pizza restaurant. Inside, it was more like I imagined a gay bar would be, except for the flat screens running sporting events with the volume off. There was a Mets game on so I stopped to watch. When a commercial appeared, I activated my darkvision so I could survey the room. Men were arranged in rows from me to the opposite wall, like Chinese terra cotta warriors. No one was watching the game; they all seemed to be looking at me. I hit shields-up as a precaution. I doubted I'd be recognized out of uniform but you never know.

"Hey, handsome. What'll it be?" a voice yelled over the loud music and louder conversations. A cute blond with a broad smile and broader shoulders winked at me from the bar.

He didn't need to shout. I have super sensitive hearing, but then he wouldn't know that. "What'll it be?" he repeated. I realized he meant alcohol. I usually don't drink–to keep my mind alert to wrongdoing–but I was off duty tonight.

I thought a moment. "Scotch on the rocks, please." That was what my father always drank. Like father, like son in more ways than one I thought, keeping the joke to myself.

"That's almost a poem," the blond said to me.

"Pardon me?"

"What you said just now. It was almost a poem. Of course, *son* and *one* aren't an *exact* rhyme." He pursed his lips a little.

Had I said that out loud? The blond stuck out his hand.

"Francis."

"Sam."

"Good grip, Sam. Jorge! *Dos whiskies escoces en la rocas, por favor!*" He shouted over his shoulder and a bartender reached for ice cubes and a bottle of Glenfiddich.

I wondered what to say next. I don't actually talk much in my line of work. Luckily, our drinks arrived before the silence got awkward.

"Cheers," Francis said, clinking his glass with mine. I took a drink and felt the alcohol go right to my head. "It's okay," Francis said quietly. "Take it slow." I must have smiled because he smiled back and asked, "Would you like to dance?"

That worried me. You'd think I'd be a good dancer, given how agile I am in the air, but no. I can fly but I can't dance.

"Don't worry, baby. You just need more practice." Francis said, getting off his stool. I decided I better not have another drink. I was already talking too much, even when I didn't think I was talking.

We went down a flight of wooden stairs to a basement. More men and louder music. Francis kept tight hold of my hand. He had a pretty good grip too. "Stick with me, baby," he shouted, winking again.

He pointed to men dancing in the middle of the room and pulled me in their direction. We squeezed into the crowd and Francis immediately started moving to the music, shaking his chest and rotating his groin at me. The room began to feel warmer. He had a great body and even I could tell he had rhythm.

I did not. I always said it's because I'm so bulky but Francis was about as bulked up as I am. I worried I'd step on his feet or he'd laugh at me.

"Shhh," he said, taking my forearms with his hands and giving me a quick kiss, which made me feel more lightheaded than the alcohol. "You're doing fine. I won't laugh. Just relax." He moved closer and put his hands on my hips. I hoped my electrometer was off. Had I remembered to change the setting?

"That's better. Think of something else instead of worrying about your dancing." He pulled me against him. His hands felt great on my ass. I looked down at our bodies. They were both moving in time to the music. How did that happen?

"You must be a magician," I told him.

Francis laughed. "Sort of. Here. Try this." Slowly, he turned around and eased his ass against my groin. "You lead."

Me? Lead? He put my hands on his hips and ground his ass into my groin. I ground back and moved my hands to his chest. His nipples were hard, like the ones on my uniform.

"You're a fast learner," he said. I felt encouraged and ground against his ass some more. His gluts were perfect, round and full and very muscular. I got an erection. I wondered if Francis could feel it.

"Whew, honey! Can I feel it? Good gracious," he exclaimed, turning in my arms so we were front to front. He felt my erection all right. I rubbed it against his. "Well! We aren't shy, are we?"

I began to think about taking him home. Would he go with me or would he rather go to his place? Did he have to get up early tomorrow? What would it be like to have sex in a bed for once?

"There you go again. Let's have another drink while you decide." He towed me across the dance floor to the bar.

After we had our drinks in hand, Francis wound his way to a seating area, with me dodging and weaving to keep up. He certainly was fleet on his feet. Miraculously, just as we arrived at an oversized leather couch, everyone sitting on it got up and left. Francis plopped down in one corner. I sat in the middle.

"Scoot over," he purred. I scooted. "That's better. Lameesh!" he said, clinking my glass with his.

"What's that mean?"

"Oh, like cheers," he said, taking another swig. I took two to catch up.

We sat together silently through a couple more sips. I wondered what was polite to ask in a gay bar? What was the etiquette? Should I ask about his work? Tell him about mine? I don't think so.

Francis laughed. "Etiquette? Oh, honey! Anyway, I'm a civil rights attorney. Queer civil rights," he emphasized. He said *queer* in all capitals, with a steely look in his eyes, which surprised me because, well, he had been so queeny.

He gave me a look. "I'll let that one go since you're so handsome. And you're a Mets fan." I was about to say thank you when he asked, "Would you like to go to my place?" I started to chug my Scotch. "Easy, baby. Plenty of time." He brought my drinking hand back to my thigh. "Don't want to dull the senses too much, right? Never know when you might need them." He gave me another wink. I opened my mouth to laugh and suddenly his tongue was in it, swishing around for the residue of my drink. The swishing felt good. I could barely remember the last time a man had swished me like that. Well, okay, I could remember exactly but then I do have a photographic memory.

After a few more sips of our drinks, he whispered, "It's time," into my ear as he nibbled it.

"You think so?" I asked as I took his short blond hair in hand and kissed him, my tongue doing the internal searching this time.

"Oh yeah," he said, gasping, when I let him go. "It's time!" Francis put his drink down and jumped up, dragging me after him. He had no trouble wending his way through the crowd and up the stairs to the first floor, but I kept bumping into people and apologizing. They looked as if they didn't mind the bumping though. More than one gave my ass a quick grope as we whizzed by.

"The boys *are* frisky tonight, aren't they?" Francis said once we were outside. "I don't live far, honey. Come on." Near, far, I wanted to pick him up and fly us to wherever he lived but didn't think I should on the first date. You never know how people will take be whisked off their feet. Literally.

The street seemed unnaturally quiet so I looked around suspiciously. Was something about to happen? Would someone need my help? I hoped not. A superhero has needs too, and right now I had a big one.

Francis seemed like he was listening and looking too, but then he smiled and started us briskly walking, his ass shaking like he meant it. He looked even more muscular in the street-lights, in his tight white t-shirt and form fitting white jeans.

"I like your tennis shoes," I told him as we rushed along.

"Don't be shy, baby. I like your body too," he said as he halted us in front of a newish multi-storey apartment building. "Here we are. And just in time," he added, looking down at my crotch with a sassy smirk.

I felt sheepish but that didn't last long. We started kissing as soon as the elevator doors closed. By the time we reached his floor, I was ready to hit the emergency button and nail him in midair if I had to but I restrained myself. I wanted sex to be horizontal tonight.

Francis pulled his shirt back down to his waist as the elevator door opened.

"Here we are," he sang out at Apartment 807. I felt more and more impatient. Open the door already.

"Hang on, baby. It's open." He held the door for me while I entered, patting my ass as I went by. That made me pause. "Don't worry, hon. I'll let you drive. Want another cocktail?" He started for the kitchen. I grabbed him before he could play hostess and reeled him back to me like we were ballroom dancing. Our chests collided.

"You're really well built," I told him.

"So are you," he said, latching onto my pecs through my shirt with both hands. I yanked his Dolce & Gabbana back up and off in one movement and grabbed his pecs too. We were now on second base. "Whee!" he warbled when I picked him up, ready to head to third. He pointed in the right direction and off we went.

Once in the bedroom, he carefully took off the rest of his clothes and I rushed out of mine. I finished first.

"Wow! How'd you do that? Trick of the trade?"

"Something like that."

"You *are* a big boy," he said, holding onto my shoulders and looking down. "Yum," he said next, seeming to shiver. I wasn't sure what was real and what was affected with him, but at that point in the evening I wasn't asking. I picked him up again, held him like a package in my arms and walked us to the bed. He chuckled. "I could get used to this picking up thing." I tossed him onto the wrought iron queen sized and jumped on top of him, making lots of squeaks.

"Ooof," he said when I landed but it didn't really seem to bother him. I took his wrists, pushed his arms over his head against the pillows and held them there while I squeezed his thighs together with mine. "Into bondage?" he asked, still saucy.

"A little," I answered, covering his mouth with mine to shut him up.

"Want to tie me down, you bad man, you?" he gargled around the obstacle. I could play along. I tied up bad guys all the time.

"Got any rope?" I asked. He started to get up. "Don't move. Just tell me where."

"In the hallway, second drawer in the linen closet."

"Don't move," I said again, looking down at him with a frown.

"Oh, you man, you," he said coyly, hands posed under his chin, legs crossed neatly at the ankle.

I trotted down the hall thinking, okay, he *is* a little queeny but what a body. And my testosterone level was full. I had to do something about that.

"Found it," I announced as I bounded back into the room. Francis gave me a look full of daggers. "What?" I asked.

"I know I'm not the butchest guy walking down 27th Street."

I dropped the rope and lay down beside him. "It's okay. I'm sorry if I said something. I didn't mean to."

"Oh, don't worry. You didn't *say* anything." His look was as arch as his inflection.

I had to coax him quite a while with my mouth and tongue and fingers to get him back in the mood. When he was moaning and compliant, I tied his arms to the bedposts, which fanned his impressive lats out perfectly. He even looked a little apprehensive, which made it better for me. Fear is something I feed on fighting the bad guys. It pumps me up. With Francis, it pumped up my cock.

"Damn, honey," he said, staring at it. "That thing is even bigger now. What'd ya do—super size it?"

I sat on his thighs, with my calves locking them in place. "Too big?" I asked. He laughed merrily. "Okay, then," I grunted as I began to slide the condom on. It took a while.

"I'd help but I'm sort of tied up here," Frank joked, with his eyes on my fumbling. I finally finished inching the plastic on. I should have bought a bigger size but this one usually fit.

I got down to business then. I pushed his legs back, stuck my cock up his ass and began banging away. In seconds I had come, taken the condom off and was lying back on the guest pillow, feeling pretty good.

"Uh, hello. I'm still here."

I looked over at him. "Oh, sorry." I untied his hands. He propped himself up on one elbow and just kept looking at me. I folded my hands across my stomach defensively.

"So, that's it?"

"Well…"

"Sammy, your wind up is terrific but your delivery needs a *lot* more practice."

Before I could say "huh?" he was on top of me, sucking my cock back into life. It didn't take long.

"There. That's better." He reached into a nightstand drawer. "We'll use mine this time. They're for big boys like us." He slid the rubber over my cock expertly and then went down on me again.

"Okay, a little lube for me and we're good to go." Francis reached back into the drawer, pulled out a tube and applied some grease to his ass. He wiped his fingers on a handy cloth and then grabbed my shoulders and rolled me on top of him. He held his legs back for me.

"First, insert cock A into hole B," he said in a teacher voice. I grinned and started to comply. "Just the tip!" he added. I stopped with just the head of my cock inside him. "Yes! Excellent. Let me get used to that big thang a minute before you stick it all the way up me. I mean, ouch. Rub it in and out a little. Yummy. Now slide another inch in and repeat. Yes. Yes! Good."

I worked my cock into him slowly, per his instructions. I enjoyed the feeling and Francis' gasps and rolling eyes indicated he did too. I felt my balls settle against his ass.

"All the way in? All righty then." I started to pump. "Wait! Just let it sit there a minute while you give me a couple smooches." I leaned through his legs, kissed him once quickly and started pumping again. "Stop! More kisses. And slow the fuck down." He moved his hands down to my ass. "Ooh, so nice. Don't get distracted, Francis," he told himself. "When I press, you pump. Okay?" I nodded. "Hold it there! Yessss."

I tried to start fucking again but he looked at me sternly. "Now pull out."

"Pull out?" I yelped.

"Don't worry, Sammy. You get to go back in. It's just fun to poke it in and out a while. Try it; you'll like it." I did, and I did.

Once Francis let me stay inside him, he gradually had me accelerate until I was really close. Before I could come he yelled, "Stop! Oh, God. I don't want you to but stop." We both were panting. "Okay, this time when you push in, wiggle it around in there."

"Like this?" I wiggled madly.

He tried not to laugh. "More slowly, baby. Slower. Slower. Oh, damn. That's it. Now, pump me again, really hard. Ahhh!" he screamed. "That's the spot, Sammmmy. That's the spot!"

I had the hang of it now and improvised. I liked Francis making me take my time. I'm used to fast, everything fast, but in this case slow was better. When I finally came it was like flying—and I should know. Francis came right after me, which prolonged my orgasm.

Between gasps he asked, "Good?"

I kissed him. "Excellent. You're a great teacher."

"Practice makes perfect," he said. "By the way kissing after is good. And cuddling." He put one hand on the small of my back and held on like a vise. The other hand settled my head on his shoulder and ran fingers through my hair. Our stubble rubbed against each other, turning me on again.

"Ready for more practice?" he asked, whispering into my ear.

"Uh huh," I mumbled into his neck. This time he took the trainer wheels off and let me ride free. He did keep talking some but I covered his mouth with long kisses and an occasional hand. After we came I collapsed on top of him.

"I'm sorry. I'm heavy," I said, trying to pull myself up. His hands clenched and wouldn't let me move a centimeter.

"Don't worry, baby. I'm strong too."

"You sure are," I agreed, feeling his muscles underneath me and around me. I wondered where he worked out. Maybe we could use the equipment at my place. It's sort of hard for me to go to 24 Hour without getting mobbed.

"Sounds like an offer I can't refuse," Francis said, grinning and running his fingers like silk up and down my back.

"What?" I asked distractedly.

"Nothing. Just a bad habit of mine. Go to sleep."

"Okay if I stay on top of you?"

"I couldn't think of any place I'd rather you be." He gave me a kiss on my forehead and kept me wrapped in his arms and legs as I drifted off. He *was* strong. He made me feel safe. No one makes me feel safe.

When I woke up, it was light and Francis was gone. I heard kitchen sounds though and could smell coffee brewing. When he came back in the bedroom with two mugs, one white and one black, I sat up. "Black, right?" he asked.

"Right. Hey, you're a good guesser."

He chuckled. "I guess I'm just intuitive. I thought. Hmm. Yes, black coffee for my superhero."

I tried not to wince at the word *superhero*. He handed me the black mug and kept the white one.

"Thanks. I was worried when I woke up and you weren't in bed with me."

Francis' eyes widened slightly. Most people wouldn't have noticed but it's my business to. "Oh, I had to go out. To get milk," he lied unconvincingly. "I drink mine white." He held his cup out for me to see.

"Did you change clothes?" His from last night were still on the floor, on top of mine. He had new briefs on, with Batman and Robin in a compromising position.

"Uh, yes. Couldn't go out in the same outfit as last night, now could I?"

His queeny expressions still got on my nerves. Hey, it's your problem, Sam, I told myself.

"Um hm, it is," Francis said between sips, like he was agreeing with my thoughts. "Drink up."

"Why?"

"Because we're going to play another inning. It's still a close game."

I laughed. So what if he had a few mannerisms I didn't feel comfortable with? Look at that body. Was a limp wrist and a few effeminate words going to make me give up on all that? No way! Besides, he was fun. The rest of my life, outside of saving people, was boring.

"Chug," Francis said suddenly, tilting his mug back. I did as instructed–following his instructions had worked out well so far–and handed him my empty mug. He set both of them on the nightstand and grabbed a condom while he was over there. As he slid the condom and his ass onto my cock, I looked at the bedside digital. There would probably be time before the automatic timer reactivated the warning device.

"Plenty of time, Sam. Oooh. Plenty of time," he repeated as he bounced up and down on top of me. I lay back and let him work for a few minutes.

"What the hell is that?"

The warning device was screaming. "Oh shit. I have to go!" I jumped out of bed. How did 11 a.m. come so soon?

"That's some alarm watch, honey." Francis got out of bed too, sorting our clothes on the floor, tossing me mine. I was in them in seconds. "You should be a model, Sammy. You can get into and out of clothes faster than anybody I know."

I wanted to laugh but didn't have time. Someone needed me. I scribbled my number on a pad near the bed. Funny, I thought, he has a pad and pen by the phone just like I do. I handed Francis the paper. "Call me tonight?"

"Sure thing, hon." He came close and held both my biceps. "I know you have to go but promise me you'll be safe."

I thought he might be kidding again.

"I'm not kidding."

"I promise then. Talk to you tonight."

I needed to fly. Literally. No time to change. They'd have to see me in my gay bar clothes. I didn't even have time for the mask. Oh, well. Maybe I could zoom through the 14th Street costume shop on the way.

After a hard day's work I got home about 5:30. My cell had been ringing all day. It rang again as I opened the door to my apartment. "Oh no," I said. "Not another one." I tossed the keys onto the entrance table. "Yes?" I answered.

"I need you," a man's voice said. It didn't sound like they usually did: excited sand urgent. This was low, slow and sultry.

"What's the address? I'll be right there." Maybe I'd have time to get into my regular outfit. The pirate's mask was shot to hell.

"Oh, you know the address but why don't I come over to your place this time? Can you turn your alarm off again for a few hours?"

I recognized the voice now. "Hey, Francis. Sure." I gave him my location. He said he'd be right over, which was good because he got me hard just talking over the phone.

I figured I had time for a shower but heard the doorbell ringing while I was still soaping up. I dried off as best I could, wrapped the towel around me and flew down the hall. Saves time. Through the peephole I could see it was Francis. How the hell did he get here so fast? I decided to give him a surprise. I dropped the towel and kicked it aside.

When I opened the door, he was smiling seductively but his eyes bugged when he saw me naked. He put one hand on the doorframe and the other on his hip. "Is that how you greet all your gentleman callers?"

"Not all," I answered, pulling him into the room and a hug and kiss. It didn't take long for me to have him out of his clothes, up in my arms and in my bed.

"Sammy," he said, as I nuzzled my way down his body. "You have this uncanny ability with buttons and zippers." I tied him down and we took up where I'd left off before the Mikowsky fire.

Afterwards, I was trying to make a decision: turn the alarm back on or ask Francis out to dinner. He looked at his watch.

"Dinner," he said, showing me the time. "You take a shower first, handsome."

"I already took one."

"You got all sweaty again, baby. Me too. Yuck."

"We could take one together," I said with a leer, which was something new. Francis must be rubbing off on me. We'd certainly been generating enough body friction.

"Good idea but we'd be all wrinkly before we got out of there. No, you first. I still need to get my heart rate down." He fanned himself and smirked. I was beginning to find the fey mannerisms weirdly sexy.

"Okay," I agreed, hopping out of bed, leaving him sprawled across the rumpled sheets. He looked so inviting I thought about skipping the shower.

"Uh uh," Francis said, stopping me with a gentle foot lunge to the chest. I wondered what those massive leg muscles could do if they really wanted to stop you. "You shower and I'll...well, I'll entertain myself." He picked up the pad and pencil by the bed, started writing and waved me off.

When I came back, still drying off, he was sitting upright, staring at the open closet. Had it been open before?

"You sure have a lot of the same Halloween costume, Sammy."

"What?"

He held up one of my Zipman outfits.

"Oh, that."

"Oh, that," Francis mimicked in a mincing tone. I cringed. "Oh, don't be that way," he said. "I'll tone down the swish. Part of it's just an act anyway. I mean, that's my name. Well, sort of." He struck a superhero pose. Information appeared on my mental screen. "That's right, honey," he said. "The Swish in the flesh, right here in your bedroom."

The Swish. Everyone knew about him. He was almost as famous as I was.

"Almost? Baby, get over your hunky self. I mean Zipman is great and all, saving people, flying around Manhattan and the tri-state area, but The Swish ain't chopped liver. For instance, remember that almost plane crash today?"

"That was you?"

"Yeah, baby. The Swish!" He spread his legs and flexed his biceps.

I tried not to zip him flat on the bed, even though my cock was ready for it again. An idea came to mind. I figured he already knew what it was but I said it anyway. "Maybe we could work together some time."

He arched an eyebrow. "You mean out of the bedroom, I'm guessing."

"Don't you know?"

"I *can* turn it off but, yes, I think we can work together. Zip and Swish. Swish and Zip. Whatever. Sounds good. Looks good too."

I didn't know what he meant until he nodded at the full length mirror. We *were* hot. I wrapped my arms around him and put my head on his shoulder, but just then there was a Donna Summer song out of nowhere. He tried to twist away from me.

"Baby, let go. That's my signal. I thought I turned it off." I released him and he checked his messages. "There's about to be a multiple car crash in the Hudson Tunnel! Let's go!"

I was in my costume in seconds. My eyes bugged. He was half way into his. It was all white and sparkly. "You brought your superhero clothes?"

Francis winked at me. "A girl has to be ready for anything." Then he opened the window and waved me over. "Come on, Zipster. Let's fly." He leapt out the window into the air. I fol-lowed close behind.

What a butt he's got I thought as we flew in close formation.

"Keep your thoughts on business, Zippy," the Swish told me. "Oh, and we're going to have to do something about that closet."

Which closet did he mean, I wondered.

"The clothes closet, silly. I'm gonna need some room for my work clothes, not to mention the ball gowns." Ball gowns? "Don't freak, baby. I'm just kidding about the ball gowns."

We were approaching the tunnel, flying in close formation. This could be a really good partnership I thought and waited for Francis to agree. He just dove for the tunnel, and I followed as quickly as I could. His body was stretched out in midair like it was in bed. I got an erection. Looked like I wouldn't be going to a gay bar again for a while, maybe ever.

"Zipster, focus. Of course we'll go out but right now, red car in the left lane. Stop it."

I did as I was told, working up a sweat. I began looking forward to a long hot shower. This time I'd make sure we were soaping up together.

# THE LATEST MODEL

"Would you like to go for coffee?"

"Robots don't drink coffee," I answered, looking up from my work.

Ridley's eyes didn't blink, even though they were programmed to. "Some of the newer models do."

"But you're not one of the newer models, are you?"

I didn't know what it was about Ridley. Something brought the bitch out in me. Anyway, I shouldn't talk. I'm not exactly one of the newer model humans.

"No, Parker. I am not."

Ridley looked hurt, which of course he couldn't be. The Alphas weren't programmed for emotions; that upgrade hadn't been allowed until the Gamma 20's. Still, he looked hurt so I said, "Okay. When?" He checked his availability and mine and suggested that afternoon at 3:15. I agreed.

I had never been asked out by a biobot before but I knew people who had. I even knew a couple of humans who dated one, although it was still frowned on. Businesses especially discouraged it. Imagine arriving at the office one morning and discovering the bot you'd been "seeing" had been traded in for a newer model. That might cause some personnel problems.

And then there was sex. My parents had warned me away from bots like they were child molesters, but everyone knew the early models were just machines. With the Gammas and Deltas though, it was becoming questionable. Gammas had emotions and it was rumored that the crazy geeks who'd built the Deltas had given them add-on sex organs and the ability to use them. And all bots since the Betas had had that skin-like sheath. Only Alphas like Ridley had been made of stainless steel, and there weren't many of them left.

I saw Ridley's stainless shining at me from a sunny table in the retro place I liked to go to. Starbucks was so 21st Century and, besides, it was the century I'd been born in. He stood when I got to the table. All bots are programmed to be respectful of humans, thanks to the conservative battle cry of Keep Bots in Their Place!

"I ordered your latte," he said just as my name was announced by the barista.

"Jason, medium latte."

It surprised me Ridley had given them my first name. I didn't know he knew it. In the office, we all went by surnames. Standard operating procedure. Don't get personal.

"I'll get it," he said, motivating before I could. I let him. Alpha 15's and above had payment cards so they could handle small purchases at outside sources. If he wanted to explain a coffee purchase to our supervisor, I wouldn't be the one to stop him.

He was back within seconds, handed me the mug and stood, towering above me. The Alpha males were all about 220 centimeters, the average height for men when they were built. I was glad when he finally sat down. I'm only about 185, which was already short when I was born.

"Thanks, Ridley."

"How is your work today?" he asked politely.

"Fine. How's yours?"

Ridley launched into a long discussion of the project he was working on. Bot social skills had been improved a lot since his time. I cut him off.

"What did you want to see me about?"

"See you about?" he repeated like it didn't compute.

"Yeah. Why couldn't we just talk in the office?"

Ridley looked at me like he found me odd, which made me uncomfortable. After all, I was the human here.

"I have nothing specific to talk about with you, Parker."

"Oh." I stirred my coffee with the spoon. Ridley was silent a moment too, then his gears lurched and he leaned forward, his long fluid arms on the tabletop, his silver hands resting like gloves. The Alpha 17's were humanoid in design, except for the joints. Appendages flowed continuously without the stops and starts of human bodies. I hadn't realized before how elegant this was, how beautiful and better. Ridley's fingers especially mesmerized me. They were like Uni-on links in how they flexed and moved. And they sparkled.

I looked up into Ridley's face but its expression, if I can call it that, made me look away. The bot seemed amused, but I knew that was impossible. I looked back to double check. Yes, amusement. I could see it clearly now.

"Have you ever gone out with a robot before?" Ridley asked with a twinkle in his visual receivers that didn't seem like a reflection.

I stood quickly, spilling my coffee across the table towards the bot but he seemed not to notice. He reached for my hand with those Uni-on fingers and held me in place. I knew Alphas were strong but this was the first direct use of that strength against me. Ridley was breaking several directives.

"Please, Jason."

My name again. I looked at his visual receivers. They were made a darker grey than the rest of him because earlier models without pupils had bothered humans. It made them think they were talking to a blind person, except of course bots weren't people. The cool touch of his hands calmed me. I discarded any idea of reporting him and sat back down.

"I'm sorry I spilled the coffee."

"It's not a problem. I'll get a cloth."

"Let me," I said quickly. "I made the mess." I slid out of the booth, asked the retro hipster barista for a mopster and soaked the liquid from the table. Some had dripped onto Ridley. I reached to clean it off his casing, and he watched me as I rubbed. A strange feeling came over me, one I didn't want to name.

Apparently, Ridley had some reaction too because he stood up abruptly and announced, "It is late. We had better get back to work. I will go first."

"I'll come with you."

He looked at me sadly. "That is not a good idea."

I watched him leave, knowing he was right.

I thought about Ridley in bed that night. Thinking about him made it impossible to sleep until I'd jerked off. It was hard to picture his metallic body on top of me but it was also exciting. I came in my hand, cleaned myself off with my come mopster and didn't think of Ridley again until I woke up.

The office was crowded when I arrived, humans and bots giving each other the greeting of the day. I heard Ridley's voice, and my eyes found him immediately. He was standing. I started to get hard, remembering last night. As soon as he was alone, I asked him if he'd like to take a walk at lunch. He said yes he would, checked our schedules and set the time for 1:10.

We met at the Arboretum, as he suggested. Trees were leafed out for spring, and early flowers were blooming. Color was everywhere around us. In a world so populated with grey, color was a deep relief.

"I like that shirt you are wearing, Jason," Ridley said, looking with his head turned in the disconcertingly right angle way Alphas have. "The blue matches your eyes."

I felt something stir and tried to ignore it. Sex with a bot was impossible, at least with Alphas. I said, "Thank you, Ridley," and kept walking. We turned down a less traveled path. It was more narrow so we bumped into each other. The something stirred again. Talk, Parker, talk. A question came to mind I'd always wanted to ask a biobot early model. I cleared my throat.

"Yes," Ridley said, stopping, understanding I was about to ask him something.

"Do...do you ever feel strange, I mean, not wearing clothes?" A sound like deep laughter came out of his upper orifice. I forged ahead. "Every model from Betas on does."

"They are built to look like humans," Ridley said, almost smiling. "But no, I don't feel strange being naked." The word banged in my brain. After a moment of sinking in, Ridley started us walking again. After a minute more, I asked my next question.

"Would you like to be human?"

Ridley looked at me as if he had been expecting it. "No," he answered, which was the only safe response for a bot. Humans all assumed bots wanted to be like them. What creature wouldn't? This assumption made people suspicious of all biobots. There were laws passed by the United Nations General Council all the time against bot manufacturers, restricting how humanoid robots could become.

We walked a few steps more. I cleared my throat again. Ridley didn't look at me or stop this time. "You seem pretty human," I said.

"That is projection, Jason, if you will excuse me for saying so. I'm an Alpha model. We are the most inhuman of the biological robotic corps. The Deltas now. I imagine you have trouble telling them apart from humans." That was true but beside the point. He was trying to deflect my interest in his humanity, real or assumed. I should have let him but I couldn't.

"You must have had modifications."

My words made Ridley freeze, turn and declare it was time to go back to work. "You will need lunch. I am sure you will find something on your way back. I will see you in the office." With that, he turned and walked hurriedly away from me. I watched his gleaming metallic body retreat gracefully along the path, his long arms and legs swinging in a natural rhythm, natural for humans anyway. The buttocks—what were they called on biobots?—particularly caught my attention. I realized I'd never looked very closely at any Alphas. It would have been like ogling the image reproducer. But now I could see that Ridley was beautiful.

I wanted to run after him. I wanted to apologize. To a bot, I told myself. He should apologize to me. It was against regulations to walk away so abruptly from a human.

Instead, I had my lunch and returned to the office. I saw Ridley across the room of humans and bots, seated at his station. He didn't look up when I went to him.

"I'm sorry," I whispered.

He said just as quietly, "There is nothing to be sorry about," and continued working on the ostralizer project he had been given. I waited a moment but he didn't look up and didn't say anything else.

Back at my station there was a note from my supervisor. "Come see me." She must have noticed I was late back from lunch.

I knocked on her office door. "Come in," she said in her command voice. She was a Delta, one of the first in our company to be allowed to manage humans as well as bots. She handed me the report I'd given her the day before. "Excellent," she said. I always expected her to mitigate any compliment with "For a human" but of course she never did. Senior management was still exclusively human and would have replaced her with a more compliant model immediately.

"Thank you."

"Please sit down, Parker."

I sat in the low chair across from her.

"I have a new project for you. It's on ostralizers. I think you'll find it challenging." Bots never said interesting. It was always challenging if it were good.

"Isn't that Ridley's project?"

"Of course. I'll ask Ridley to join us." She went into communication mode.

"Is he being replaced?" I asked before she began to hum.

She looked at me curiously. I wondered what bots thought about inter-being relationships. They wouldn't tell you the truth of course. The truth could get them in big trouble.

"No," she said benignly. "It has been his project but it's become too complex. He's an excellent Alpha, the best I've ever seen, but ostralizers need a human touch." She smiled at gracious level and went into full communication mode. In seconds, Ridley was with us in the wide office. "Sit," she told the Alpha. Ridley looked at me before taking the chair next to mine. Our arms almost touched.

Matsumoto explained to Ridley her creation of a team, as she phrased it. Ridley hesitated after she finished, not looking at me.

"Excuse me, Matsumoto, but is my work inadequate?" I understood his worry. Biobots were replaced when they were no longer up to the evolving tasks we were given.

"Your performance is perfectly adequate. In fact, superior. However, your work has reached a stage at which an additional mind is required. You know Parker, don't you?"

"Yes," Ridley muttered. It was strange not to hear a bot speak forthrightly. In fact, his whisper to me after lunch was unusual.

"Good. Now, the two of you will meet immediately to begin work. Ridley, you will need to bring Parker up to date on the project. Bernstein?" she asked, going back into communication mode. "Is there a conference room available?" Her assistant must have said Number 7 because that's where Matsumoto directed us.

Ridley walked ahead of me down the hall. I admired his broad shoulder plates and narrow middle housing. I watched the syncopation of his pneumatic mounds–that's what the buttocks were called–shifting up and down with the easy weight of his steps. My cock began to harden, and I wished I were somewhere else.

Ridley held the door for me, as bots were always supposed to do for humans. As I eased past him, I felt the heat manufactured by all the mechanisms inside his structure. My cock hardened more. I sat quickly in the middle seat on the right side of the table, hoping Ridley didn't see. He sat on the left side directly across from me and began to sum up his project, our project.

I interrupted his long monologue. "Why did you ask me out for coffee?"

Ridley looked angry, which was shocking. Anger was an emotion Gammas and Deltas never showed, at least not to humans, and Alphas supposedly didn't even have. "Why did you ask me to take a walk?" he said, his voice level rising.

I had never discussed feelings with a bot, even with ones who had them. Were they really feelings if they were manufactured? Of course, I understood that my feelings were also manufactured, chemical reactions in the brain, but at least mine were organic. I snorted at the word.

"You suspect me of something," Ridley said after my snort. I suppose he thought it was directed at him.

"No, I don't. But I am interested in you." I hadn't been "interested" in anyone for several years.

"Interested?" Ridley echoed and something like hope appeared in his visual receivers. He nodded as if he had encountered this before. Perhaps he had. He was a handsome machine, very handsome.

His head was very humanlike in design. Of course all his features were simplified and he was bald, if that's a word you can use to describe a being which has never had hair. His facial plate was like some classical African sculpture, sleek and smooth, with high bulges which would be called cheekbones on humans and metallic jaws hinged at the aural orifices, jutting down to an abrupt ending. If he were human, people would say Ridley had a strong chin. His visual receivers were far apart, made for 270 degree vision. His unnecessary nose was long and straight. The upper orifice had no lips though, which was a strange inconsistency. A nose but no lips: why?

Ridley's body was in excellent condition, mimicking a human's except of course for genitalia. There wasn't a dent on him. His coating gleamed. Stainless still stains but Ridley's was as shiny as new. I calculated his age and came up with a spread of twenty-five to thirty. In robot years that meant he was old, far older than I was. At fifty-seven, I was still on the young side of middle age.

I had been a child once; Ridley never had. He came into the world as an adult, had lived his whole life as an adult. He had been the latest model when he was…what? Made? Created? Everyone must have thought he was really something. He still was.

My erection became extremely uncomfortable. Perhaps, if Ridley had been another human or even one of the modified Deltas, we could have had a quickie in the conference room but he wasn't so I decided we might as well get back to what the government was paying us for.

"We should probably get back to the project."

"Yes," Ridley agreed, sounding as reluctant as I did.

Over the next few weeks, we worked together eight hours a day, five days a week. The UN had decreed that bots couldn't be worked any more than humans. The close contact was frustrating to me and not relieved by jerking off, during the day or at night. I wanted to hold Ridley's elegant hands, to stroke the sleek contours of his body. And then what, I always asked myself. There was no then what, which only made my sexual frustration worse.

For years I had avoided sex. Relations with women were repugnant and sex with men pointless. Men were so undependable and, ultimately, unloving. Biobots were absolutely dependable but, then, they were bots. Were they any more capable of love than humans? I doubted it. As far as I knew, no program for love had been developed.

It was five weeks before Ridley asked me out again. I was startled by how happy I was.

"I'd love to," I said. My smile was reflected in Ridley's face.

We were back at Starbucks, at the same table. I drank my coffee meditatively.

"What are you thinking?" Ridley asked quietly, as if he really wanted to know.

I looked up. "It's silly."

"Tell me anyway."

I took a breath and looked directly into his visual receivers. "I was wishing you could drink coffee too."

Ridley reached across the table to touch my hand with his Uni-on fingers. "That is very sweet, Jason."

My heart and cock swelled at the same time. He hadn't called me Jason since the Arboretum. One of my hands left the coffee cup and took his in an embrace. He stared at it as if he didn't know what to do, as I'm sure he didn't. I tightened my grip but he wasn't letting go anyway. We sat holding hands, staring from organism to machine and back, wordless for I don't know how many minutes. At last, the muscles of my arm ached from being in the same position for too long and I withdrew my hand. His stayed in the same position, as if waiting for mine to return.

We had a conversation back in the conference room Bernstein had booked ad infinitum for us.

"We have to be more careful," Ridley said. I nodded. "You could be reassigned and I could be…"

"Replaced," I finished grimly, my eyes locked on his. Now he nodded.

"It's impossible anyway," I said, slumping in my chair. Ridley took my hand under the table. I had given up sitting across from him. We sat together now, facing the door.

"The evidence so far," he said in a joking way I didn't know Alphas had, "Shows that it is not."

I felt his cold metal grow warm in my hands. I knew what he meant. But sex I thought, chiding myself for being so human.

"Say it," he said softly.

"I can't."

"Sex," he said for me.

"Yes."

"I can't."

"I know."

"Isn't this enough for you?" he asked. I dreaded disappointing him but I shook my head. He tried to release my hand, but I tightened my fingers around his. We sat watching the door, me wishing I could kiss him, Ridley maybe wishing he could kiss me back.

A few days later, we agreed to spend the evening together. He would come to my building. I wondered what I could do for him? He didn't need food or drink. In the end all I could think of was to wear the blue shirt he liked.

He noticed when I opened the door. His visual receivers lingered on my chest and his upper orifice opened in what must have been a smile. "You look very good in that shirt, Jason." My nipples tightened at the sound of my name in his mouth. I wondered what his "mouth" would feel like on them.

I showed him around the rooms. He appreciated my taste in furniture and art in the living room and noticed all the utensils in the kitchen.

"You like to cook then?"

"Yes," I agreed, feeling instantly sad. I would never cook for him.

I led him past the bathroom but he stopped to look in. "I've never seen a home evacuation facility."

"Haven't you looked at the one in the office?"

"Oh yes. But this is different." He looked around the small space, turning on taps and opening doors like he was thinking of buying the place. He picked up the hand soap and smelled it. "Lemon," he said.

"Yes," I confirmed. Later Alphas had been given an olfactory program to help in their work. I felt insanely glad I still used old fashioned bars of soap. My ejecting wells were always empty.

I wiped the slight soap residue off his beautiful fingers, remembering when I'd wiped the coffee off his groin shield. Was he remembering too?

We looked in the mirror at ourselves, standing shoulder to shoulder, me tanned and dark haired, Ridley all shine and silver. What had I been thinking? I moved away but he brought me back. I smiled when he put a silver arm around my blue shoulders.

"Would you show me the bedroom now?" he asked, his facial plate continuing to look impassively at mine in the mirror.

I nodded and we walked out of the bathroom and down the hall single file, me first. I wondered if Ridley were admiring my pneumatic mounds.

When we entered my bedroom, I saw it through Ridley's eyes: small and spare. We both looked at the bed and then Ridley turned me to him and began to pull up my shirt. Many men had done this for me but never a bot. His flexible fingers brushed my nipples up and down.

"Do you like that?"

"Yes," I told him hoarsely. He rubbed and tweaked and pulled them gently, the touch of his Uni-ons strange but wonderful. I kicked off my shoes, slipped out of my pants and underwear, discarded my socks and we were both, as Ridley phrased it, naked. Slowly, he reached for my cock, sending shivers up my body. A silver digit traced its length. I jumped when all five of his metacarpals encircled it.

"Cold," I gasped out as he began to jerk me off but he didn't let go. His palm guards warmed, and my body ached with wanting.

"Let's get in bed," I managed to say, leading us there.

I slid in first but Ridley hesitated at the edge. "I...," he began.

"Don't talk," I told him, throwing open the covers. As if in slow motion, he lowered himself onto the bed next to me. I brought the bed coverings over us and scooted next to him. His body parts were chilly against mine but they would warm, like his hands had. I put my mouth against his facial orifice and felt for lips and tongue which were not there. He let me explore the metal pieces inside his orifice. It was like tracing dental work with my tongue.

Bot sex was preliminarily discouraging but I kept at it gamely. I rolled Ridley on top of me and pulled his head towards my nipples. The edges of his orifice clamped on them to bite and massage. I squirmed my cock up against him and felt the absence of his. Don't stop I told myself and slid my hands down the smooth blandness of his back plate to his bulging pneumatic mounds and pressed him against me. Ridley got the idea and rubbed up and down along my cock until I ejaculated. I moaned and yelled incoherently. He watched as I came.

When I was calm again, I started to fetch a clean mopster, not wanting Ridley to see my filthy one, but he said "Stay" and added "Please" so I relaxed back into place. We watched one another across the divide.

"I wish I could do something for you," I told him.

"You did."

"What?"

Ridley's visual receptors focused on mine. "You gave me joy. That's what you humans call it."

"Bots feel joy?"

He grimaced at the slur and rolled onto his back, looking for all the world like he'd love to have a cigarette.

We continued like this for weeks, working together all day, being together all evening, having a sort of sex together at night. Ridley knew I needed sleep to regenerate and I knew he didn't. Each night, after I came, he monitored my sleepiness and always said "good night" before I went unconscious. When I asked what he did while I slept, he said he went into idle mode. That seemed terribly sad to me.

Our work progressed as rapidly as our relationship. I said it was because we were so well attuned and Ridley didn't disagree. We finished the research phase and prepared our report for presentation. I became more and more anxious but didn't share my anxiety with Ridley. When we finished what would use there be for an obsolete Alpha?

The day of our presentation, I woke up alone. Ridley had left a note.

"Had to go to the office early. Meeting with Matsumoto. See you there." He had signed it "Love, Ridley," the first time either of us had used the L word. It didn't register at the time; all I felt then was fear. A meeting with Matsumoto? It could only mean one thing. I rushed into my clothes and ran to the transporter tube.

At the office Ridley's station was empty. I hurried past the few early biobot arrivals without a hello and burst into Matsumoto's office. She was alone and smiled up at me.

"Where is Ridley?" I almost yelled at her.

She rose. "Sit. Please." I sat.

"Your report is excellent." To the question in my eyes, her answer was, "Ridley gave it to me."

"Where *is* Ridley?"

Matsumoto looked at me with simulated regret. She even hesitated over her words. "Ridley is gone."

I jumped up. "Gone?" Matsumoto waved me back into the chair.

"For modification. He will be back. Such an unusual biological robot. His abilities are outstanding, inconceivable for his model, but somehow he has evolved. His emotions seem so real."

"Alphas don't have emotions," I said automatically, worrying about the modifications. Usually, that meant the scrap heap or so many changes the biobot wasn't the same. Sometimes they came back with a completely different personality.

Matsumoto stood, edged around her desk and leaned against it, folding her arms. "You humans made us but you don't understand us at all. I wonder if God has the same problem with you." It sounded like a joke but I wasn't sure. I had never heard Matsumoto make one before.

She reached for my hand. I stared at hers, so human, so unlike Ridley's.

"Ridley," she began, "Has gone away but he will be back. He requested modification."

"Requested?" I repeated dumbly.

"It's not the first time. He has had many upgrades over the years, as many as there were for Alphas."

"Was there a new one?"

"No. There have no new upgrades for Alpha 17s in two years. The model is considered obsolete."

I winced at the word. "But then…"

"Ridley asked to be modified into a Delta. It was only approved because inter-model modification has never been attempted before. Think of the cost savings if it works!

"If?"

Matsumoto took both my hands in hers now. "If, Jason. If." She looked at me directly, with something like real empathy.

I was assigned a new project and my work life went on, but every night I went home to loneliness. I didn't hear from Ridley or anything about him. Matsumoto said I wouldn't. As the weeks stretched on, I began to expect the worst, to have Matsumoto call me into her office one morning and tell me the experiment had failed, that Ridley was gone, gone forever. I had experienced death—I was human—but not this death, not the death of the beloved. How could I survive that?

I didn't survive very well. I spent my weekends in bed, eating very little and nothing nutritious, watching mindless entertainment on my animation activator, ignoring the invitations and entreaties of family and friends. I could work without Ridley but I couldn't live, at least not the everyday. I breathed and ate and slept. I longed for sleep because Ridley came to me in dreams, in all his shining beauty. We worked, talked, had sex. I would wake up wet.

One Saturday, I woke from my dreams of Ridley to a loud knocking at my door. I tried to ignore it but it continued unabated. Thinking it was my brother or my parents finally taking action, I crawled out of bed, grumbling, and picked up a wrinkled wraparound from the floor.

"Who is it?" I said through the communicator, attaching the wraparound.

"Ridley," came the reply.

I ripped the door open. It wasn't Ridley. It was a man the size of Ridley in height and breadth but a human, not a biobot. The man was handsome: blond, with brown eyes and red lips, strongly built, dressed in blue. I tried to shut the door. What kind of awful joke was this?

A strong hand reached out to hold the door open. "It's me, Jason. It's me." I listened now. The voice did sound like Ridley's. I dropped my head, ashamed of how I looked to whomever–or whatever–this was.

"Come in," I muttered, opening the door wider, but he just stood at my threshold, this stranger claiming to be the man I loved. Man? Somehow, the robot I loved didn't sound right either.

"Come in," I said again, more firmly. The man still hesitated, human visual receivers just watching mine. They were a lovely warm brown. So beautiful, just like the rest of him. Then, he reached out for my hand and I felt human fingers grasp mine. It didn't feel like Ridley at all but I led him into the living room anyway, towards the couch where Ridley and I had sat together and made love.

"You're wearing clothes," I said when we were seated. I tried not to sound disappointed.

Ridley looked embarrassed. "I have to now." My eyebrows went up. He blushed, which was sweet and definitely something Alpha Ridley could have never done. I touched his cheek reflexively and felt stubble. Delta Ridley shaved. Alpha Ridley had just polished himself with a mopster.

He took my hand again. "I missed you." My heart lurched, as if it were trying to agree with my brain that this really might be Ridley.

"You'll be safe now," I replied, feeling shy in front of this handsome stranger with a familiar name.

"I didn't do it just to be safe," Delta Ridley said, tipping my chin up and making me look at him. He smiled, his red lips parting, exposing white regular teeth. "Don't you like the Delta me?"

"Oh, of course. It's just…"

"Different."

"Yes," I agreed, grateful we were still finishing each other's sentences. "But it looks great. You look great."

"Thanks. I tried to pick your type."

I laughed unconvincingly. "My type? Do I have one?" Ridley nodded and of course he was right, at least partially. Previously, I'd been attracted to blonds but since I'd met Ridley I'd been partial to stainless.

"Besides," he said, settling heavily against the couch. "I would have been replaced. I was the oldest Alpha 17 still working. Matsumoto told me that."

"When?"

"A week before I left."

I reminded myself that Deltas were not to be trusted. So human and so not. But Ridley was a Delta now. Could I trust him?

"Ridley…" I began. "Ridley," I repeated, so happy to say his name again. He stood up then and led me to the bedroom. That was new, the strength of his body tugging mine urgently along.

Arriving at the bed, we stood staring at one another, holding hands. Ridley seemed uncertain. I took off my shirt and put his hands on my nipples. They began to squeeze, the feel of human skin strange against mine. I missed Alpha Ridley's Union digits. He stopped squeezing.

"Remove my clothing, Jason," Ridley said in a husky voice.

I began, slowly at first, then hurriedly, like I was unwrapping a present, until all his new skin was open to the air. His cock was flaccid. I wondered if it was difficult to engorge. He turned around slowly, showing me a spectacular human ass. "Thank you for that," I said.

"What?"

"Your ass. I always loved your pneumatic mounds."

Delta Ridley laughed, which sounded like Alpha Ridley, and I felt more reassured. I came up close and wrapped my arms around him, gripping his gluteous maximi like I'd clutched his pneumatic mounds.

"How does it feel?" he asked, breathing into my ear, scraping his warm rough jaw against mine.

"Different," I told him honestly. "But different good," I added.

"I'm still me," he said as he pulled my wraparound open and off my shoulders. He embraced me again as the garment fell onto the floor.

I felt his cock grow before I saw it, the length and width generous. If you were going to choose a cock for yourself, would you choose otherwise?

We held onto each other, feeling two cocks together where there had only been one. "I like the cock," I said over his shoulder.

"I thought you would," he said over mine. I started to laugh but it was cut short by Ridley gripping my ass hard and moving his groin side to side, our cocks playing in a way Ridley's metallic sheath and my aching hard-on never could. I leaned my neck back in ecstasy and Ridley's mouth kissed it.

A kiss! Lips warm and full implanting a wet mark and electric feeling on my skin. Lips against mine, melding them together, a tongue entering my mouth, exploring it as unknown territory.

Delta Ridley seemed good at this. Had he practiced in the laboratory? Was it practice if it were only with other Deltas? With humans? I couldn't ask, engulfed as I was by his mouth and engorged by his tongue, and, when mouth and teeth and tongue moved on to my chest, I was beyond speech except for a breathy "yes" or inarticulate moaning.

I felt us moving down, towards the bed. Would this work? My body was screaming that it hoped so. I opened the bed covers and slid in, holding them open for Ridley. He stood for a moment, looking down my body, and I took the opportunity to take his cock in my mouth. I could do something for him now.

I slid down every inch of him, wanting him to love it, wanting him to know the risk was worthwhile, for us as well as for him. I held his perfect ass with its sparse coat of natural-feeling hair and ran my fingers over the hard muscles beneath the warm human skin. I sucked his cock in and out of me rapidly.

"Slow down, Jason. I don't want to come yet."

"You can come?" His cock fell out of my open mouth and bobbed in front of my face.

Ridley smirked, a look no Alpha could imitate. "I'm fully operational."

I took him back in my mouth eagerly. He pulled out of me again.

"I want to feel you come in my mouth!" I protested.

He pushed me back onto the rumpled covers. "Later," he promised and settled on top of me, cock to cock and chest to chest. I could hear his magneto pulsing against my heart. He kissed me with mouth and tongue and spread my legs with his, lifting mine onto his shoulders with his jointed arms. His cock prodded my ass and found the hole. A cool liquid squirted into it. Was he coming already?

"Are you...."

"Lubricant," he explained as he slid inside me.

Oh those programmers, I thought and then stopped thinking. This might be programming, but whatever it was it worked. His pseudo penis made its way up my colon. His cellulose balls pressed against my ass when the man-made shaft had gone as far as it could go. I felt the joy we had once so clinically discussed. Ridley was inside me!

And then he began to fuck. I knew the cock was pushed in and pulled out by complex hydraulic muscles which mimicked my own. I knew they weren't real, but the feeling they gave me was. I appreciated engineers like I never had before. I told Ridley how good it felt. My exact words were, "I've never had a fuck like this!"

"I hope not," he growled in a very human way as he slammed harder and harder against me, holding my arms flat against the bed. I felt very human groans reverberate into my chest as Ridley pressed against me. I felt him shoot inside me, the liquid warm and generous.

"Jason!" he yelled each time he spurted. I loved hearing his voice say my name over and over, loved feeling his come inside me. I freed my hands to keep him close.

I thought of a question while our breathing/oxygen pumping slowed and our heart/magneto rates decreased. I waited to ask it until he had softened inside me. "What's your first name?" I whispered into his ear beside my jaw. I couldn't hear his answer so I repeated the question. Ridley lifted his head.

"I don't have one," he said, audible again.

"You will now. What should it be?"

"What would you like it to be?" he asked, hands on my chest, mouth back on mine.

"You decide. It's your name," I answered, in between kisses and gropes.

He stopped, lay back and thought a great while. I worried that maybe he'd accidentally slipped into idle mode. Would he still do that? Questions to ask.

At last he turned to me, his neck no longer making a full 90 degree twist. "Isaac," he announced.

"Isaac?" I asked. "Why Isaac?"

"Because of Isaac Asimov."

"The novelist?" And then it clicked. "*I, Robot!*"

Ridley grinned like a happy parent. "Exactly. I've read nearly all his novels." That was quite an achievement—there were so many of them—but, then, biobots did read at exceptional speed.

I looked at Isaac's eyes; I was beginning not to miss the grey. "Are you sure?" He leaned over and kissed me very softly, a grazing of adapted skin against adapted skin. I saw love in his eyes. Maybe that could be programmed after all.

"I love you," he confirmed.

"Can you?"

He frowned at me. "What, do you think it's just electronics?"

"Isn't it?"

Isaac took me in his arms and held on until I had my answer. When he felt me hug back, he rolled himself on top of me. I settled happily into the softness of the bed underneath me, feeling his hard human body above mine. I rejoiced in it now. Ridley was a biobot with no first name. Isaac was a man, my man.

I said his name over and over as I came.

# TICKET TO RIDE

It was just an unpainted wooden box, with vertical slats holding up a pale blue sign. Sometimes the sign read "Lemonade 50 cents," only there wouldn't be any lemonade. Other times it commented on current affairs.

I almost didn't look that morning since I was hurrying to buy something I couldn't live without at Cliff's Hardware. But the message drew my eyes and slowed my steps. "Time machine rides 5 cents, return trip 25 cents." I put down three dimes and continued towards Cliff's in a much better mood.

On the way back, my dimes weren't there but an envelope was, hand addressed to me. After looks over both shoulders, I shrugged and tore it open. Inside were two rectangles of yellow construction paper. The first said in pencil: "To Wherever." The second said in ink "From Wherever. P.S. don't lose." Each had a disclaimer printed in tiny, precise letters on the back.

"Ticketholder may go to wherever he/she chooses. No time limit on stay. Must have From ticket to return. (Or else it's not my fault.)"

I thought what a good joke it was until I remembered to wonder how they knew my name. I pondered that awhile, slapping the tickets against my palm. Anyway, if I *were* going to wherever, which wherever would it be?

The answer came to mind immediately. I would go back 30 years, to Chico. I closed my eyes and pictured myself there but nothing happened, of course. I heard someone say, "Try again." I looked around but no one was nearby or even grinning from a window. "Out loud," the voice prompted. I stared at the tickets to ride. If I were going crazy, why not go all the way?

"I want to go back to Chico when I was 18 before..." In the middle of the sentence my head jerked and I saw my room in Chico and me lying on my rumpled bed, breathing heavily. I had just come. And then I was there.

"Aaron," I heard my father call, which almost made me cry since he'd been dead nearly twenty years. Next, he'd bang on the door and yell "breakfast!"

Bang, bang, bang! "Breakfast!" I jumped out of bed, pulled on my boxers and opened the door.

"Dad!" I yelled, grabbing him in a bear hug.

"Hey, big guy!" he said in surprise. "What's the occasion?" I held on until he pulled away, hands on my shoulders. "What's wrong, son?"

"Nothing, Dad," I told him, pulling him close again, smelling his aftershave, feeling the scratch of his stubble on my cheek. He patted my shoulder. Neither of us knew what to say. Neither of us ever did. Finally, Dad pulled away again and I let him go.

"You better get dressed, son. Your mother's chomping at the bit. Remember we're going to the coast today after breakfast. You sure you want to stay here on your own? It's gonna be a scorcher."

"Yeah," I said uncertainly. Why exactly was I staying home?

"You and Kevin don't tear up the place, okay? No wild parties." Oh, right. It was *this* weekend.

I went across the hall to the bathroom I used to share with my little brother. And there he was, brushing his teeth. He looked back at me in the mirror. "Don't say it," he mumbled through the toothpaste.

"What?"

"You always ask, 'Why ya brushing your teeth *before* break-fast?' and then you mess up my hair."

"Okay, I won't ask. Anyway, Ben, it's your mouth." He was still staring at our faces in the mirror. "What?" I asked again.

"You called me Ben."

"That's your name, isn't it?"

"A million times I ask you to stop calling me Benny and you never do. Why today?"

He was right. I didn't call him Ben until he went in the Army. "Yeah? Must be your lucky day…Benny." He made a face, showing me all the toothpaste in his mouth, and went back to brushing.

I hopped in the shower. When I opened the door and reached for my towel, it was gone and so was Ben. Funny guy. I dried off as best I could with the hand towel.

The mirror was all mine. Damn, I used to have a lot of hair! Now I was about as bald as Dad and Grampa. *Grampa.* He was gone too. I combed my long luxurious hair and ran to get dressed.

When I walked into the kitchen, my family was eating pan-cakes, like we did almost every Saturday back then. I sat down to mine, wondering what chores my dad would have for me while they were away. On cue he said, "Be sure to mow the lawn today, son."

"I will, Dad," I promised, glad to say the word *Dad* again to him.

"Then and only then can you and Kevin go for a swim in the pool." That's right. Dad had the pool put in that spring, in time for summer.

I got the mower out of the garage and yanked the cord to get it going. The noise was louder than I remembered. I had almost finished the section between the two crape myrtles when my family came trooping out the front door. I cut the motor and brushed the hair out of my eyes. I still did that sometimes, even if it was just phantom hair.

"Here's the number of the motel we're staying at," my mother said. I stared at her hand. It was so smooth and pale. Now it was wrinkled and mottled with liver spots.

Dad handed me some money. "Enjoy yourself." I pocketed the bills, realizing my wallet was 30 years ahead of us in San Francisco.

"We'll be back late Sunday," Mom said as she got in the front passenger seat of the old Buick. Benny slid in back. I waved goodbye and stared after them. Dad was dead, Mom was in a retirement "village" and Benny lived in Massachusetts. Maybe I should have gone with them. But that wasn't why I came back. I cranked the mower up again.

Once I'd finished the backyard, I reached in my pocket to let Kevin know my family was gone. Oh, right. No cell phones yet.

"Hello?" Kevin's voice answered after I called him from our house phone. My brain couldn't get my mouth to work. "Aaron, is this you?" he asked after I just kept breathing into the handset.

I wanted to shout "I love you! I'm sorry!" over and over but all I said was, "Yeah. How ya doing?"

"Great. Your folks gone?" Kevin was always a get down to business kind of guy.

"Yeah."

"Okay. See you in 10. Bye!"

The dial tone buzzed in my ear. I was about to see my dead lover. What would I say to him after what I'd done? Only, I hadn't done it yet.

It seemed like only seconds before the Mustang's tires screeched when Kevin hit the brakes in our driveway. The car door slammed, his big feet slapped along the sidewalk, the doorbell rang and there he was, all 6'3, 220 pounds of him, in sleeveless shirt, baggy shorts and flip flops. I resisted the urge to throw my arms around him and cover him in kisses. Neighbors in a small town are always watching and I wasn't out back then.

"Why'd you ring the doorbell?" I asked, hands inserting themselves into my jeans pockets.

"I always ring the doorbell." Something else I'd forgotten. That said, he closed the door behind him and leaned down to kiss me with those soft full lips no one could forget. "You wanna?" he asked, wiggling his eyebrows.

"Uh, let's go for a swim first."

"Huh?" He looked at me like I was crazy. Maybe I was. I mean, was any of this really happening? But he felt real when he put his arms around me so I wiggled my eyebrows yes.

"That's better, baby," he said and led me off to the bedroom. We got undressed and into bed. Kevin took his time. Nobody was home to knock or walk in on us.

After sex, we lay naked on top of the bed, him smoking those damn cigarettes, one arm around my shoulders, my head against his.

"I wish you weren't going away this summer."

I was going away? Oh, right. The Forest Service. Oh, no! Geoff! "I have to make money for college," I said, like there hadn't been a pause. "And you've got football camp anyway." We were going to UCLA. Kevin had a football scholarship. I wanted to go to Berkeley but he had talked me out of it.

"Yeah, I know, but that's not til August. You coulda still taken the road trip with me."

The past came back to me with a thud. After this weekend I had spent that summer cutting brush with a machete and chain saw and fucking Geoff. Kevin had ridden the Harley around 11 Western states before he went off to UCLA. I had gone to Berkeley after all, with Geoff.

"Come visit me in Arcata," I suggested.

"I am. Hey, what's with you today?" He stubbed the cigarette out on an empty coke can and turned towards me, his fingers automatically attaching themselves to my left nipple. "You're gonna miss this, baby. And this." He put his other hand on my cock and started jerking.

"I sure have," I said, gasping.

He laughed. "You talk like it's been years or something."

"Yeah," I agreed, making myself laugh too.

I spread my legs when his hand slid between them. He fingered my ass, then pushed both legs up. I didn't stop him this time and suggest we use a condom. Neither of us had one anyway. AIDS hadn't entered Chico's consciousness yet.

It always amazed me that the All North State quarterback fucked me on a regular basis. "You close, baby?" he asked in a hoarse croak. I gasped out a yes and Kevin went into overdrive. He started grunting, that uh, uh, uh that always made me come. We shot at the same time, me onto my chest, Kevin up my ass.

He looked down at me, leering. "You sure are horny today, babe." He wiped us up with the cum rag we always used. "Whew," he said, flopping against the mattress. When he reached for another cigarette, I tried to stop him. He slapped my hand away, lit up, took a puff and asked, "So, what do you wanna talk about?"

I gulped. My ticket to ride had brought me back to Wherever all right, the last minutes before I'd ruined my life, before I told Kevin I didn't want to go to UCLA, that I thought we should break up. What should I say instead? Kevin smoked while I thought.

"Knock, knock," he said, rapping his knuckles against my forehead.

"Uh…well…I just thought maybe we should make some plans for your visit. To Arcata, I mean." Good save, Aaron. Everything would be all right now. It had been so simple. I could go back to 2014 soon.

"Oh, yeah. We should decide when and where. I gotta fit it into the ride."

We settled on a date. As for where, I said, "I have a room," remembering Mrs. Grundy's big, white, two storey house. "I'll give you the address."

"Yeah, I'll need it to drive you up there like we planned." He took a drag on the cigarette and blew the smoke away from us. It hovered in the air at the foot of the bed like the specter it was. In 18 years he'd be lying in a different kind of bed. I yanked the cigarette out of his mouth and pushed it down the Coke can.

"Hey! Why'd you do that?"

"You know why. Cigarettes are going to kill you."

Kevin slumped and stared up at the ceiling. "Yeah, I know. I *know*," he said, looking me. "I've tried to quit. I don't know if I can."

"You can. You will. Otherwise, you're dead at 36."

"What, you have a vision or something? Sounds like you know the exact date."

I did. Where was a nicotine patch when you needed one? Not invented yet. I could probably "invent" all kinds of stuff. We could be millionaires.

"Earth to Aaron. Come in please." Kevin was waving his hand in front of my face. I blinked. We were still on my bed, totally naked, his big football body still muscular and full of life. And his beautiful hair. I ran my fingers through it. He closed his eyes and hummed happily.

"Baby, when did you start doing that?" His eyes opened. "Okay, let's make our plan." It was back to business.

Kevin drove me the 200 miles to Arcata in the Mustang, with me playing GPS. Mom and Dad offered to take us but I needed to be alone with Kevin as much as possible before I met Geoff for the second time.

The house was at the end of a cul de sac. Huge blackberry bushes filled the lot behind the gravel parking area next to the kitchen porch. I was looking forward to seeing Mrs. Grundy, remembering how nice she was to me that summer. I'd been so unhappy when I arrived. The Mustang sent the gravel flying as Kevin stomped on the brakes just before he ran over the blackberries. He hopped out, popped the trunk and hoisted both my bags out.

"Let me take one."

"Nah. I got em." He looked towards the porch and turned on his Mr. Popularity smile. A friendly looking older woman smiled back at him.

"Aaron?" she asked, looking at Kevin.

"I'm Aaron, Mrs. Grundy," I said, moving towards her. "This is my friend Kevin."

"Welcome to Arcata! Let me show you to your room. It's upstairs," Mrs. Grundy said in her always optimistic-sounding voice. We followed her into the house and up the narrow flight of steps, down the equally narrow hall. At the farthest room, she turned the knob. "I'm sorry there's just the one bed."

"That's okay," Kevin said. I was glad Geoff wouldn't arrive until the next week.

Mrs. Grundy opened the door and showed us the one bed, which was occupied at the moment by a large dark haired person about my age. Geoff was here already! I must not have remembered correctly.

Mrs. Grundy looked flustered too. "Oh, Geoff! I'm sorry. I was just showing...oh well, Geoffrey Freudlich, this is your roommate, Aaron Cohen. You're both working for the Forest Service this summer."

Geoff stood up in his tidy whities, displaying a body I definitely had not forgotten. He rapidly covered it with a robe, shook my hand, then reached out to Kevin, whose mouth was wide open.

"Uh, this is my friend Kevin Roberts." I tried to look at Geoff like we were strangers.

Kevin closed his mouth, put my bags down and shook Geoff's hand, squeezing hard enough for Geoff to wince. They locked hands like two bulls competing for the same cow. Finally, Kevin said, "I gotta go," and lurched away. I followed, trying to talk to him as he tromped down the hall and pounded down the stairs. He finally answered me outside by the Mustang.

"Where am I going to stay, Aaron? In bed with you and your roomie? I don't think so."

"We could get a motel room. Please Kevin. Don't be mad. Geoff wasn't supposed to be here until next week."

"Oh, it's Geoff already, huh?"

Damn. Blew it already. "Don't be jealous," I said, trying to recover.

"I'm not jealous," he said automatically. He leaned against the car. "Okay, I'm jealous." A big sigh lifted his big chest. He looked up at the second floor.

"It's a long summer."

"Don't worry," I said, giving him a hug and kiss out in public. "I love you, remember?"

"Wow," Kevin said. "Who are you and what did you do with my boyfriend?" I pulled away fast and he grinned. "Yeah, I remember. I love you too, babe," he said, socking my shoulder. "I'll come through on the bike like I promised. Then, we'll be together at college and next year we can get our own place. What's one summer anyway?" Kevin had life planned out for us, down to his career and mine. He would play in the N.F.L., and I would be a doctor. I knew the N.F.L. wouldn't be ready for an openly gay quarterback in 1988, but we wouldn't have to face that situation anyway. Kevin would become a copier salesman after college and work his way up at Xerox. He was their youngest district manager when he died.

"Right," I agreed, trying not to picture his funeral.

"Don't look so sad, baby. I saw a phone in the kitchen. We'll talk." He gave me another hug and a kiss with plenty of tongue before he hopped in the car and drove away, honking three times like always. When there was only empty street and settling dust, I wiped my eyes and turned around to face the house. No one was staring or calling the police. I went inside.

Mrs. Grundy was in the kitchen, too obviously stirring a pot. She looked around at me. "Is everything all right, dear?"

"Yes," I assured her—and myself. "It's just that my friend had planned to stay the weekend." The lie the words *my friend* told hovered in the air between us.

"Oh, I'm sorry. I wish I had another room but when the Forest Service called I told them I only had the double bed. I thought they'd tell you." I said it was okay even though it wasn't and began trudging up the stairs to start avoiding my summer fate.

The door was open and Geoff was sitting on the bed when I walked in. He stood up, wearing shorts and a tight tee shirt now. I remembered what he looked like naked, how his cock felt, how sweet….

"I hope everything is okay, Aaron."

I focused again on the past present. "Don't worry about it."

"I'm sorry about the bed. I didn't know either until I got here. I called the Forest Service but they said basically take it or leave it." I thanked him for trying.

He moved to the chest of drawers. "I saved half for you. You want the top or bottom?"

"Huh?"

"Do you want the top two drawers or bottom two?"

"Bottom, I guess."

He smiled. "Good. I'd rather be on top anyway." Then he gave me that lopsided grin I had loved so much the two years we'd dated at Berkeley.

"Uh, okay," I said, looking away towards my luggage.

"Here. Let me help you with those." He yanked both bags onto the bed as if they were Ziplocs. I bent over and started unpacking, trying not to sweat. He stood behind me and the room temperature went up even higher. I kept unpacking and not looking at him.

"Well, I guess I better get out of your way," he said after several minutes of mutual silence. I said okay without turning around. Once I heard the stairs creak, I sat on the bed and asked myself how I was going to do this.

That night, Geoff made it harder when he invited me to dinner. Mrs. Grundy cooked breakfast for her boarders, but at lunch and dinner we were on our own. I tried to say no to the invitation but Geoff wore me down.

At Angelo's, we sat across from each other like we were on a first date, which in 1984 we had been, as it turned out. Geoff was a good listener and matter of fact about himself. He was a sophomore at Berkeley and on the baseball team, no scholarship. His dad owned a chain of department stores. I recognized the last name. He asked lots of questions about Kevin, except the one I knew he really wanted the answer to.

Back at the house, Mrs. Grundy was watching "Family Ties" on her new Sony in the living room. I thought about Michael J. Fox's Parkinson's in the future and felt sad for him. Geoff and I said good night to her and went upstairs.

"You want the bathroom first?" he asked. "Hey, you like hiking? There are some great trails around here." I said no. We had fucked and sucked on some of those trails. I collected my toiletries and took my turn in the bath. Back in our room, Geoff was sitting on the bed with a towel wrapped around him. His chest was everything I remembered.

"All done?" he asked, hopping up.

"Yep."

I waited for him to leave, only he didn't. He just stood there in his towel, watching me standing there in mine. His started to tent. So did mine.

"I can't," I said quietly.

"Boyfriend?" he asked and I nodded. "The guy today?" I nodded again. "Too bad." He rewrapped his towel so his erection was against his body, took one more look at mine and left for the bathroom. I exhaled, slipped back into my Jockeys and got into bed. When Geoff came back, he turned off the light. I heard the towel drop and his underwear slide on. I remembered how good his ass felt.

"Ouch!"

He must have bumped into something.

"You can turn the light back on."

"It's okay."

I listened to him settle into bed and not say anything for several minutes. I was drifting off to sleep when I heard him whisper, "I wish you didn't have a boyfriend."

I wanted to say, "Me too," but just pretended I didn't hear.

The next morning we were spooning when I woke, my ass against his erection, his arm holding me close. That summer, Geoff and I fell asleep like that almost every night and woke up in the same position almost every morning. We fit together well, but then so did Kevin and I. *Kevin.* I tried to pull away but Geoff mumbled something in his sleep and his arm tightened around me. I tried again and woke him up.

"Oh, God! I'm sorry. I was asleep. Really!"

"I know."

The second night it happened, I said, "I could get a sleeping bag."

He leaned over me. "Maybe we could put pillows down the middle of the bed or something."

"That won't leave much room, especially for you." I sat up while Geoff considered that. "Look," I said. "We can do it. We don't have to have sex."

He gave me his crinkly smile. "Won't it be more like not doing it?" So, we spent the weeks before Kevin came back not doing it, although anyone who saw us and knew from gays, assumed we were. We worked together, ate all our meals together, shopped together and slept together, his cock against my ass every morning. Mrs. Grundy treated us like a couple. People in Arcata stared at us. The surveyors we worked for made insinuations frequently.

By the time Kevin called to remind me when he'd be back in Arcata, I was so horny I was ready to jump him in the blackberry bushes. I booked a motel room instead.

"Hey, this is a nice room," he said as he opened the door. I closed it behind us and started kissing him fast and furiously, then went down on him and sucked him hard. "Wow! I missed you too, babe!" he yelped.

We fucked twice before coming up for air. Post second coitus I lay on his chest, waiting for him to light up, but he didn't.

"Three weeks, no smokes," he said, grinning down at me. "Do I get a reward?" I laughed until he rolled against me, cock to ass. I froze immediately.

"What's wrong, baby?"

"Nothing," I assured him, rubbing my ass against his hard on.

"That's my hot man," he whispered into my ear, teeth nibbling the lobe, one hand guiding his cock back inside me, the other starting to jerk me off. I'm ashamed to say I closed my eyes and pictured Geoff some of the time, but at least I didn't yell the wrong name when I came. Tuesday morning, when I woke up spooning with Geoff, I tried not to think of Kevin's cock up my ass and what Geoff's would feel like up there. Anyway, I remembered how it felt. I pulled away, Geoff woke up and we began our new workday.

Another month passed, with Kevin in Chico working for his dad and me in Arcata working for Uncle Sam. We talked every day, which really ran up my phone bill since I usually dialed the numbers, but reminding myself I loved Kevin was the only way I couldn't fall in love with Geoff again.

When we all turned the calendar to August, Kevin flew south for football camp at U.C.L.A., no cars allowed. Phone calls got fewer. Geoff and I got closer. When he told me about his life at Berkeley, I remembered more than he said. It had been our life after all, once upon a time.

Not having sex became increasingly difficult for both of us. One Saturday morning it became impossible. I got a sleeping bag after that. Geoff said he'd sleep on the floor but I made sure we took turns.

At the end of August, my last day in the Forest Service and taking turns on the floor finally arrived. Football camp was over and Kevin was flying north to pick up his car, pick up his boyfriend and drive both of us back to Westwood. I was going to be a tennis team walk-on so he and I could be roommates in the jocks dorm.

Geoff and I said goodbye at a gas station off 101 in Arcata. After they gassed up, he and the surveyors were driving to Gasquet for the rest of the week.

"Thanks for everything!" he said, with what looked like tears in his eyes. The surveyors glanced at each other like, yep, homos. I didn't care anymore. I leaned across the seat and gave Geoff a long hug. I wanted to say let's keep in touch but just got out and waved goodbye.

The green Forest Service SUV pulled out of the gas station, and I ran up the overpass sidewalk. From the center of it, I watched the SUV merge onto 101 north. I waved again, in case Geoff was looking back. Then, I walked the long sad blocks to Mrs. Grundy's.

Kevin was waiting outside the house. I tried to smile for him. He looked so happy and healthy. He hadn't smoked all summer. Seeing him, I knew I'd made the right decision coming back, not changing our plans, not screwing up my life and his.

"I put your bags in the trunk already," he told me. "You good to go?"

"I'll just say goodbye to Mrs. Grundy."

"She had to leave. She told me to give you a big hug." I hugged him back, so tightly I could feel his heart beating. He gave me a kiss and I didn't worry about the neighbors.

"I'll just go in and take another look around," I said after he let me go.

"Okay, babe. Take your time." Old Kevin would have pulled his pack out then and had a smoke while he waited, but New Kevin just settled his bubble butt against the Mustang, folded his arms across his chest and smiled.

The house was locked so I used my key. I wrote a note to Mrs. Grundy and then wandered around, saying goodbye to my summer. In my room with Geoff, I looked at the bed we'd slept in and, once, made love in. I felt a tsunami of regret and, for better or worse, also wrote him a note, with my address and phone number. In the final moments, I couldn't face not knowing him. And anyway, I'd be safe and sound in Los Angeles with Kevin. It wasn't like I'd be living in that funny old house on Channing Way.

On my way out, I stopped at the kitchen window. Through the curtains I could see Kevin still leaning against the Mustang, trying not to be impatient. I could also see Geoff's MG farther away where he always parked it. What would their lives be like, now that I had changed the past? Would I still know Geoff? Would Kevin start smoking again? And my dad. If he just ate healthier food, got more exercise and had his cholesterol checked, he wouldn't have his stroke, at least not so soon.

I pulled the return ticket out of my wallet and read the words again. I had come back to change my life and I had. The thing was though, I would never actually get to live it. But I could. I only had *not* to do just one more thing. I heard Kevin honk the horn, a bugle call to action.

Without another thought I tore my return ticket in half and quarters and eighths and let the pieces flutter into the trashcan under the sink. My stomach dropped with them. What had I done? Kevin honked again. I looked outside. He was walking towards the door.

"I'm sorry," I said, opening it for him.

"No problem," he lied, one foot tapping.

I locked the kitchen door behind us, slipped my key through the mail slot and took my first steps into the next 30 years. I wasn't sure what would happen through all those years but I was ready to find out. Kevin opened the passenger door on the Mustang and I slid in. He popped the gearshift into reverse, backed up and off we roared, leaving dust and gravel flying behind us. I settled back. I no longer had a ticket, but I was ready to ride.

Richard May

Richard May

# About the Author

Richard May's short fiction has been published in his collections *Inhuman Beings* and *Ginger Snaps: Photos & Stories* (with photographer David Sweet), his series *Gay All Year* on Amazon Kindle, in anthologies like *Never Too Late*, *Best Gay Erotica*, and the Lambda Literary nominated *Outer Voices Inner Lives*, and in literary journals, including *Bay Laurel*, *Chelsea Station*, and *Hyacinth Noir*.

Rick also organizes the monthly Perfectly Queer book reading series with his partner Wayne Goodman in Oakland at Nomadic Press: Uptown and in San Francisco at Dog Eared Books Castro, individual LGBTQ Pride Readings at Laurel Books in Oakland and Dog Eared Books Castro, the annual literary festival Word Week at Folio Books and other locations in Noe Valley, and an online book club, Reading Queer Authors Lost to AIDS.

Rick is from Sacramento and Brooklyn and now lives in San Francisco. He has red hair and truly believes in all things ginger. Please follow him on social media at facebook.com/richardmaywriter, @rickmaywritr on Twitter, and richard.may1313 on Instagram.

www.ingramcontent.com/pod-product-compliance
Lightning Source LLC
Chambersburg PA
CBHW070436120726
47910CB00003B/811